FIRST
OFFENSE

ALSO BY MARTI GREEN

The Innocent Prisoners Project Series

Unintended Consequences
Presumption of Guilt
The Price of Justice

Happy reading –
Marti Green

FIRST OFFENSE

Marti Green

THOMAS & MERCER

Published by Thomas & Mercer, Seattle

www.apub.com

Amazon, the Amazon logo, and Thomas & Mercer are trademarks of Amazon.com, Inc., or its affiliates.

ISBN-13: 9781503934702
ISBN-10: 1503934705

Cover design by Cyanotype Book Architects

Printed in the United States of America

Dedicated to Rachel, Joshua, Jacob, Sienna, and Noah.
You light up my life.
and
To my aunt, Edith Beiles, who always made me feel special.

Jessica Bishop sat slumped on the floor, her arms wrapped tightly around her body. She'd been unable to stop the flow of tears ever since the two soldiers, in their freshly starched uniforms, had left her home. Lt. Col. Alex Bishop was missing in action, the soldiers had told her. She couldn't wrap her head around it. She'd begged her husband to retire last year, when he'd reached twenty years in the army, but he'd insisted on waiting two more years so he could collect his maximum pension. "Don't worry," he'd reassured her. "We're just doing training of the Afghan army now. We're not going out on active patrols anymore. I'll be safe." Each week he'd Skype her from his dust-filled base in Laghman Province, surrounded by mountains. He was training his Afghan counterparts on the use of heavy-duty, long-range weaponry.

"It's going well," he'd told her on the last call, before mentioning that he and another officer were heading by helicopter to a different outpost in a few days. "I'll be home before you know it," he'd promised. Only now he might never come home.

She wiped her cheeks with the back of her hand, then dried her hand on her pants leg. *I'm an army wife. I've always known it was possible. I should be stronger.* But there was a wide gulf between possibility and reality. She called out his name with a low moan, then buried her face in her hands. How could she tell the boys? Especially Frankie. Bobby was most like his father. Stubborn like him. He looked like him; he'd joined the military like him. Maybe that's why they always seemed at odds with each other.

But Frankie? He idolized his father. When Alex was deployed, Frankie seemed lost without him. Especially now, when they were living off-base for the first time in years, in a new city with a new school and new challenges. How could she tell him that his father might not come home this time? How could she go on if he didn't come home?

The only person she knew in her new city was her mother. That's why they'd moved to Key Vista, Florida—so she could be closer to her. She was getting older, more forgetful. She'd fallen in her apartment two months ago and broken her hip. That's when Jessica made the decision to move. But she couldn't turn to her mother for comfort. It would be too distressing to her. Instead, Jessica picked up the phone and dialed her brother-in-law—Alex's half brother.

"Help Innocent Prisoners Project, Bruce Kantor's office," his assistant said when she answered the phone.

"Is he in? It's Jessica Bishop."

"I'll put you through."

In another instant, Bruce was on the line. "Jessica, is everything all right?"

She'd expected he'd be surprised at her call. She'd never phoned him at the office. They'd talk occasionally but always when he was at home. She tried to answer him but couldn't speak. Instead, she began sobbing.

"Jessica, what is it?"

Finally she brought herself under control. "Alex is MIA."

"Oh, God!" There was silence on the other end of the phone for a minute, and then Bruce said, "Tell me exactly what they said."

"He was in a helicopter, and it crashed. Maybe from a missile. They're not certain yet. They found the wreckage, along with the pilot's body. But Alex and another soldier are missing."

"So—that's good. It means he's probably alive."

"They don't know. He could have been badly injured, wandered off, and died someplace where they haven't found him." Jessica began crying again.

"I'll fly down there tonight."

"No, you don't need to. I just needed someone to talk to."

"I want to come. You shouldn't be alone."

"I'm not. Frankie's here."

There was silence again. "Does he know?"

"Not yet."

Bruce sighed. "This will be especially hard for him."

"I know. But he'll just have to get stronger. We're an army family. It's what we do."

Frankie Bishop had been angry ever since learning a week ago that his father was MIA. Angry at his mother for having moved him to Florida, angry at his brother for leaving them last month to join the Marines, but mostly angry at his father. And he knew that was wrong. He knew his father was brave and strong and loved him. But still he felt angry, and he couldn't say why.

The new school was part of it. He was tired of being the outsider, tired of always being the new kid. Four moves in the seven years since he was old enough to start kindergarten. "It's part of the job of being a soldier's son," his mom always said. Well, he didn't choose the army; his dad did. But he was the one who always got the brunt of it. The name-calling, the cold shoulder, the pitying stares of his teachers, even when he wasn't one of just a few black kids in the school, but especially when, like now, he was. Months later, they'd come around. They always came around when they saw how good he was at sports. Even though he was small for a seventh grader, he could run faster and hit a baseball farther than all but a few high school kids.

He didn't want to wait months, though. Last night, he'd found something, rooting around in his brother's drawer while his mother was downstairs watching TV. Frankie had been looking for loose change but found something much better.

"Hurry up, Frankie, you're going to be late," his mother called up to him.

"In a minute." He stashed the prize from the night before in his pants pocket, then flew down the stairs. Before he even entered the kitchen, he could smell his favorite breakfast waiting for him—chocolate-chip waffles and a glass of milk. He glanced at his mother and saw her red-rimmed, puffy eyes. Every night this week, as he lay in his bed, he'd heard her crying in her room next door.

"Come on, now," she said. "The bus will be here in ten minutes."

Frankie poured syrup over the waffles and wolfed them down, then drank the milk. His mother wiped the milk mustache off his face, then brushed back the wisps of hair that had fallen on his forehead. He'd inherited his mother's golden-brown curls—a white person's hair, not his father's tightly coarse, dark-brown hair. He grabbed his backpack, kissed her good-bye, and ran out to the bus stop. At least they were living someplace warm now, he thought, as the sun beat down on him. For the first time, it wasn't army housing. So now, not only was he the new kid in school, but he was in a place where people weren't used to military kids. At least the house was nice, he thought. Nicer than army housing. And he liked the palm trees, especially the way the leafy fronds swooped around in the wind.

The bus came, and he took a seat in the back. Twenty minutes later, he arrived at Parkwood Middle School. He moved with the sea of students inside the building, ignored by all of them, and made his way to Miss Mather's classroom. He liked this teacher. She was young and pretty and, like him, had mocha-colored skin.

"Settle down, everyone," she said after five minutes had passed and kids were still twisting in their seats, talking to their friends—all except Frankie, who'd yet to find anyone to even say hi to in the hall in his first three weeks. Slowly the room quieted, and all eyes turned to the front. They began with the Pledge of Allegiance, and when they were back in their seats, the lessons started. Miss Mather taught them math and science. Then they would change rooms and go to

Mrs. Cromwell's class for English and history. Frankie loved math and science. He wanted to be a doctor one day.

"Frankie, are you with us today?" Miss Mather asked.

Only then did he realize that he'd been called on for an answer. The students around him giggled, and one boy muttered, "Dope." Frankie wasn't stupid—he was smart, very smart, his teachers had told his mother—but today his mind was on the prize in his pocket. He blushed and looked up at the board where an equation waited for its solution. Quickly he calculated the answer and then gave it to his teacher.

"Very good. Now tell the class how you solved it."

Frankie halfheartedly explained. It was easy for him, yet it was that very ease that kept him an outsider in the class. He forced himself to pay attention for the rest of the morning, just waiting for the lunch recess to finally arrive. When it did, he headed to the cafeteria. Instead of sitting alone at a table in the corner, as he usually did, he approached the group of boys he'd already identified as the cool kids in his class. They were the ones who pronounced whether a newcomer was okay or a pariah. He slid into a seat next to Tony Cuen, the leader of the group.

"Hey, what are you doing here, dweeb?"

"I got something," Frankie said, ignoring the insult. "Thought you guys might be interested."

"You don't have anything we'd want." Tony laughed, then turned away from him.

Frankie glanced around the room, careful to make sure no teacher was watching, then pulled a plastic bag from his pocket. Inside were two rolled-up joints. "You smoke one of these before?"

Tony shot a look at what Frankie had in his hand. "Sure, lots of times."

Frankie didn't know whether that was true or not. He'd never smoked weed himself. Thought it was stupid. But he could always pretend to inhale. "Want to smoke it after school?"

Tony looked at his friends sitting around the table, and Frankie caught him winking at them. "Sure," Tony said. "We'll meet you over in Windham Park when school lets out."

Frankie didn't know what the wink meant. He figured he'd find out when he got to the park.

—

An hour later, Frankie sat in the principal's office, tapping his foot nervously as drops of sweat trickled down his sides. He'd never been in trouble before, not in any school he'd attended, and felt ashamed to be sitting before this woman whose mouth had been turned down in a frown ever since he'd walked into her office. He shuddered to think what his mother would say when she found out.

"I realize you're new to this school, Frankie," Mrs. Whitman said, "but we're no different from any school nowadays. We have a zero-tolerance policy when it comes to drugs. I'm afraid I'm going to have to notify the police."

Now the tears he'd struggled to hold back ever since nice Miss Mather had frowned at him and sent him to the principal flowed freely down his cheeks.

"Of course, we'll call your mother as well," Mrs. Whitman continued. She shook her head and said, almost in wonderment, "I'd heard such good things about you from your teachers. You're the last one I expected to be fooling around with drugs."

Frankie sat on the chair, numb, all feeling in his arms and legs gone. All he could think about was how he'd been tricked by those boys, the ones he'd wanted to become friends with.

"Do you have anything to say for yourself?"

Frankie shook his head.

"Well, you'll have to talk to the police."

He wouldn't talk to the police, of that he was certain. He definitely wouldn't tell them where he found the marijuana. If he did, the Marines might kick Bobby out of the service before he even finished basic training, and Frankie wouldn't risk that happening to his brother. Bobby had talked of nothing else his senior year of high school. It had been his dream to serve his country as a Marine, and he'd finally left three weeks ago for basic training. No, Frankie wouldn't talk. No matter what it meant for him.

———

"Jessica Bishop's on line one," Bruce Kantor's assistant said on his intercom.

Bruce quickly pressed the key for line one. "Any news?"

"Not about Alex. Frankie's been arrested."

That was the last thing Bruce ever thought he'd hear. "For what?"

"He brought marijuana to school."

"Frankie? He's smoking pot?"

"He insists he found it in the street. And Bruce, I'd know if he was using. I saw it enough with Bobby."

"Okay. Where's he now?"

"They sent him to a detention center."

"You need a lawyer. He'll get him out."

"Can you represent him?"

Bruce thought about it. It would be easy to hop on a plane to Florida. Arrange for Frankie's release. Return when a hearing was held. But he truly believed the old warning that a lawyer who represented himself had a fool for a client, and he thought that applied to representing family members as well. He was too close to them to be objective, and that's what a lawyer had to be. If something went wrong, he'd always blame himself, and they'd always blame him.

"You don't want me. You need someone who's in juvenile court all the time. I'll check around and call you back with an attorney's name."

"Thank you, Bruce."

"It'll be okay. Don't worry." As Bruce said that, he knew it would be impossible for her. Still, Frankie was a good kid with an unblemished record. A good lawyer would get Frankie off with a stern warning. He was certain of that.

TWO MONTHS LATER

D ani Trumball sat on the edge of the bathtub and stared at the blue-and-white stick in her hand. *It's not possible. It can't be.* She'd been sitting in the same position for five minutes, her eyes fixed on the digital readout, unable to move. "Pregnant—3+ weeks," it said. *It must be wrong. I'm in early menopause, that's all.* Even as she thought this, she knew she was kidding herself. Morning nausea didn't accompany menopause. She shook her head. Jonah was almost fourteen. She and Doug were long finished with sleepless nights and dirty diapers.

Once, she'd wanted a big family. Growing up an only child, she'd longed for brothers and sisters. But when Jonah was diagnosed with Williams syndrome, a disorder that caused cognitive difficulties, she and Doug decided they needed to focus all their attention on him. *Oh, Lord, what's Doug going to think? And Jonah? And HIPP—how much can I cut back before it just makes more sense to step away entirely?* Questions without answers swirled through her mind, rooting her to the bathtub edge. Doug had already left for work, Jonah for school. She was alone in the house, alone with her worries.

Finally she forced herself up and finished readying herself for work. She drove into HIPP's East Village office, a luxury she could indulge in from her suburban house in Bronxville only because she left home after the morning rush hour and left work before the evening one. She worked from home during the evenings to make up for time not spent in the office.

She pulled into the parking garage forty minutes later, then stopped at the corner deli for the best coffee in Manhattan—even if it now had to be decaf—and a jelly doughnut, her craving for something sweet overpowering her vow to reduce her sugar intake. Once she stepped off the elevator and entered HIPP's offices, Bruce Kantor ambushed her before she even got to her own office. She took one look at his sunken eyes and knew immediately something was wrong.

"Can you come in my office?" he said, his voice low.

"Of course." Dani stepped inside, placed her coffee cup and doughnut on his desk, and removed her coat. "What's going on?"

"I got a call from my sister-in-law last night. My nephew was sent to a juvenile prison two months ago. In Florida—it's where they live. Every Saturday she visits him, but she went this past Saturday, and he wasn't there."

"Where was he?"

"That's just it. No one would tell her. She's called every day since then and gotten the runaround each time. Since my half brother's still MIA, she's all alone. She's frantic."

"I would be, too. What can I do to help?"

Bruce kneaded the back of his neck, then stood up and walked to the window, the only one in their entire office space. He stared outside for a moment, then turned back to Dani. "It's my fault. She asked me to represent him, and I turned her down. Thought I'd be too close to the situation. Instead, I gave her the name of an attorney I'd heard was good."

"That was the right thing to do. It's never a good idea to represent family."

Bruce shook his head. "I was just so upset about my brother, I didn't want to deal with another problem. And now this."

"It's probably just some mix-up with the records."

"I should be down there. But I'm starting a trial tomorrow, and we've already had one continuance. The judge won't permit another."

Dani understood all too well how it felt to be pulled in opposite directions by work and family. "I have nothing pressing now, Bruce. Would you like me to fly down to Florida and find out what's going on?"

Dani could see Bruce's body physically relax. "Would you? I'd really appreciate it. I'll pay for the airfare."

"Of course. Tell me about your nephew. What did he do?"

"He's only twelve and got caught with marijuana in school. He'd been having a hard time since learning his father was MIA, but Jessica insists he's never been in trouble before, and I know he's a straight-A student. I can't fathom why he was sent away for that. It should have been supervision at most. I spoke to Frankie's attorney about an appeal, but he thought it would be pointless. And it was just four months. Jessica had been so distraught about Alex, and then Frankie . . . I thought it'd be better to just let him get the sentence over with, and maybe by then we'd have some word on Alex." He shook his head again. "I should have known better."

"I'll fly down tomorrow. Nothing else is on my plate." *Nothing but a pregnancy I'm unprepared for.*

"Thanks, Dani. And see what Tommy's schedule is like. It might be good for him to go with you."

———

It was nine o'clock—"honeymoon hour," when Dani and Doug set aside whatever they were doing and retreated to the living-room couch. No television, no work, just time to spend with each other. Dani had put off telling Doug until now. She wasn't sure how he'd react. It had taken all day for her to come to grips with how she felt about it.

"I have some news," Dani said.

"Good news, I hope."

"I'm not sure."

"Well, now you have me intrigued. Spill."

Dani turned to look directly into Doug's eyes. She loved his eyes. Large, deep set, cerulean blue. She couldn't help but be drawn into them. She took his hands in hers. "I'm pregnant."

A flicker of something passed over Doug's face. Was it displeasure? Happiness? She couldn't tell. Maybe confusion, like she'd felt.

For a long while, he said nothing, then finally asked, "Are you certain?"

"Well, I haven't been to the doctor yet, but the home test was positive. How do you feel about it?"

"We made the decision a long time ago to stop with Jonah."

"Yes, but look where he is now. He's doing so well, thriving even." An image popped into Dani's mind of the symphony Jonah had composed, recently performed by the Westchester Philharmonic. Thinking about it still gave her goose bumps. Like many Williams syndrome children, Jonah had demonstrated very early extraordinary musical talent.

"So . . ." Doug paused again. "You want this baby?"

"I think I do."

"What about work?"

"I'll take time off. Not nine years, like I did with Jonah. Maybe six months. We have Katie now. I'm hoping she'll agree to work longer hours and care for the baby during the day. And maybe I can do more work from home. Go back to just appeals, instead of handling cases from inception."

Doug sighed deeply. "I'm forty-seven, Dani."

"And I'm forty-five," she said with a smile. "Believe me, I'm aware."

His answering smile wasn't a strong one. "Well, you've had a chance to think about it. I haven't yet, but I have to tell you, I'm worried about being able to deal with the demands of an infant all over again." He looked away. "I don't know that I want to."

Dani felt a rise of anger, then tamped it down. "Then don't. I'll do it all."

That earned her a look. "The baby would have its own ideas about that," he said, "and you know it. But that aside, it's not that simple."

"Why not?"

"Because we're finally at that stage of our lives when we can have more freedom, Dani. Last winter was the first time we've taken a vacation with just the two of us since Jonah was born. I want that. I want to know that complete freedom is within sight, not twenty years away."

"You want me to have an abortion?"

After what felt like an impossibly long, still moment, Doug said, "I don't know. Just . . . it's something to consider."

Dani began to cry. Hormones starting in on me already, she thought. Doug pulled her close and wrapped his arms around her. "Just think about how disruptive a baby will be," he whispered in her ear.

"Yes. A baby is disruptive. And I'll think about that. But only if you promise to think about how wonderful a baby is, also."

"I will."

Dani couldn't remember the last time she and Doug had disagreed; it had been so long ago. Probably over something minor, she thought. Not something as important as this. Dani had started the morning unsure of how she felt about the pregnancy. But now, she realized she had no doubts at all. She wanted this child.

4

The next morning, Dani and Tommy Noorland, her favorite investigator at HIPP, flew to Tampa International Airport. She always felt safe in Tommy's presence, and not only because of his years with the FBI. With his six-foot-two-inch frame and muscular build, he could take on almost anyone who threatened them. After they landed, they drove their rental car north to Key Vista, a small community near the Gulf where Jessica Bishop lived. She was waiting for them in front of her home when they arrived, and she grabbed Dani's hands as soon as Dani exited the car.

"Thank goodness you're here. I don't know what to do. I'm so frightened."

Dani looked over the thin woman dressed in jeans and a T-shirt. Her thickly lashed eyes had dark circles underneath, and her face, although pretty, looked pale. "Let's go inside, and you can fill us in. Bruce didn't tell us much."

"Of course, of course, pardon my manners," Jessica said as she led them into the two-story stucco home. It was in a gated community, with winding roads lined with feathery palm trees and tropical plants.

Once inside, she offered them drinks.

"No, thanks," Dani said. "Let's just talk first."

Jessica led them into the living room, furnished simply with a rattan couch and two chairs, a wooden table in between. The windows were covered with sheer white curtains. "I rent this house. It's just temporary," she said as she took one of the chairs. "At least I hope so. We've only been here a few months."

"It's very nice," Dani said. She sat back on the couch. "Why don't you start from the beginning, with your son's arrest? I understand he brought some marijuana to school."

"It was so stupid. He just wanted to fit in. That's all."

"Was this the first time?"

"Of course. He'd only been in the school a few weeks. He'd never even smoked pot."

Tommy cut in from his seat beside Dani. "Sometimes kids do things we don't know about. They can be pretty secretive when it comes to parents."

"Trust me, I know what a kid looks like when he's smoking pot. Or any other drug. My older son, Bobby, he was another story. I caught him high plenty of times."

"Could Bobby have shared it with Frankie?" Dani asked.

"My boys couldn't be more different, but the one thing they have in common is their devotion to each other. Bobby would never do anything to hurt Frankie, and that includes giving him drugs."

"Where is Bobby now?" Tommy asked.

"He just finished basic training at Camp Lejeune, and he's been assigned to remain there. He joined the Marines one week after we moved here."

Dani leaned forward. "I'm surprised Frankie was adjudicated a delinquent and sent away. Bruce told me he'd never been in trouble before." Dani had wondered if there was more to the story than Jessica had let on—even to her brother-in-law. Despite Jessica's protestations, perhaps Frankie *had* been using pot. Perhaps even selling it. She knew that many states, including Florida, imposed harsher penalties when drugs were sold near a school. Inside a school would certainly set off alarms.

Jessica had been nodding as Dani spoke. "That's what his attorney said. He promised me that it would be dismissed, maybe not immediately but after a few months of good behavior." Her hands fluttered as she spoke but now stopped to brush back one of the golden-brown curls that had fallen over her eyes. "Only, when we got to court for the hearing, he changed his tune. Said this judge was known for being harsh." Jessica dropped her head into her hands, and Dani could see tears falling onto her shirt.

When Jessica looked up, she said, her voice strained, "I'm afraid something terrible has happened to Frankie."

Dani rose from the couch and moved to Jessica, sitting down in the chair next to hers. "I'm sure it's just an administrative error. Probably some new clerk mistyped the list of names. We'll get it straightened out this afternoon."

"You don't understand."

Dani looked at her quizzically and waited.

"Things have happened there. Bad things."

"What do you mean?"

Jessica ran her fingers through her hair. "The last time I visited Frankie, he told me what went on there. I wanted to go to the State, report them, but he begged me not to. Said they'd just take it out on him."

Dani went back to her briefcase on the floor by the couch, took out a legal pad and pen, then returned to Jessica. "I need you to tell me everything Frankie said."

"There was a boy. Older than Frankie. In the room across the hall from him. He was having trouble breathing and begged the guard to let him see the doctor. The guard laughed at him and called him a sissy, then shoved him down to the floor and made him do push-ups. When he collapsed the guard kicked him, over and over again."

"How does Frankie know this?"

"He saw it. Their doors were open. Frankie didn't want to talk about it, but I could sense something was bothering him. I kept pushing him until he finally told me. Or whispered it to me. He clearly was afraid. He said the guard made Frankie and a group of kids in the hall watch him kick the boy, and when he finished, he told them that's what happens when they don't obey him."

"How awful."

"There's more. The next morning, Frankie's stomach bothered him, so he didn't go to breakfast. He saw two guards go into this boy's room, and a few minutes later they carried him out, wrapped in a sheet. He was dead. Frankie heard through the grapevine that they said he died of pneumonia."

Dani's hand flew up to her mouth. How could such barbarism exist, especially in a facility for children? It seemed incomprehensible to her. She felt the stirrings of nausea and wondered if it was the story or her pregnancy. Without thinking, she dropped her hands to her stomach, as though they could protect the growing child within her.

"Have you spoken to Frankie's attorney about his disappearance?"

"He was the first person I called. He suggested I phone the state Department of Juvenile Justice."

"And did you?"

Jessica nodded. "They checked their records and said Frankie should be there." Jessica gazed up at Dani, a pleading look in her eyes. "What if they've done something to Frankie?" she asked, her voice choked by a sob. "What if they've killed him?"

"Don't think like that. We'll get this straightened out. I'm sure Frankie's okay." Dani fervently hoped it was true, but hearing Jessica's story, she feared that a guard who would do what Jessica described was capable of anything. Even killing a twelve-year-old boy who'd brought marijuana to school in the hopes of winning a friend.

———

Two hours later, Dani, Tommy, and Jessica walked into the visitors' entrance of Eldridge Academy. A strange name to call a juvenile prison, Dani thought. *Makes it sound like an elite private school.* Still, the fenced-in building with locked doors left no doubt that its young residents were deprived of their liberty. Dani walked up to the visitors' desk and identified herself to the matronly woman in a guard's uniform who was seated there. She handed the woman her card. "We're here to see Francis Bishop."

"Visiting is on Saturdays only. Come back tomorrow."

"I'm here as his attorney. Visiting-day rules don't apply."

The woman turned to her computer and typed in his name, then looked back at Dani. "Sorry, he's not available."

Dani could feel her temper rise, then consciously strove to control it. Getting angry with this woman wouldn't get her anywhere. It was doubtful she had any authority. "Can you tell me what that means? When will he be available?"

The woman shrugged. "I only know what it says here. Next time, I suggest you call before making the trip."

"I'd like to see Warden Cummings."

"You have an appointment?"

Dani smiled at the woman sweetly. "I'm going to assume you're just following standard protocol. But here's what's going to happen. Either you buzz the warden and let him know we need to speak to him, or I head straight to federal court and file a petition for habeas corpus." Dani figured the woman already knew this compelled the facility to produce a body. "From there, I'm going to hold a press conference and say that a boy under the warden's charge was brutally mistreated by one of the guards and died as a result."

Dani could see the color drain from the woman's face. Dani knew this was a dangerous gambit. Frankie had been afraid the guards would overhear him tell Jessica about the incident, no doubt because of retaliation. Now she was making it clear he'd reported it to his mother. But something was going on with Frankie. Maybe they'd already retaliated. Better to let the warden know that an attorney was on board and would hold him responsible if anything happened to the boy. She turned around and saw that Jessica looked just as pale as the guard.

"I'll see if he's available. Wait over there." The guard motioned toward a group of chairs near the front door, and Dani headed over there, along with Tommy and Jessica.

"It'll be okay," Dani whispered to Jessica while they waited.

The woman picked up a phone. She hung up a few moments later, then motioned Dani back. "Someone will come and bring you to his office."

Two minutes later, a male guard entered the reception area. The woman pointed to Dani's group, and he came over to them. "I'll take you to see Warden Cummings, but he's a very busy man. You'll have just five minutes with him."

They passed through an X-ray machine, first emptying their pockets and placing their bags on the conveyer belt, then through a locked door into a hallway. The guard led them to the end, then knocked on a door before opening it and stepping inside. Dani, Tommy, and Jessica followed him. Seated behind a desk was a woman dressed in civilian clothes. Her gray hair was cropped short, and her black-rimmed glasses covered her eyes. A nameplate on her desk read "Anne Hancock." She looked up at them and, without a smile, said, "You can go on in. Warden Cummings is expecting you."

Dani opened the door and entered, the others following right behind. The room was large but barren. Minimal furnishings and walls bare of pictures. Warden Joe Cummings stood up from his desk and held out his hand.

"Thank you for meeting with us," Dani said as she shook it, then handed him her business card and introduced him to the others.

Cummings turned to Jessica. "I understand your son is supposed to be here."

"He was here for two months until last week, and now no one can tell me where he is."

"I'm sure it's some clerical error. I suspect he was transferred to another facility."

"But why?"

"There are lots of different reasons why someone is transferred. I'll check into it and find out for you where he is? I'm sure I can get an answer for you in a day or two."

Dani looked over at Jessica, who nodded tentatively at her. "I think one day should be sufficient for you to locate a twelve-year-old boy," Dani said to the warden.

"There's one other thing, Ms. Trumball," the warden said.

"Yes?"

"I understand you've made some allegations about abusive behavior by one of our guards."

"Yes. I did."

The warden's eyes hardened as he glared first at Dani, then at each of the others. "I don't tolerate that behavior in my facility, and the staff knows that well. The residents who end up here are troubled children, prone to making up stories. I wouldn't look kindly on anyone who went around repeating them."

The threat in the warden's words and his tone of voice were clear. Mess with him, and there would be repercussions, if not for Jessica, then for her son.

His smile returned. "Now, Mrs. Bishop, leave your phone number with my assistant outside, and I'll give you a call as soon as I locate Francis."

They left the warden's office and stopped at his assistant's desk. The guard who'd escorted them there was waiting by the door.

"Warden Cummings asked me to leave my phone number with you," Jessica said to the assistant. She reached into her purse and took out a business card, then wrote some numbers on the back. "Here's my cell phone number and home number."

The assistant picked up a card that she'd had by her hand. "And here's Warden Cummings's direct phone number, in case you need to call him again." She handed it over to Jessica, still unsmiling.

Dani held out her hand. "Why don't you give it to me? I think it's best if I'm the one who calls the warden." As Jessica handed it over, Dani glimpsed scribbling on the back. She brought it closer to her eyes and read, "Check local hospitals." She swung around to look at the assistant. She sat upright in her chair, her face expressionless, although her eyes seemed to say, "Don't say a word."

As soon as they cleared the compound, Dani showed Jessica and Tommy the message on the card, then watched as Jessica's face drained of color.

"What have they done to him?" Jessica's hands were wrapped tightly around her body, as though they could control her shaking.

"Do you know where the closest hospitals are?" Dani asked.

As Jessica shook her head, Tommy announced, "Got it." He held his smartphone in his hand and read off from it, "Mercy Hospital and Emporium General. Mercy is the closer of the two."

The three practically ran to the car. Tommy hopped in the driver's seat and set the GPS on the dashboard for Mercy Hospital. They arrived twenty minutes later. Once inside the three-story building, they approached the receptionist seated behind a window.

"Do you have a Francis Bishop here?" Jessica asked.

The receptionist typed his name into a computer. "Sorry, he's not at this hospital."

"How about Frankie or Frank Bishop?"

"Nope. Not here."

Dani put her hand on Jessica's shoulder. "Don't get discouraged. We'll try Emporium."

As Jessica and Dani started to walk out the door, Tommy stopped them. "Maybe we should call over there first. Give them Frankie's name."

Dani nodded, and Tommy dialed the number, first moving away from the door to a quieter spot. A few moments later, he returned. "No one by that name there either."

Jessica began to cry, first just tears streaming down her face, then loud, heaving sobs. She sunk down to the ground, cradling her body with her arms. Dani bent down next to her. She knew it was pointless to try and comfort this mother. No amount of soothing words would erase the terror she no doubt felt over her son's safety. Instead, Dani sat next to her until the sobs subsided.

"I'm sorry," Jessica said, as she stood up.

"I'm a mother, too. I understand."

Tommy had stayed off to the side as the two women were collapsed on the walkway. Now he approached Jessica. "Do you have a picture of Frankie with you?"

Jessica nodded, then took out her cell phone, clicked on "Photos," and scrolled to one of Frankie.

"Let's go back inside and speak to the receptionist again." Tommy took the cell phone with him, and when he reached the window, slid it over to the woman. "Is it possible you recognize this boy?" he asked. "He would have been brought here from Eldridge Academy."

The woman took the phone in her hand and stared at it, then slipped it back to Tommy. "I'm sorry. If he came in through the emergency room or admitting, I wouldn't have seen him."

Tommy nodded, then started to walk away.

"Wait a minute," the receptionist called after him. "Let me call up to the pediatrics floor. Maybe they know something."

Tommy stood by as the woman spoke to someone at the nurse's station. When she hung up, she said, "No one was brought in from the detention center."

Tommy thanked her, then walked back to Dani and Jessica, shaking his head as he approached. "He's not here."

Dani looked closely at Jessica. Her eyes were swollen from crying, her face was flushed, and her hands still trembled. "It's almost six o'clock. I think we should go back to your home. We can make a list of all the hospitals within a two-hour radius of Eldridge Academy and call them. If we get a hit, we'll leave early tomorrow morning and drive there. If we don't locate him, then I'll have someone from my office draw up papers for a motion in federal court."

Jessica nodded, but said nothing. Dani slipped her arm inside Jessica's and led her to the car. They drove back in silence.

—

As soon as they arrived, Jessica ran into her house and made a beeline for the computer. It was already dark outside, past dinnertime. Although she hadn't had anything to eat since breakfast, the thought of food made her nauseous. During the entire two-hour drive back from the hospital, she'd felt like she couldn't breathe. The fear that had gripped her the past six days now exploded in her chest. Quickly, she turned on the computer, tapping her foot restlessly while she waited for it to boot up. Once it was ready, she did a Google search for all hospitals within eighty miles of Eldridge Academy. There were six.

She printed out three copies of the listing, then gave one page each to Dani and Tommy. *Thank heavens for Bruce. Thank heavens he sent me help.* Although she'd always thought of herself as a strong woman, she was grateful for the presence of the two HIPP representatives. They were resolute in their assurances that they'd find Frankie, that they wouldn't give up until they had. She thought she might have collapsed in a heap without them and stayed frozen in that spot, unable to face her greatest fear of all.

They each took two hospitals to call. Jessica dialed the first and pressed the numbers prompted by the recording for patient information. When she reached a live person, she asked, "Do you have a patient there by the name of Francis or Frank Bishop?"

"Hold on, I'll check."

A minute later, the woman was back on the line. "We have no one listed by that name. Were you told he was here?"

"I was told he's in a hospital, but not which one. Do you have any children who were brought there from Eldridge Academy?"

"I wouldn't have that information. I'll put you through to the pediatrics floor."

After four rings, the phone was answered. "Pediatrics."

"My name is Jessica Bishop. My son was taken to a hospital from Eldridge Academy, but I don't know which one. Do you have a twelve-year-old boy who came from there?"

"Sorry, Mrs. Bishop. We don't have any twelve-year-old boys here right now."

"Thank you," Jessica mumbled as she hung up the phone. She looked over at Dani and Tommy, and they shook their heads at her. They, too, had struck out with the first calls they'd made. She dialed the next number and went through the same routine, with the same results. As she hung up, she glanced at Dani and saw a beaming smile as she held the phone to her ear. Jessica ran over to Dani's side, and Dani held up her thumb.

As soon as Dani got off the phone, she said, "We've found him. He's at Crescent Hills Regional Hospital."

"What happened to him?" Jessica asked, as she steeled her body for the news.

"He was in a fight at Eldridge. He had internal bleeding and a ruptured spleen. Also has some broken ribs and a lot of bruising."

"Did they operate to remove his spleen?" Tommy asked.

"No. The nurse said they kept him in the hospital, confined to a bed, and monitored him. It seems the bleeding has finally stopped, and he should be released in another day or two."

"We have to go there, right now," Jessica said.

"How far is Crescent Hills from here?"

Jessica paused as she tried to picture it on a map. "About three hours. Maybe a little more."

"It's too late. We wouldn't get there until after eleven. They won't let you in at that time. We can leave early tomorrow morning."

"Then I need to call his room, speak to him, right now." Jessica reached for her phone. but Dani's hand on hers stopped her.

"I asked them to patch me through to his room," Dani said. "Because he's confined at Eldridge Academy, the phone in his room isn't activated."

"But I'm his mother." Jessica knew she sounded like a pleading child but couldn't help it. None of this made sense to her. Frankie wasn't a fighter, never had been. Why would another child have done this to him? She needed to be by his side, cradle him in her arms, protect him from further harm. "I'm going tonight. I'll wait in the lobby if I have to."

"I know you're worried, but you look exhausted, you haven't eaten, and I bet you haven't slept much lately. I don't think it's safe for you to get back in the car and drive three hours," Dani said. "We can leave early in the morning and drive you there. I promise, you'll see him tomorrow."

Reluctantly, Jessica agreed. She was too tired to fight them.

Frankie had struggled to stay awake, but with all the medicines coursing through his body, he had succumbed. He awoke with a start and saw it was still dark outside. The clock on the wall read 4:10 a.m. Two hours later than he'd wanted. Still, he could make it work.

When the doctor made his rounds yesterday, he'd told Frankie he was healing nicely. Frankie already knew that. He no longer had pain on the left side of his stomach, or in his left shoulder. Two days earlier, the nurses had started to let him get out of bed when he needed to go to the bathroom, and his light-headedness was gone. It still hurt when he took a deep breath, but the doctor had told him it would take six weeks for his ribs to heal. They wouldn't keep him in the hospital for that long, Frankie knew. No, if his spleen had healed, they would send him back to Eldridge. And if that happened, Frankie feared he wouldn't leave there alive.

Frankie had learned how to get by during his two months at Eldridge Academy. After his hearing, he'd been held in custody at the courthouse before he'd been transferred to Eldridge. He'd heard stories about the place then, about what some of the older boys did to the smaller and weaker ones. But they'd let him alone. It hadn't taken long for them to realize he was smart, even smarter than the older boys. He began doing the homework of a few of the strongest ones, and they put the word out that he was to be left alone. They couldn't help with the guards, though. Some were nice, but most were mean. Frankie tried his best to stay out of their way.

Everyone inside had nicknames. He was called Einstein. He sort of liked that. Cougar was his roommate, a year older and many years wiser when it came to the operations of Eldridge. Unlike Frankie, he'd been in and out of trouble for years, getting suspended from school three times and landing on home supervision twice. Cougar, taller than Frankie by four inches, with thirty more pounds on his bones, had taken Frankie under his wing, teaching him how things worked at Eldridge—how to stay away from the eyes of the older boys, and how to curry the guards' favor.

Frankie had come back from a visit with his mom two weeks earlier and told Cougar what she'd said about Munchie, the boy who'd died. "My mom said the guards who kicked him could go to prison for what they did." As soon as the words came out of his mouth, Frankie knew he'd made a mistake. A serious one. Cougar had taught Frankie to keep his eyes open and his mouth shut, no matter what he saw. He'd realized too late that applied to what he told Cougar as well.

Frankie had seen plenty. He saw kids kicked and punched by guards while they were handcuffed and helpless. He saw kids stripped naked and marched to solitary confinement, not to resurface until weeks later. He saw a kid who'd refused an order to throw his cup in the trash on his way out of the cafeteria get his elbow broken in a guard's stronghold. He saw another guard attack a fifteen-year-old boy by slamming his head to the floor and punching him. Frankie heard the kid complain that he couldn't breathe, and watched as the guard placed his hand over the boy's mouth. None of the guards tried to hide their abuse. They only made sure it was done out of sight of security cameras.

Sometimes, instead of inflicting abuse themselves, the guards used older boys to send a message. When they did, the boys were rewarded. Sometimes with extra food, sometimes with drugs, sometimes just more TV time.

Until his blunder with Cougar, Frankie had stayed out of their way. He obeyed their instructions and did his work. He went to drug-counseling sessions and pretended he'd smoked weed, not because he had, but because refusing to admit it subjected him to deprivations. The already meager portions of food at mealtimes would be reduced. He wouldn't be allowed to watch TV in the communal room. His time outside the building, shortened. So he gave them what they wanted, and he got along.

The day after admitting to Cougar that he'd told his mother about Munchie, he was cornered coming out of counseling by four older boys, members of the Latino group. There were only two groups at Eldridge: Latino or black. There weren't enough white boys there to make up a third group. They were more than six feet tall and bursting with muscles. "Hey, shrimp," one had called to him. "You got a big mouth, I hear."

Frankie tried to shrink away from them, but he was quickly surrounded.

"Momma's boy couldn't keep his mouth shut, could he?"

"I made a mistake. But she won't say anything. She promised," Frankie had told them.

"Maybe. Maybe not. Big Joe don't like what you did, though. Says you need to be taught a lesson."

Big Joe was the warden. Frankie knew he was in trouble. The biggest of the four threw him to the ground, then they all started kicking him in his stomach, his chest, his face, his legs. He didn't think he'd survive, but suddenly, he heard a voice behind them say, "That's enough." They left him on the ground, bleeding, barely conscious. He lay there, he didn't know how long. After some time, through the fog that was his mind, he heard footsteps approach, then felt hands lift him onto a gurney that rolled out of the building and into an ambulance. He heard a voice say, "Not the local hospitals. Take him to Crescent Hill." Before the ambulance pulled away, the voice leaned over him and whispered in his ear, "Snitches don't survive inside here." It was the last thing he heard until the bright lights of the emergency room awakened him.

—

Now, ten days later, Frankie knew he couldn't return to Eldridge. He also knew he couldn't return to his mother. That would be the first place they'd look. His only hope was getting to his brother somehow at Camp Lejeune, in Jacksonville, North Carolina. Bobby would know what to do.

Since being allowed out of bed, Frankie had first checked the closet to see what clothes were there. The ones he'd worn when brought to the hospital were covered with blood. Someone must have brought over a new set, though, because a fresh pair of chinos and a T-shirt emblazoned with the words "Eldridge Academy" were hanging there. He could turn the shirt inside out to hide the words. It would get him by until he got a new one. The past two nights, he'd strolled by the nurse's station at midnight. One nurse sat there, not the four or five who usually bustled about. Each night her head was buried in a book. Each night, Frankie stealthily crept down the hallway in the opposite direction to the staircase marked "Exit." She never noticed, not when he left, or when he returned.

He climbed out of bed and shed his hospital gown and pulled on the clothes hanging in the closet. His sneakers were on the floor, his socks tucked inside them. There was no jacket, and he suspected it might be cold outside. Although temperatures in early spring usually warmed up to the seventies and eighties, it could dip into the fifties at night in this part of Florida. He knew just where he was. Yesterday, when the nurses were busy elsewhere, he'd made his way to the visitors' lounge and logged on to the computer there. With a few clicks, he'd located the hospital's town on a map and figured out his route north.

Frankie eased his head out of the doorway and glanced down the corridor toward the nurse's station. Peggy was on duty overnight, and as usual, her head was bent over a book. He crept silently past the other hospital rooms, and once he reached the end of the corridor, quietly opened the door to the stairs. The tricky part, he knew, would be once he got to the lobby. He walked slowly down the three floors, the pain from his broken ribs still sharp. When he reached the bottom, he opened the door just a notch to get his bearings. He breathed a sigh of relief when he saw that it emptied out into a quiet corridor rather than the lobby itself. He stepped out, glanced around, and saw at the end of the hallway a door with a lit "Exit" sign over it. He walked toward it, then stopped. What if an alarm went off? He couldn't take a chance. He'd need to go through the lobby. As he followed the signs to the main entrance, he passed a door marked "Maintenance." He put his hand on the doorknob, and it opened to a small room filled with cleaning-equipment trolleys. On each was a bucket and a mop, a broom, and dustcloths. Against one wall were shelves. On one were neatly folded pants and shirts with the insignia of Acme Maintenance. He stepped inside and closed the door behind him, then sifted through the clothes looking for the smallest sizes. When he found what he needed, he put them on over his own clothes, rolled up the pants legs so they wouldn't drag along the floor, then headed back out. As he turned the last corner, he saw the brightly lit lobby with a reception desk. An elderly man sat behind it.

Here goes, Frankie thought as he walked confidently into the room.

"All finished?" the man at the desk said as Frankie walked by.

Frankie nodded and waved, too afraid that if he spoke, his child's voice would give him away. As he approached the large glass doors to freedom, he kept expecting to be called back. Instead, the doors opened automatically, and he walked outside into the cool evening air.

I'm free, he thought. *I'm free.*

"Sir, Crescent Hills Regional Hospital is on the phone," Joe Cummings's assistant told him.

"What do they want?"

"It's about Francis Bishop."

Cummings shooed his assistant out of the room, then picked up the phone. "This is Warden Cummings."

"Good morning. This is Dr. LaGrange. I'm sorry to tell you, but Francis Bishop has disappeared. Apparently, he snuck out of the hospital sometime between eleven p.m. and seven this morning."

"What the f—?" Cummings stopped himself before completing the expletive. "How the hell did that happen?"

"His spleen had healed, and he would have been discharged this afternoon. He no longer needed to be hooked up to monitoring equipment, so the nurse's station wasn't alerted when he left his room."

"Are the people working there incompetent? You let a twelve-year-old boy outsmart you? He was in juvenile detention for a reason. You were supposed to secure him."

"We're a hospital, not a prison. If you needed him watched over, you should have camped someone outside his door. Our job was to heal him, and we did that."

"All right, all right. Look, do you have cameras that can tell you exactly when he left?"

"We do, and you're welcome to send someone over to look at them. Our staff doesn't have the time to do that."

"Fine. Someone will be there this morning."

"Just one other thing. I'm told his mother called last night and learned he was here. She's planning on driving in this morning."

Now Cummings didn't hold back. "Fuck," he said, then slammed down the phone.

—

There were few things that scared Joe Cummings. He'd always been big for his age, stronger than most, and not shy about showing it. As he grew up, the confidence he'd had as a child continued into adulthood. When he spoke, others listened. All except Roger Wilcox. The man frightened him. Reluctantly, Cummings picked up the phone and dialed his boss.

When Wilcox got on the line, he said, "You must have bad news for me. It's not the day for your weekly update."

"I do. It's something I probably should have told you earlier, but I thought I had it handled."

"Go ahead."

"The kid, the one who died of pneumonia?"

"Yeah."

"He was helped along by a few of the guards."

"What does that mean?" Wilcox asked, his voice stonily cold.

"He kept asking to see the doctor. I thought he was faking it, so I put it off. Figured a few days wouldn't make a difference. But two of my men forced him to do push-ups, to test him. They may have roughed him up a bit, too. Some kicks, I understand."

"Shit." There was silence for a few beats. "Yes, you should have told me. Paperwork just says he died of pneumonia, right?"

"Of course."

"So, that's our story."

"There's more. A bunch of kids saw him being kicked around by the guards. One of them told his mother."

More silence. Then, "Have you taken care of the kid?"

"I did. He received a strong lesson on keeping quiet. A bit too strong. He ended up in the hospital. I figured, when he returned, I'd reinforce the message with a stern warning."

"What do you mean, 'you figured'?"

"He's gone. Ran away from the hospital during the night."

A litany of shouted curses erupted over the phone. When Wilcox calmed down, he asked, "Wasn't there a guard posted outside his room?"

"The kid is only twelve, inside for drugs. It's not part of standard protocol to post a guard in that situation."

"What were you thinking? This wasn't a standard situation! How could you let a squealer alone like that?"

"Look, even if I'd posted someone there, he could have told his doctor or one of the nurses how he got his injuries. He didn't. I'm pretty sure he understood my message."

"'Pretty sure' doesn't cut it with me. Find the kid, get him back, or start looking for another job."

———

Jessica was on the road to Crescent Hill Regional Hospital by six a.m. She, Dani, and Tommy pulled into its parking lot three and a half hours later. They went inside the main entrance together and stopped at the reception desk. "I'd like the room of Francis Bishop," Jessica said.

The woman at the desk typed his name into the computer. "Room 302. Take the elevators to the left."

Jessica's anxiety was palpable. Ever since they'd left home, her heart had been racing. Only seeing her son could calm it down. They rode the elevator in silence, and when they stepped out on his floor, they followed the signs on the wall to his room. Jessica ran ahead of the others as she rushed to her son. When Dani and Tommy joined her inside Room 302, they found her staring at a neatly made empty bed. She turned and looked at Dani. "Where is he?"

"Reception must have given us the wrong room. Let's go ask at the nurse's station."

They retraced their steps and stopped before three nurses, two on the phone and one writing in a chart. Jessica waited for her to look up, tapping her foot the whole time, then said, "We're here to see Francis Bishop. Can you tell us what room he's in?"

"And you are?"

"I'm his mother."

The nurse glanced at the other two at the nurse's station, hesitated a bit, then looked Jessica directly in her eyes. "Why don't you wait in Room 302 just a minute? I'll get his doctor."

Jessica's hands began to tremble. "What's happened to him? Where's Frankie?"

Dani took her hand and, with her voice soft, said, "Let's go wait in the room." She led Jessica back there, and then she and Tommy took seats. Jessica couldn't sit down, not until she knew her son was okay, so she paced back and forth in the small space.

Ten minutes later, a balding man with tortoiseshell glasses and dressed in a sports jacket and tie entered the room.

"Mrs. Bishop?"

Jessica stopped her pacing and stared at him. "That's me. Where's Frankie?"

"Why don't you take a seat?"

"Just tell me. What happened to my son?"

"First, my name is Dr. LaGrange, and I treated Frankie. He's fine now. He came in with a seriously damaged spleen, several broken ribs, and considerable bruising. We were able to save the spleen, and once his ribs heal, he'll have no lasting injuries."

Jessica sunk down on the bed and grasped her hands together to stop their shaking, then quietly exhaled. "Thank goodness. But where is he?"

"I'm afraid I have some bad news. Frankie ran away this morning. We don't know where he is."

The first thought that ran through her head was, *Thank God he's not going back to that hellhole.* It was quickly replaced by fear. What would happen to him if the authorities found him before she did? What would they do to him? An image of Frankie, alone and scared, flashed through her mind. She needed to find him. She needed to protect him.

"Has Eldridge been notified that he's missing?" Dani asked Dr. LaGrange.

"Yes, they're aware of it."

"Do you have any idea when he left?"

"No. But Warden Cummings is sending someone over to review our security tapes."

Dani thanked the doctor, then sat down next to Jessica, who was hunched over on the bed, staring straight ahead. "Let's go home. That's probably where Frankie is headed."

"What if . . . what if he doesn't go back there? He'll know that's the first place they'd look."

"Where else could he go?"

Jessica looked up at Dani, then drew her close, so she could whisper in her ear. "He might try to get to Bobby. That's the only other place I can think of."

Dani turned to Dr. LaGrange and asked him for privacy. When he left the room, Dani asked Jessica why she thought that.

"Bobby always looked out for Frankie. He'd figure Bobby would know what to do." Suddenly, Jessica stood up and pulled at Dani's arm to raise her off the bed. "I've got to call him. I have to let him know. But not here. Not if they could be listening."

They quickly left the hospital, and as soon as they exited the lobby, Jessica called Bobby. He answered on the first ring.

"Everything okay, Mom? You usually don't call me this early."

Immediately, the tears began to stream down Jessica's cheeks. "Frankie's been hurt. He was beat up, they sent him to the hospital, and now he's run away."

Dani listened as Jessica filled Bobby in on everything she knew. When the call ended, Jessica heaved a sigh and said, "If he turns up there, Bobby will look out for him."

Dani and Tommy had come here to help Bruce's sister-in-law find out what happened to her child. Now Jessica knew. They drove her home, then headed to the airport for a flight back to New York. There was nothing more they could do in Florida.

Assistant Warden Fred Williamson finished looking at the hospital's security tapes, then placed a call to the warden. "Looks like he left the hospital at four twenty-two a.m."

"So that gives him about six hours on us. He can't have gotten too far."

"Unless he thumbed a ride."

"Could you see what he was wearing?"

"Looked like a cleaner's uniform. Probably has his prison clothes underneath."

"Well, if he caught a ride, we're out of luck. We've got to start creating our own narrative."

"What do you have in mind?"

There was silence for a few moments before the warden spoke again. "He was a troubled kid from the start, always picking fights with other boys, making up tall tales about them. He started a fight with a smaller boy, and others jumped in to stop it. That's how Francis landed in the hospital."

"You think that will fly?"

"It will when I tell the boys to back it up."

Sometimes Fred felt a twinge of guilt about his job. He'd worked his way up from one of the low-paid guards to his current position, a better job than he'd find elsewhere with just a GED diploma. It wasn't just that after ten years, he finally had decent pay. Being the warden's go-to man came with perks, and he didn't want to give them up. "You going to notify the Department about his escape?"

"I'll send in a report. In the meantime, why don't you take a ride around, see if you can spot him? His home is southeast of here, but he's a smart boy. Probably knows that's the first place we'd look. If I were him, I'd head to Ocala National Forest, try to hide there a few days."

"Okay. I'll drive that way. Maybe alert the ranger's office to keep an eye out for him."

"Good. And I'll start creating the paperwork to back up our story."

As Fred hung up the phone, he had a moment of pity for the child. But it passed quickly. He got in his car and drove to the forest.

———

Frankie knew he needed to head west, then north. That's where the Ocala National Forest lay. Thousands of acres of green cover, mostly wild. In his pocket was the map he'd printed off the computer, along with directions from the hospital. But he didn't need to look at it. Once he'd studied something, it remained imprinted in his mind. Late at night, when the nurse thought he was sleeping, he had studied all the maps he'd printed out, from Florida to North Carolina, and committed the route to memory.

If he could get to the forest before the light came up, before the day nurse made her rounds, before the alarm was sounded of his escape, then maybe he'd have a chance. He thought he could hole up there a few days, maybe find some berries to still his hunger. Only, he'd wanted to leave by two in the morning, not close to four thirty. He'd need to run, even if with every step he felt shooting pains in his chest.

He walked the few blocks from the hospital to State Road 40, then headed west. The road was sparsely traveled in the early morning hours, and the few cars that passed ignored him. Even so, when he saw the lights of a car from up ahead, or heard the motor of one from behind, he hung his head. He ran as long as he could, then walked until the pain subsided, then ran again. Run, walk, run, walk. The sun had already started to rise when he saw the forest up ahead. If he kept on the roadway, he'd reach State Road 19, the major north-south road through the forest. He had no intention of going that far. Instead, he turned north into the forest well before, and with one last sprint, he was inside, blanketed by a mass of scrub pine. He stripped off the maintenance uniform, then rolled it up and carried it under his arm.

Frankie slowed down now. He tried to stay off any trails, but still make his way north. Up to North Carolina. Up to Bobby. There were a few forest roads, and numerous trails and waterways of all types: more than six hundred lakes, rivers, and springs. This time of year, the waterways were used for fishing, or to kayak or canoe. And that meant people. There were developed campgrounds along with primitive campsites. Or, visitors could just set up a tent anywhere they wanted. The forest was risky for him but still safer than the roads.

He watched the rising sun to set his course. Not ten minutes after entering the forest, a man dressed in tattered clothes jumped onto the path ten feet ahead of him. His facial hair was too dense for Frankie to guess his age.

"Whatcha doing here, boy?" The man's eyes were wide and glaring, his mouth set in a snarl. The fingers of his right hand were wrapped tightly around a large stick, the end chiseled to a sharp point.

"N-nothing. Just walking." Frankie remembered a newspaper article he'd brought into his new school for a current-events project. It described how the forest was populated with homeless people, many of them veterans who had returned from various wars with post-traumatic stress syndrome, too fragile to hold a job, their minds too far gone to live with other people. He briefly thought of his father and wondered if he were wandering a forest somewhere in Afghanistan, lost and confused. He preferred that picture to believing his father was dead.

"These here are my trees. You don't belong!" the man shouted. He took a step toward Frankie, his makeshift spear at the ready, then stopped suddenly when Frankie saluted.

"Sir, yes, sir! Permission to retreat?"

The man hesitated, then laughed heartily. "That's a good one, boy. You're a clever one." His arm swept across his body, motioning Frankie onward. "Go ahead. I won't hurt you."

Frankie ran past the man as fast as he could, then stopped when the pain in his side made it too hard to breathe. He bent over, gasping for air, until he recovered. Frankie continued northward, now walking more slowly, trying to conserve his energy. He kept a sharp lookout, hoping to avoid any other confrontations. He was lucky with the last. He might not get away so easily if he ran across another homeless person.

As the sun continued to rise in the sky, Frankie's stomach began rumbling. He had no food, no water. He tried to visualize the map of the park he'd seen online. If he didn't find one of the natural springs, he'd never make it. It was too slow staying off the trails, skirting around the trees and scrub. He decided to chance it and made his way back to one. After two more hours, he saw a group of elderly men and women walking toward him.

When they neared, he asked, "Do you know where the closest spring is?"

The man who seemed to be the leader pointed west. "There's one just past the rise. Turn left and go about three hundred feet."

"Thanks," Frankie said and started to walk away.

"Are you all right?" the leader called after him. "Did you get separated from your parents?"

"I'm fine. I'm with a Young Adventurers group, and it's a contest to see who finds fresh water first."

"Well, you won't have any trouble. It's just where I said."

Frankie thanked them again, then headed to the spring. When he reached it, he scooped up water in his hands and guzzled it down thirstily. When he'd had his fill, he moved on, back to the trail, back heading north. As he walked, he kept his eyes peeled for berries but found none.

By late afternoon, he couldn't walk anymore. He left the trail and headed deeper into the forest until he came to a clearing where he could bed down. He found a grassy area, then rolled the pants of the maintenance uniform up to make a pillow. He set aside the shirt to cover him when the sun went down and the mild temperatures dropped to the fifties. He hadn't eaten anything all day and was hungry. Very hungry. But he couldn't do anything about it, so he willed himself to push aside the hunger pangs.

At the first sign of darkness, he decided to try and sleep. Yet no matter how hard he tried to find a comfortable position, his ribs ached. The only sounds he heard were the wind rustling through the leaves and, occasionally, the howling of a coyote, far enough away that it didn't frighten him. He thought his hunger, his pain, and the coyotes would keep him awake all night, but eventually he drifted off, only to be awakened a few hours later by the sound of crunching branches. He shot up, looked around, and with the light of the full moon, spotted a black mass about a hundred feet away, its back to Frankie. Was it a man? Another homeless guy? He watched, careful to make no noise. When the mass moved from the tree into a clearing and dropped down onto its four legs, Frankie realized it was a black bear. A large one. He recalled what he'd read about the forest. *Bears generally don't attack people. Generally. Which means sometimes they do.* As quietly as he could, he stood and walked backward to the shelter of a tree, then leaned his body into it, hoping to make himself invisible. He waited what felt like an endless amount of time, holding his breath as the bear meandered around the trees, rooting for food. It seemed like forever before it wandered away from Frankie's makeshift bed. He remained trembling, under the tree, until he was certain the bear was gone. He thought about continuing his march north, but he was too hungry and too tired. He returned to his bed, closed his eyes, and prayed the bear wouldn't return.

—

The sun woke Frankie the next morning. He didn't think he'd ever been so hungry, and his throat was parched. He'd need to find another spring soon. When he stirred, he gasped at the bolt of pain from his ribs. There was no way to get up from the ground without it hurting, so he finally just had to force himself through the pain and onto his feet. He caught his breath, then gathered up the maintenance uniform and started walking.

After no more than a few minutes, he stopped suddenly at the sight of a tent up ahead. To the side of the tent, about twenty feet away, was a thick, plastic bag up high in a tree, attached to a pulley rope. Food, he realized. Placed out of the way of bears. He walked as silently as he could to the tree, then grabbed the rope and slowly brought the bag down.

"Hey!"

Frankie spun around and saw a man, maybe in his twenties, with brown, wavy hair that fell almost to his shoulders. He had on a pair of jeans, and his muscled chest was bare. Fleetingly, Frankie thought of running, but the sharp pain in his side when he'd turned made it clear that this man could catch him easily.

"What do you think you're doing?"

"Um. I was hungry."

A slim woman emerged from the tent, also in her twenties, her long hair disheveled.

"What's going on?" she asked, her voice husky from sleep.

They stared at Frankie until finally the man asked, "Are you in trouble?"

Frankie didn't know what to do, what to say, so he stood frozen in his spot as tears started to roll down his cheeks.

"Oh, honey, don't be scared," the woman said. "We're not going to hurt you." She turned to the man. "Give him some food, Bill. He's obviously hungry."

Bill nodded, then finished bringing the bag of food down from the tree. He handed Frankie a box of doughnuts. "Go ahead. Pick one. Take two if you want."

Frankie hadn't had doughnuts in two months. At the sight of them, his mouth began watering. He lifted out a chocolate one with rainbow sprinkles, and a powdered one.

"I'm Bill, and this is Ivy. Why don't you tell us what's going on with you?"

Frankie's mouth was full with the doughnut, which gave him time to think. Could he trust this couple? Would they bring him back to Eldridge? Maybe he was being stupid. How far could he really get on his own? He swallowed the last bite in his mouth, then told this young couple everything, from the day he'd brought marijuana to school to his escape from the hospital.

"Man," Billy said. "When I was back in school, if we'd gotten busted just for a couple of joints, my whole class would've been behind bars. Two joints? Really, that's all it was?"

Frankie nodded.

"We have to help him," Ivy said.

"He's a fugitive. You know what they'd do to us if we're found with him?"

"We can't just leave him here."

"Hell, yes, we can. We won't turn him in, but that's it. Stay out of it, Ivy. He's not Seth."

Ivy walked over to Bill and placed her hand on his arm. "Maybe if someone had helped Seth, he'd still be alive."

Frankie wanted to ask who Seth was, but figured it best to remain quiet.

"It was different with your brother. He wasn't running away from jail."

"But he was running away. And scared. And if someone had shown an interest in him, then maybe he would have returned to our family before . . . before—"

"Before he was murdered," Bill finished, his voice soft. He turned to Frankie. "Okay, we'll help you. But, if we get caught with you, you need to deny telling us you came from Eldridge. We just picked you up hitchhiking, and that's all, okay?"

Frankie nodded.

"We better leave soon. We'll pack up, hike back to the car, and then we can drive you as far as Savannah. You're on your own after that, but at least you'll be out of Florida."

Frank couldn't believe his good fortune. He picked up the second doughnut and stuffed it in his mouth.

Jessica sat on the bed in Frankie's room, unable to move. She'd entered twenty minutes earlier, needing to feel his presence, and she had, in every Little League and soccer trophy on his desk, in every certificate of achievement hanging on his walls, in the sports posters and lined-up textbooks. Frankie had always been tidy. She'd never needed to pester him to put away his toys. He seemed to relish order on his own. And he hated the messiness of fighting.

It wasn't that Frankie hadn't been faced with aggression. Moving from school to school, always being one of the smaller boys, always smarter than everyone else, always needing to prove himself. He did it with his wits, not his fists. He always averted fights, but never once had he been called a coward. So she couldn't understand how he'd ended up in the hospital, seriously injured. "He was in a fight," the doctor had said. Jessica knew better. He'd been attacked, maybe even by more than one boy. What she wasn't sure of was what she should do now. Call the warden? He must have known what had happened to Frankie, yet he'd looked her straight in the face and lied to her. No, she wouldn't believe anything he said now. If Frankie ran from the hospital, it had to be because he didn't believe they would protect him from another beating, or worse.

She shuddered to think of what Frankie faced now, all alone, still injured, no money or food. *Call home, Frankie. Please call home. I'll protect you, no matter what it takes.*

—

Frankie helped Bill and Ivy break down their tent and pack up their supplies in their backpacks. When they were finished, Bill said, "Okay, kid. We've got about a two-mile hike to the car. You up to it?"

Frankie had walked for hours just to get to the forest. He was exhausted and hungry, and had shooting pains when he took a deep breath. "Yeah, I can do it."

They started out, Bill leading the way, and after forty minutes, Frankie could see the clearing up ahead with cars parked. He also saw a park ranger near the cars and knew that was trouble. "Bill, stop."

Both Bill and Ivy came to a halt.

"There's a ranger there."

"So? They're usually around."

"But, what if he was told to look for me?"

"You're being paranoid, kid."

"Maybe," Ivy said. "But we shouldn't take a chance. Why don't I go out first and try to distract him? I'll ask him for directions. When he's turned away from the car, come out of the forest. I hate to do this to you, Frankie, but I think you need to go in the trunk, at least until we're on the highway."

Frankie nodded. He would ride in anything if it got him closer to Bobby.

Ivy walked into the clearing first, then sauntered over to the ranger. Frankie couldn't hear what she said, but saw her maneuver the ranger so that his back was to the cars.

"Hurry," Bill whispered, as they ran out of their cover to Bill's car. Quickly, he popped open the trunk, and Frankie climbed in. Bill's backpack went in after him. When they were set, Bill slid into the driver's seat, and when Ivy returned, they drove off.

Frankie could feel every bump in the road and, for once, was grateful that he was small. He could almost stretch out his legs. Still, it was dark and smelled musty, and he hoped they'd get to the highway soon. He called up the image of the map he'd memorized and knew they had more than an hour's ride before they reached I-295.

The sudden stopping of the car startled him awake. He had no clue as to how long they'd been driving. A moment later, the trunk popped open, and a smiling Ivy held out her hand for him. He climbed out of the trunk and slid into the backseat. Frankie looked around to get his bearings, then realized they were at a truck-weighing station off I-95. One truck was parked far away from them, and the rest of the area was devoid of other vehicles.

"You're looking kind of pale," Bill said into the rearview mirror. "You okay?"

"Yeah, sure."

Two minutes later, they were on the highway, speeding along with the other cars. "So, do you have a plan for how you're going to get to your brother?" Bill asked.

"Um. Maybe hitch a ride?"

"On I-95?"

"I guess."

"First of all, cars going along at eighty miles per hour aren't likely to stop for a hitchhiker. Second, the cops patrol that roadway all the time. What if there's a bulletin out for you?"

"Maybe I'll stick to the smaller roads, then."

"And what, take three months to get there? Cars using the smaller roads aren't going long distances."

"I'll figure something out."

"Don't you think you should call your mom? Tell her what happened to you, and I bet she can do something to keep you from going back there."

Frankie wished that were true, but she hadn't been able to keep him from being sent there in the first place. He didn't want to think about what was ahead. He didn't want to think about what he left behind. Instead of answering Bill, he eased down onto the seat, waited for the pain in his ribs to subside, then breathed in the seat's worn-leather smell and fell asleep.

———

"Wake up, Frankie," a disembodied voice said. It sounded like the voice in a dream, faraway and not quite real. He felt a gentle push on his arm and opened his eyes. A pretty woman standing by an open backseat door looked down at him. Slowly, it came back—his escape from the hospital, his rescue by Bill and Ivy.

"I thought you were going to sleep forever," Ivy said when he'd sat up.

"Where are we?" As he looked around, he saw that Bill's car was parked in the driveway of a small ranch house, nearly identical to all the others around it.

"Our home. We thought it would be better to bring you back here instead of leaving you on the road. You can have a good meal, sleep on a real bed tonight, and tomorrow get started toward your brother. How does that sound?"

Frankie wanted to weep, he was so grateful to them. A real meal. Not watered-down slop that had no taste and often had dead bugs buried in the center. Maybe they would even have ice cream. His mouth watered at the thought.

"That would be really nice," he said. He followed them inside, helping to carry their gear. Their house had pretty flower boxes on the front windows, and comfortable furniture inside.

Ivy led him into a small bedroom, pointing out the bathroom on the way. "This is our guest room. You can sleep here tonight."

The room was painted a warm beige, and the queen-size bed was covered with a navy-and-beige quilt. He sat down on top of it and felt the cushioned mattress that reminded him of his own home, not the thin mattress on the cot-size bed he'd slept on for the past two months.

"Thank you," he said. "You and Bill are really nice." He wondered for a moment if he should be frightened of them. "Never talk to strangers," his mother had always warned him. "Never get in a car with people you don't know." Well, he'd done both now. Somehow, he knew that it was the right thing for him to do.

"Here," Ivy said as she handed him a thick towel. "In case you want to take a shower. You won't get much of a chance while you're traveling north."

Frankie nodded, then headed for the bathroom. He turned the faucet on in the tub to let it heat up, and when it was warm enough, flipped the nozzle for the shower. He stepped inside and let the hot water fall on him, ecstatic that he wasn't standing in a row with four other boys, a guard watching nearby. He soaped himself clean, then turned off the faucet, stepped out of the tub, and when dry, put back on the only clothes he had.

When he entered the living room, Bill looked him over and made a face. "We need to do something about those clothes. There's bound to be a description of what you're wearing. Even though your shirt is inside out, you can see the lettering through it."

Ivy nodded. "Why don't I stop at Kmart when I'm out and pick up a few things? What size are you, Frankie?"

"Size ten."

"We're going to bring food in tonight. Which would you prefer, pizza or Chinese?"

Frankie smiled, already thinking about the treat. "Pizza."

After Ivy left, Bill invited Frankie to play a game. "I have Monopoly, Sequence, and Scrabble. And an Xbox 360."

Frankie's eyes lit up. His situation kept getting better and better. He pushed away thoughts of what he'd been through the past few months, and what still lay ahead, and asked, "What video games do you have?"

"Pick your sport. I've got Madden NFL, NBA 2K, MLB 2K, and FIFA."

"Just sports?"

"Nah. I've got others—Grand Theft Auto, Gears of War 3, others like that. I'm just not sure your mom would want you playing something violent."

Frankie thought about it. He was probably exposed to the reality of war more than other kids his age because he'd grown up on military bases. He'd had friends whose fathers returned from action with missing arms or legs, or didn't return at all. Even so, Bill was right about his mother. She didn't let him buy violent video games. Sometimes, though, he played them at his friends' homes.

"Let's play MLB," he said, giving in to his mother's voice in his head.

Two hours later, they were still at the game when Ivy walked in, carrying a large pie and two bags for Frankie. "Go ahead, open them up."

One bag had a backpack; the other had two pairs of jeans, three T-shirts, a jacket, and two packages of underwear. She'd also bought him a toothbrush, toothpaste, and a comb.

"I promise my mom will pay you back for all this."

"Don't sweat it, kid," Bill said. "We just feel bad we can't drive you all the way. But we have to get back to work tomorrow."

Ivy pulled her wallet out of her purse. "There's one more thing. Here's $200 for you. That way we won't worry about you starving, and maybe you can find some cheap motels along the way."

Frankie hugged Ivy first, then Bill. This is a sign, he thought. Maybe it meant he'd make it to Bobby and never have to go back to that prison. Yes, definitely a good sign.

W hen Dani arrived at the office Monday morning, she grabbed Tommy, and they headed into Bruce's office. "I'm sorry we couldn't do more to help your nephew," she told him. "Has Jessica heard from him yet?"

Bruce shook his head. "She's spoken to Bobby, so if Frankie contacts him, he'll loop her in."

"I still don't get it," Dani said. "Why was he sent away for a first offense of possession of marijuana? That wouldn't have happened to an adult. At most, he'd get probation. Maybe not even that. Just an ACOD." Dani didn't need to explain to Tommy that it meant adjournment in contemplation of dismissal. As a former FBI agent and an investigator at HIPP for more than ten years, he was fully familiar with legal shorthand.

"Jessica said it's because of the school's zero-tolerance policy, and I get the policy," Bruce said. "But I don't get sending away a twelve-year-old boy who's never been in trouble. It's lunacy."

Dani nodded. "I thought zero tolerance meant a kid would automatically get suspended for an infraction, maybe even expelled. Why did the school even bring in the police?"

"Apparently, Frankie's school district goes a step beyond what others do. They call the police for anything that violates their no-drugs, no-weapons, no-violence policy."

"But for a twelve-year-old, straight-A student who's never once gotten out of line?"

Tommy shook his head. "Some crazy things have happened since schools began adopting zero tolerance. Did you hear the one about the kindergarten kid who was suspended for making a finger gun?"

Dani shook her head in wonderment.

"And the third grader who was expelled for a year because her grandmother sent a knife along with a birthday cake to school, in order to cut the cake?"

"That sounds more like zero intelligence than zero tolerance to me."

Tommy and Bruce both nodded their agreement.

"Boss, do you mind if I look into Frankie's case a bit?" Tommy asked. "I can work it around the other stuff I'm handling."

"I'd really appreciate that."

"I'd like to do a little digging myself," Dani said. "Something doesn't seem right about this case."

"Both of you, I'm really grateful, but you're paid by HIPP to work on innocence claims. I can't use their resources for personal matters."

"Well," Dani said, "you know we both put in much more than a forty-hour week. Not that we're counting, but we have to have accumulated a couple hundred hours of comp time. It's got to be okay now and then to make up for that by working on something important to us. And Frankie has become important to us."

Bruce shook his head. "You're both amazing. Thank you."

As they stood up to leave the office, Bruce called Dani back. "I have a transcript of Frankie's hearing. I got it when I thought we might appeal the ruling." He opened up a file drawer and pulled out a folder. "Here it is." He shrugged. "We should have appealed. But all we could think about was Alex. Was he alive? Had he been captured? It was all both of us thought about. Frankie's problems just seemed like background noise then."

He handed Dani the folder, and she took it back to her own office, got settled in her chair, and began reading.

JUDGE HOWARD HUMPHREY: "Ready?"

CAMDEN: "Yes, sir. Assistant State Attorney Warren Camden for the State."

KNICKERBOCKER: "Burtram Knickerbocker for the respondent."

HUMPHREY: "Let's get started then. Call your first witness."

CAMDEN: "I call Tony Cuen."

Dani skipped over his swearing in.

CAMDEN: "Do you know the defendant, Francis Bishop?"

CUEN: "Yeah. Only everyone calls him Frankie."

CAMDEN: "How do you know him?"

CUEN: "We're in the same class."

CAMDEN: "Are you friends?"

CUEN: "You kidding? He's a dweeb."

CAMDEN: "Did you ever have a conversation with Frankie?"

CUEN: "Just once. He came over to me in the lunchroom and showed me some joints. Asked if I wanted to smoke it."

CAMDEN: "And what did you say?"

CUEN: "Well, I don't do that stuff, but I thought I'd string him along, so I said, 'Sure.' I said we could meet at the park after school."

CAMDEN: "Did Frankie say anything else?"

CUEN: "He told me he could get as much of the stuff as he wanted. That he had a good source. He could even get some for me at a good price."

CAMDEN: "And did you meet Frankie at the park?"

CUEN: "Nah. As soon as lunch was over, I found our teacher, Miss Mather, and told her about it."

CAMDEN: "Thank you, Tony. I have no more questions."

KNICKERBOCKER: "You don't hang out with Frankie, do you?"

CUEN: "Nah."

KNICKERBOCKER: "Other than this one time, have you ever seen him with illegal drugs?"

CUEN: "No."

KNICKERBOCKER: "Have you ever seen him smoke marijuana?"

CUEN: "No."

KNICKERBOCKER: "I gather you don't like Frankie."

CUEN: "Like I said, he's a dweeb."

KNICKERBOCKER: "So, you wouldn't care if Frankie got in trouble."

CUEN: "Why should I?"

KNICKERBOCKER: "And, maybe you'd like to see him in trouble."

(Witness shrugged.)

KNICKERBOCKER: "Maybe you'd even lie to get him in trouble."

CUEN: "I'm not lying. He had two joints. Miss Mather took it from him."

KNICKERBOCKER: "But we have only your word that he said he could get more. As much as he wanted. That he could get some for you at a good price. And you don't like him, you've said."

CAMDEN: "Is there a question?"

KNICKERBOCKER: "I have nothing more."

Dani skimmed the testimony of Frankie's teacher, Miss Mather; the principal, Mrs. Whitman; and the policeman who came to the school. Mather and the principal testified on direct examination that two marijuana cigarettes had been found in Frankie's possession. Two joints seemed like an awfully small amount to Dani. It must have been Tony Cuen's testimony that Frankie had said he could get more that swayed the judge. She returned to the transcript.

When Camden finished with the teacher and the principal, Knickerbocker asked each if they'd ever observed Frankie under the influence of drugs. Both answered no. He asked each if Frankie had ever been in any other trouble in school. Both answered no.

The policeman testified that the cigarettes taken from Frankie were tested and determined to be marijuana. At the end of his testimony, Camden rested.

HUMPHREY: "Do you have any witnesses, Mr. Knickerbocker?"

KNICKERBOCKER: "Yes, Your Honor. I call Jessica Bishop to the stand."

Again, Dani skimmed over her swearing in and the preliminary questions.

KNICKERBOCKER: "Do you work outside the home?"

(Witness nodded.)

KNICKERBOCKER: "You need to speak up for the court reporter."

J. BISHOP: "I do. Part-time. I'm always home to send Frankie off to school, and I'm back when he returns."

KNICKERBOCKER: "And what is it that you do?"

J. BISHOP: "I'm a graphic designer. What I don't finish at work, I do at home, after Frankie's asleep."

KNICKERBOCKER: "So, you're around Frankie a good deal."

BISHOP: "Yes. Except when he's at a friend's house, although he hasn't made any friends here yet. We've only been in this house six weeks. He will, though. Make friends, that is. It's just hard when you start school in the middle of the year."

KNICKERBOCKER: "Do you know what someone looks like when they're high on drugs?"

J. BISHOP: "Of course I do."

KNICKERBOCKER: "Have you ever seen Frankie look that way?"

J. BISHOP: "No. Never."

KNICKERBOCKER: "Have you ever found drugs in his room?"

J. BISHOP: "Never."

KNICKERBOCKER: "Does Frankie earn money from a part-time job?"

J. BISHOP: "No. He's a very good student. He spends a lot of time studying."

KNICKERBOCKER: "Have you ever found money missing from your wallet?"

J. BISHOP: "No."

KNICKERBOCKER: "Does Frankie get an allowance?"

J. BISHOP: "Yes. Five dollars a week, for helping around the house."

KNICKERBOCKER: "So, as far as you know, Frankie has no other source of income."

J. BISHOP: "That's right. So he couldn't have money to buy drugs."

CAMDEN: "Nonresponsive. Move to strike."

HUMPHREY: "Sustained."

KNICKERBOCKER: "Thank you. I have no further questions."

CAMDEN: "Mrs. Bishop, you said that you're familiar with how someone looks when they're using drugs. How is it that you know that?"

J. BISHOP: "I was a teenager once."

CAMDEN: "And did you use drugs when you were a teenager?"

J. BISHOP: "Once or twice. Just marijuana."

CAMDEN: "And how about now? Do you still smoke marijuana?"

J. BISHOP: "Of course not."

CAMDEN: "Has Frankie ever seen you smoke marijuana?"

J. BISHOP: "Look, I said just once or twice. When I was in high school. That's it. Of course Frankie hasn't seen me smoke anything. I don't even smoke cigarettes."

CAMDEN: "Is your husband here?"

J. BISHOP: "He's a lieutenant colonel in the army. He went MIA a month ago, while stationed in Afghanistan."

CAMDEN: "I imagine that must create a lot of stress in the household."

J. BISHOP: "He'll be rescued. It just takes time. Frankie understands what it means to be a military family. He's confident his father will return."

Dani looked up from the transcript. No doubt, Camden wanted to suggest Alex Bishop's disappearance created stress in the family, leading Frankie to turn to drugs to alleviate that stress. Jessica had handled the question well.

CAMDEN: "No further questions."

KNICKERBOCKER: "I call Francis Bishop to the stand."

Like the other witnesses, he was sworn in, spelled his name for the record, and gave his address.

KNICKERBOCKER: "How old are you, Frankie?"

F. BISHOP: "I turned twelve two months ago."

KNICKERBOCKER: "Have you ever taken any illegal drugs?"

F. BISHOP: "No, sir."

KNICKERBOCKER: "Not even marijuana?"

F. BISHOP: "No, sir, no drugs at all."

KNICKERBOCKER: "Before this, had you ever been in any kind of trouble?"

F. BISHOP: "No."

KNICKERBOCKER: "Now, you heard Tony say you showed him some marijuana cigarettes. Is that true?"

F. BISHOP: "Yes, sir."

KNICKERBOCKER: "How many did you have?"

F. BISHOP: "Two."

KNICKERBOCKER: "Were they yours?"

F. BISHOP: "No. I found them in the street, by the school bus stop."

KNICKERBOCKER: "Have you ever purchased marijuana?"

F. BISHOP: "No."

KNICKERBOCKER: "Tony said you told him you could get as much as you wanted. Did you tell him that?"

F. BISHOP: "No. I never said anything like that."

Dani stopped again. Two versions of the same event. She wondered why the judge found Tony to be more credible. According to the impartial witnesses—his teacher and principal—before this Frankie had always been a model student.

KNICKERBOCKER: "Why did you show Tony the two cigarettes you found?"

F. BISHOP: "Because I wanted him to like me and maybe stop picking on me."

KNICKERBOCKER: "Thank you, Frankie. I have no more questions."

CAMDEN: "Now, Frankie, you know what it means to tell the truth, right?"

F. BISHOP: "Sure."

CAMDEN: "Even if it gets you in trouble, you understand that you have to be honest, right?"

F. BISHOP: "Yes, sir."

CAMDEN: "Now, I don't want to hurt you. And the judge doesn't want to hurt you. We both want to make sure that if you have a problem, we get it cleared up. And if you need help, we'll get you that help. Do you understand?"

F. BISHOP: "Yes."

What a crock, Dani thought. The whole purpose of this proceeding was to hurt Frankie.

CAMDEN: "Now, isn't it true that you didn't find the marijuana cigarettes in the street?"

F. BISHOP: "No, sir. That's where I found them."

CAMDEN: "Remember, Frankie, you've promised to tell the truth."

KNICKERBOCKER: "Objection. The witness has answered the question. Mr. Camden is just harassing him now."

HUMPHREY: "Sustained. Move on, Mr. Camden."

Dani read through the rest of Frankie's cross-examination. Question after question, Camden tried to move Frankie from his story. Answer after answer, Frankie remained firm. He found the cigarettes in the street. He'd never used drugs. He just wanted to get Tony to like him. Finally, Camden gave up and sat down.

HUMPHREY: "Any more witnesses, Mr. Knickerbocker?"

KNICKERBOCKER: "No, sir."

HUMPHREY: "Any rebuttal, Mr. Camden?"

CAMDEN: "No."

HUMPHREY: "I've listened carefully to the witnesses. On the one hand, Francis is a good student and hasn't been in trouble before. His mother is a stable influence in his life, but his father's job, although doing something we are all grateful for, can't help but create stress in the household. It's not uncommon, when young lads are faced with that kind of stress, to turn to drugs. Although Francis denies using drugs, the evidence is clear that he brought marijuana to school and offered it to other boys. It is not believable to me that someone who would do that has never partaken of those drugs. To compound matters, Francis refuses to acknowledge that he needs help. There is also some evidence that Francis may be involved in the sale of marijuana. Although the amount in question is less than twenty grams, the fact that Francis possessed cannabis in a school, and offered it to other children within the school, exacerbates the offense. In this situation, both to protect other students at the school and to help Francis overcome his drug use, I find that he is guilty of possession of a controlled substance and that he is a delinquent. He is hereby committed to the Department of Juvenile Justice for placement in a residential program that offers drug counseling for a period of four months."

Dani put the transcript down. It was clear the judge had credited Tony's version of the events without any corroboration. Even so, she thought the sentence was harsh. She would have guessed probation a more likely sentence, given Frankie's age and lack of priors. Especially with only his hunch that Frankie was a dealer. Perhaps Humphrey wanted to set an example for other students in the school that there were no second chances. Still, she couldn't get past the fact that he was only twelve years old. Even if the verdict was justified—and after reading the transcript, it certainly wasn't a slam dunk—it just seemed cruel to lock up such a young boy.

Finished with the transcript, Dani turned to her computer and began researching juvenile prisons in Florida. An hour later, she sat back in her chair, stunned at what she'd learned. One hundred percent of the juvenile prisons in Florida were operated by private, for-profit companies, paid for with taxpayer dollars. Dani knew enough about business to appreciate that the way to maximize profits was to reduce overhead. That meant hiring lower-paid staff than government-operated prisons, and along with lower pay came lower skills and greater turnover. In Florida, one private contractor stood out from the rest: ML Juvenile Services, Inc., the operator of Eldridge Academy. It operated six of the sixty-one juvenile residential centers, despite a string of complaints against the company.

One incident in another ML Juvenile Services facility, described in a grand jury report, involved a sixteen-year-old boy who died in his cell because the guards believed he was faking his behavior and refused to call for an ambulance. Peter Limone had been suspected of carrying contraband. The guards threw him against a wall, and he struck his head on the concrete. When he stood, he was unsteady and had difficulty walking. That evening, he awoke during the night screaming about hallucinations. He was out of bed, crawling, unable to stand, and crying, saying as he held his head, "It hurts, it hurts." As he tried to stand, he fell and hit his head once more. The guards got him back in his bed, but an hour later, he woke up again and vomited. The guards didn't bother to call 911 despite this alarming behavior. When he hadn't awakened by ten the next morning, the guards discovered him dead in his bed.

When Dr. LaGrange told them Frankie had run away, Dani had cringed. No matter how minor his original infraction, running away would be viewed seriously. He would be found, whether by the authorities or by Jessica. Either way, he wouldn't be able to remain hidden. Now, as she read of the atrocities that went on in juvenile prisons in general and ML Juvenile Services facilities in particular, she wondered if Frankie was right to escape. Maybe it would give Dani time to find a way to prevent the courts from sending him back to Eldridge Academy. And she knew, now, she had to try to do just that.

—

Dani headed home, her head filled with the thoughts of children sent to juvenile facilities in order to help them, to provide services to turn their lives around, and once there, cruelly, heartlessly abused. She fervently hoped that the facilities she'd read about were anomalies, a few bad detention centers out of thousands across the country that worked well. But she suspected that wasn't the case. She also suspected that as more and more states moved to private, for-profit prisons, both for juveniles and adults, the abuses would increase.

She pulled into her driveway and was happy to see that Doug was already home. On days like this, she'd usually greet Jonah, hear about his day, then, as she and Doug prepared dinner, they'd pour glasses of wine for themselves and unwind. Only she couldn't drink any alcohol now. No magic elixir to loosen the knots in her neck. Instead, she made herself a cup of decaf tea. They still had unfinished business to resolve, but it would have to wait until Jonah was asleep. Instead, she filled Doug in on what she'd learned about ML Juvenile Services.

"It's so wrong," she complained when she'd finished.

"What Frankie reported to his mother about the boy who died is certainly terribly wrong. It's sickening. And what got him confined definitely does sound like a one-off, understandable bit of misbehavior for this kid. But it's also true that there have to be consequences when people violate the law, even for young people."

"Sure. And if a kid commits a violent crime or a string of minor offenses, then he should be locked up. But look at Frankie. Two joints. Perfect record. No adult would be locked up for that. And, to make it even worse, more minority children are incarcerated than whites, for the same offenses."

Doug nodded and sighed. "I have no doubt," he said, then took her shoulders in his hands and guided her back onto a stool at the kitchen counter. "How about you sit here with your delicious, relaxing, decaffeinated tea and fix all of society's wrongs while I fix us dinner?"

Dani smiled at him. "How did I get so lucky to marry you?"

"If I remember correctly, you kept chasing after me. I didn't have any choice but to marry you."

"Hah! I think there's some selective memory going on there." Dani handed Doug the peeler she'd been holding, then sat back in her chair. "Did you know that eighty-eight percent of the schools in America have a zero-tolerance policy for drugs?"

He smiled as he pulled a bag of carrots from the refrigerator. "I do now. And isn't that kind of a good idea? Shouldn't schools send a message to their students not to bring drugs there?"

"On paper, it makes sense. But locking up a twelve-year-old for it doesn't."

Doug put the peeler on the counter and sat down next to Dani. He took her hand in his. "I know you're worried about Frankie Bishop. I understand that. But I was just kidding a minute ago, Dani. You can't change the world. Just concentrate on saving one boy."

———

Later that night, during "honeymoon hour," Dani turned to Doug. "We need to decide what to do about my pregnancy." Dani saw Doug's back stiffen.

"Can't that wait awhile longer?"

"I have an appointment with my obstetrician after work tomorrow. I'd like to know what to tell her."

He sagged into the couch. "Okay," he said. "Let's talk about it. I'll start: You've struggled so much with your conflict between working and being a mother. And now, now that you're finally accepting that Jonah's okay despite your leaving for work every day, you want to put yourself through it all over again?"

Dani knew that Doug was right. It had been a constant battle within her—the feeling that she was depriving her son by not greeting him when he stepped off the school bus each afternoon, by not being the parent who accompanied his class on school trips, by not devoting 100 percent of her time to his well-being. Yet, she'd finally come to recognize that despite not being at home with Jonah all the time, he'd still managed to thrive. He was a happy boy, and not just because it was the nature of his disability. Would her self-doubt resurface if she began anew, leaving an infant at home with a sitter? She'd thought a great deal about that the past few days, and realized she had gotten past that. Deep down, her yearning for this baby far outweighed her past insecurities.

"I do want to do it again," she told Doug. "I really want this child."

Doug kept shaking his head, a solemn look on his face.

"I know we didn't plan for this," she pressed, "but sometimes the unplanned events are the most fulfilling. Besides, a baby will keep us young."

"Hah. I'm afraid it'll be just the reverse. A baby will age us fast."

Dani stared into his face, her eyes silently pleading for him to come to terms with the idea of another child. "Remember how much fun it was watching Jonah at the beach when he was just a toddler? Remember how much we enjoyed the Saturday morning soccer games, even though Jonah often ran the wrong way?" Dani could see the tightness in Doug's face begin to soften. "Remember how good it felt when Jonah cuddled in our lap at night before going to bed, and then when we'd tuck him in, he'd plant kisses all over our face? He's too old for all that now, but I miss it. Don't you?"

Slowly, a smile began to form on Doug's face. "Those *were* nice times." He took a deep breath. "I'm surprised you're not mentioning the strongest argument for another child."

"What's that?"

"When we're gone, Jonah will have a brother or sister in his life. He won't be all alone."

"So, you're okay with this?"

Now Doug's smile broadened. "I suppose I am. But you've got all the four a.m. feedings."

11

Jessica hadn't slept much. She was too worried about Frankie. Bobby had promised to call if he'd heard from his brother, but the phone had remained silent. As she paced her kitchen floor, she realized she couldn't simply stand by and do nothing any longer. She needed to act. She picked up the phone and dialed the number she'd been given for the Department of Juvenile Justice. After several attempts to reach the appropriate person, she was finally put through to Oscar Martinez, an analyst at the agency.

"I'm frantic, Mr. Martinez. My son was at Eldridge Academy, and he suddenly went missing. No one there would tell me what happened to him. Finally, six days later, I learned he had been severely beaten and was at Crescent Hills Regional Hospital. When I got there, I was told that he'd run away during the night."

"Hold on, Mrs. Bishop. Let me see if I have anything on that."

Jessica waited what seemed like an interminable time until he finally came back on the line. "We received a report this morning. According to Warden Cummings, your son has been acting out since he arrived, and he was the instigator of the fight that landed him in the hospital. In fact, the warden believes your son has some serious mental-health issues."

"We can't be talking about the same person."

"Francis Bishop, born December 15, 2003?"

"That's Frankie, but he's the gentlest boy you'd ever know. He'd never start a fight. And whoever thinks he has mental-health issues must be crazy themselves." Jessica heard the note of desperation in her voice.

"Children often hide their real tendencies from their parents."

Now Jessica's desperation turned to anger. "Then he hid it from every teacher he ever had, from every athletic coach, from every friend, and even from every enemy. No, Mr. Martinez, I know my son, and that report doesn't describe him."

Jessica heard a loud sigh on the other end of the phone. "I'm not sure what you want from me. Your son ran away. If he's picked up, he'll be brought back to Eldridge, and we can arrange for a psychiatric examination at that point."

"No!" Jessica shouted. "Not Eldridge. Anyplace else. Something's going on there. I don't know what, but they lied to me about where Frankie was, and they've lied to you in that report. If Frankie ran away, he had a good reason to. Please, please, don't send him back there."

"Well, at this point, we're not sending him anywhere. We don't know where he is, and we don't exactly send out the posse for something like this. I have to warn you, though. If he returns home and you don't notify us, you might face criminal charges yourself."

"And if you don't investigate what's going on at Eldridge, you might just face civil charges, with a lawsuit for millions in damages."

Jessica slammed down the phone and continued her pacing.

—

Why is there always a wait in doctors' offices? Dani wondered. She'd left work early for her appointment with her OB/GYN, and Doug had joined her. They'd been sitting in the waiting room for forty minutes.

She'd done more research into Florida's juvenile prisons. Her dismay had increased when she learned the problem was widespread. A myriad of complaints had been filed against for-profit privately run juvenile prisons across the country. "I can't get past why he was sentenced to prison," Dani said.

"Then that should be your starting point. Figure out why."

Dani chuckled. "It's so easy for you to say that. You teach law school students from cases that were already decided, where the facts are nicely laid out. It's not so easy in the real world. Especially with juvenile court, where the records are sealed." Dani was quiet for a moment, then said, "Thank goodness I have Tommy on my side. Somehow, he always manages to work a miracle. I'm going to have him start with the judge who did the sentencing. Maybe he can find someone willing to talk."

Just then, Dani's name was called, and she and Doug entered Dr. Kaplan's office.

"So, you think you're pregnant?" the doctor said when they'd taken seats opposite her desk.

Dani nodded. "The home test was positive."

"Well, let's take a look."

A nurse led Dani first to a bathroom for a urine sample, and then, with Doug, into an examining room. She pointed to the paper gown and told her to put it on with the opening in the front. When Dr. Kaplan came into the room, she announced that Dani's urine test was positive for pregnancy. She performed a pelvic examination, then a sonogram. "Looks like you're ten weeks along."

Dani sat up from the examining table and looked over at Doug, who had a smile on his face. He's come around, she thought, with a sense of relief. *It's not just for me. He's happy.*

"I'm forty-five," Dani said to the doctor. "Should I be worried about the baby's health?"

"Well, no question your age is a factor. But we'll do a number of prenatal tests. And nowadays, women your age are having babies more and more often. They want to be established in a career first, then all of a sudden realize their biological clock has an end date."

Dani didn't know what she would do if the testing showed a problem with the baby. She hadn't needed prenatal testing for her pregnancy with Jonah, and so they were unprepared for his diagnosis of Williams syndrome. His special needs made him different, sometimes in ways that made her heart ache, sometimes in ways that made her heart soar with pride. But always her intense love for him triggered a need to protect him.

How could so many children languish in prisons where the profit motive outweighed compassion? she thought. Who was protecting them? Where was the community outrage? Where were the government overseers? She wasn't naive. She was well aware of the abuses that took place in adult prisons. But these were children, she wanted to scream. No one should accept a twelve-year-old boy—who'd brought to school only two joints in an effort to make friends—ending up in a hospital with severe damage to his spleen. Frankie's mother wouldn't accept it. And neither would Dani.

12

Frankie awoke the next morning to the smell of bacon sizzling. He slipped on his new jeans, pulled a new T-shirt over his head, and headed into the kitchen.

"Morning," Bill, still in his pajamas, said as he stood over the stove. "In the mood for some bacon and eggs?"

Boy, was he ever. Cold cereal or lukewarm oatmeal was all he ever got at Eldridge.

"Have some for me, too?" Ivy asked as she entered the kitchen behind Frankie. She was all dressed up in a skirt and blouse, with her red, wavy hair pulled back in a ponytail.

"Sure, sweetie, pull up a chair."

"Um, can I help?" Frankie asked.

"You can get the orange juice from the fridge."

Frankie did as he was asked, then sat down at one of the place settings. When Bill finished cooking, he scooped out scrambled eggs onto each of the three plates, then placed four strips of bacon next to the eggs. He sat down to join them.

When they finished eating, Ivy turned to Frankie. "Bill and I have done some investigating. There's a train that goes from Savannah up to Raleigh. From there, it's only about a hundred and twenty miles to the base. There probably are taxis at the train station. Take one to the airport, and from there, you can get a shuttle that goes to Camp Lejeune. The money we gave you will cover the fares. We think that's what you should do."

"Will they let me on the train alone?"

"Just pretend you belong there. Don't look like you're doing something wrong. If anyone asks, say you're on your way to visit your father."

"Won't they think I should be in school?"

"Say your father is shipping out, and you got special permission to take a few days off to visit him."

"Okay."

"Here's the thing, though. There's only one train a day, and it leaves at one thirty in the morning. So we think you should hang out here today, and we'll drive you there when it's time."

Frankie was fine with that. They had a big-screen TV on the wall, and he could also play video games. When they were ready to leave for work, they showed him the food in the refrigerator and pantry and offered suggestions for his lunch. He was happy making a peanut-butter-and-jelly sandwich for himself. Before she left for work, Ivy implored him once more to call his mother. "I'll think about it," he said.

Once he was alone, he settled himself on the couch, looked over the Xbox games, then pulled out FIFA—a soccer game—and popped it in the console. Two hours later, he finished playing games, then turned on the TV. It was a treat to watch what he wanted to watch, rather than what was playing on the communal TV. He flipped through the cable channels, found a *Fast and Furious* movie that was about to start, then settled back and watched it.

After a while, he thought about Ivy's plea to phone his mother. He knew she would have come to see him for her regular Saturday visit, and wondered what the guards at Eldridge had told her. Maybe she was worried. He reached out for the phone, began dialing, then hesitated. What if they'd bugged it? What if they could find him from his call? No, he would stick to his plan. He'd get to Bobby by tomorrow, and then he could figure out the rest.

Dani arrived at work armed with her cup of decaf coffee and freshly baked doughnut from the corner shop. As she got settled in her office, Tommy stopped by. "I found out some things about the owner of ML Juvenile Services."

"Spill."

"His name is Roger Wilcox, and apparently he's wreaked havoc wherever he's gone."

"What do you mean?"

"Well, he leads the pack in complaints of abuse, both physical and sexual. He pays rock-bottom wages, so it's no surprise that he has the highest turnover of staff of any prison in Florida. And since no one is there very long, no one has much experience."

"Why is he still in business?"

"Not only is he still in business, but his company is thriving. He keeps getting new and renewed contracts."

Dani shook her head in disgust. "How does he get away with it?"

"By not reporting incidents and scaring the kids so they won't report abuses themselves."

Dani wondered if this is what landed Frankie in the hospital. He'd told his mother about a boy dying through the neglect of the guards. Was the warden trying to cover up the incident? Had the guard done it at the warden's behest? If so, then once Frankie was found—and she fervently hoped that would be soon—she might have success in convincing a court to overlook his running away and, at the very least, move him to a different prison.

"This is helpful, Tommy. Keep digging."

Dani turned to the appeal she was working on for a HIPP client. There was nothing more she could do for Frankie Bishop until he was found.

At 12:45 a.m., Bill woke Frankie. "Time to get ready to leave."

Frankie opened his eyes, still groggy. His backpack was ready, filled with snacks in addition to his clothes. He'd gone to sleep already dressed for travel and now slid out of bed and laced up his shoes.

Bill looked him over. "You going to be okay?"

Frankie pulled his shoulders back and stuck out his chin. "Sure." Even as he said it, he knew he was bluffing. He'd never traveled on his own before. Yes, he'd traveled lots with his parents. All over the United States and in Germany, too. But never alone.

"Okay, let's get going."

Frankie had already said good-bye to Ivy when he went to sleep earlier that night. Now just he and Bill got into his car and drove the twenty minutes to the train station. Bill bought him a ticket from the automated machine. The platform was empty, and Bill waited with Frankie for the train to arrive.

"Remember, give the conductor your ticket, and ask him to wake you when the train gets to Raleigh. Then, go to sleep. Don't talk to anyone."

As the train chugged into the station, Frankie turned to Bill and hugged him. "Thank you. And Ivy. For everything."

"Just remember, when you get to the base, call us. We need to know that you got there safely."

Frankie nodded, then boarded the train. He found a seat away from the other passengers, placed his backpack under the seat in front of him, and settled in. Within minutes of the train pulling out of the station, a uniformed man came around and asked for his ticket. Frankie handed it to him, carefully averting his gaze, then scrunched down on his seat and closed his eyes. He wouldn't arrive in Raleigh until almost nine a.m. He'd certainly be awake then. No need to ask to be awakened.

Within minutes, Frankie fell soundly asleep. The bright sunlight streaming through the window woke him, and he wondered what time it was. It had to be morning. He looked around, hoping to see a clock, and instead saw a middle-aged man across the aisle. He was dressed in a suit and tie and was staring at Frankie. He quickly turned away from him and leaned his head against the window. His body stiffened when he felt someone sit down next to him, but he didn't turn around to look. A moment later, he felt a tap on his shoulder. Slowly, he turned to face the middle-aged man.

"You're awfully young to be traveling by yourself."

"I'm old enough."

"Shouldn't you be in school?"

Frankie had his answer prepared. "My father is being shipped out from Camp Lejeune soon. I got permission to go see him."

"Why isn't your mother with you?"

"My mother died. I live with my grandmother, and she's too weak to travel."

"Still, I have a son myself, around your age. I'd worry about him being all alone on a train."

"I'm okay."

"My boy plays soccer. How about you?"

"Yeah."

"What position?"

"Forward."

"That's what my son plays. He's high scorer for his team." The man took out his wallet and pulled out a picture of a boy in a soccer uniform, holding a soccer ball in his hands.

Frankie fell into an easy conversation with the man, about school sports and professional sports and life in the military and even what movies he liked.

After a while, the man said, "This train doesn't stop near Jacksonville. Do you know that?"

"I'm getting off in Raleigh and taking a shuttle from the airport to the base."

"I'm headed to Camp Lejeune myself. On business. I have a car waiting at the station. If you'd like, I can drive you there. It'll save you time and a lot of money. I'd like to think that if my son was traveling alone, someone would help him out."

"What kind of business?"

"What?"

"You said you're going to Camp Lejeune on business. What kind?"

"Oh. My company has the contract for cleaning the uniforms. Every now and then, I stop in to make sure things are going smoothly."

Frankie had lived on or near army bases most of his life. He knew many of the services were provided by outside vendors. Still, his mother had drilled it into him over and over—don't talk to strangers. Don't get in cars with strangers.

"Don't come along if you're not comfortable with it. I have the utmost respect for our soldiers and wouldn't want your father angry at you for hitching a ride with a stranger."

Frankie had trusted Bill and Ivy, and it had worked out well. This man seemed nice, too. He smiled at him and said, "That would be great."

—

When the doorbell rang, Jessica knew who it would be. She opened it to the policeman, standing outside with a sour look on his face.

"Good morning, ma'am. I'm Officer Garcia. I understand you're aware that your son Francis ran away."

"I am. I'm also aware that he was badly beaten while incarcerated."

"That may be, but my job now is to bring him back to Eldridge Academy. May I come in?"

"No."

"Excuse me?"

"You heard me. Unless you have a warrant, you don't have permission to enter my home."

Now the sour look changed to one of annoyance. "You're making a mistake here. It'll only be harder for your son when I come back."

Jessica couldn't believe he was threatening her. Was the whole world crazy, with anger fueling more and more violence? "Good day, Officer." She closed the door and began to shake. How long would it take him to get a warrant? An hour? A day? She wanted him to believe that Frankie was at home. That way, they wouldn't look for him elsewhere. But she had no intention of being here when Officer Garcia came back. She'd already decided that she couldn't wait at home any longer.

It drove Jessica crazy, not hearing from Bobby, not knowing if Frankie was okay. It was different from her worry over her husband. Every day, she brushed away images of him being shot by a sniper, or ambushed by a troop of Taliban. But she had no control over what happened to him, so she needed to rely on her belief that he was highly trained and exceptionally careful. After months of all-consuming worry about his safety, she'd decided she simply wouldn't allow the notion that he was dead to linger in her thoughts.

A mother was supposed to be in control of her child, though. To always know where he was and what he was doing. How had she lost that control?

She knew the answer. In her distraction over Alex, she'd allowed herself to be lax, to rely on Frankie's strength instead of her own. She'd assumed that because he was so smart, he wouldn't do something so stupid. She'd forgotten that he was still a child. And because of that, he'd ended up in juvenile prison. It was her fault, not Frankie's. And now he was missing.

She picked up the phone and placed a call to Bobby, leaving him a message when he didn't answer. An hour later, he called back.

"Any news?" he asked.

Jessica could hear the worry in his voice. "Nothing. It's been days. He should have gotten home by now if he was coming here."

"Yeah. I think so, too."

Jessica tried unsuccessfully to hold back her tears. "I'm afraid, Bobby. I'm afraid something's happened to him."

"Don't think that way. Look—like you said, if he were coming home, he would have gotten there by now. I think you're right—he's heading up to me. He knows I'm finished with basic; he knows he can always count on me. It makes sense that he wouldn't have gotten here yet. It's a good distance if he's hitchhiking. And that's what he must be doing. It's what I'd do."

"But why hasn't he called? If not me, then you?"

"I don't know, Ma. He's a kid. A scared kid, and he's probably not thinking too clearly."

Jessica made an instant decision. She couldn't wait at home by herself any longer. "I'm coming up there. To Camp Lejeune. I'm leaving right away." As soon as she hung up, she threw a few clothes into an overnight bag and headed out to the car. If Frankie did reach Bobby, she wanted to be nearby, not hundreds of miles away.

—

The train pulled in to the Raleigh station on time, and a number of passengers stood up to leave. Frankie and the man sitting next to him, who'd introduced himself as John, exited the train. Once on the platform, John motioned for Frankie to follow him. It was colder here than it had been in Savannah, so Frankie opened his backpack and pulled out the jacket Ivy had bought him. When they reached John's silver-gray Mercedes, John opened the passenger door for Frankie, then got in the driver's seat. Frankie gazed out the window. He didn't need to check the map stashed in his backpack; he'd memorized the route he'd needed to take to get to Camp Lejeune. And so when the Mercedes turned in a different direction, he said, "Hey, this isn't the way."

"I know a shortcut."

Frankie sat back and tried to visualize the map. It didn't seem right to him. A shortcut shouldn't be going west when they needed to go east.

"I think you made a mistake, John. We're going in the wrong direction."

John turned and looked at him, with eyes that narrowed and lips stretched in a thin smile. "Don't think so, Frankie. I think maybe you're the one who made a mistake."

Frankie's heart sank. He knew this was trouble. Bigger trouble than Eldridge. Bigger trouble than he'd ever faced.

13

T he buzzer on Dani's intercom sounded. "He's here," her assistant told her when she picked up the phone.

"Good. Let Tommy know, and bring him into the conference room."

Tommy had tracked down Brian Bismark, a man who'd previously worked for the Florida Department of Juvenile Justice, monitoring conditions inside the for-profit juvenile prisons. He'd agreed to talk about his experiences.

"Thanks for coming in, Mr. Bismark," Dani said when she entered the room. She looked Bismark over. He was a small man, with a receding hairline and sad eyes. "I'm Dani Trumball, and this is Tommy Noorland."

"Please, call me Brian. And I'm glad if I can be of help. I've been disturbed for a long time about what's going on in those facilities."

"Is that why you left?"

He shook his head. "I was forced out. Because I reported the truth."

Dani steeled herself for what she expected to hear from him. Each time she read about the atrocities that occurred in juvenile prisons, she felt an overwhelming sense of despair. Doug had reminded her once again last night that she couldn't fix all the wrongs in the world by herself. That she should take comfort in the fact that she'd chosen a career where she made a real difference in the lives of innocent men and women, wrongfully incarcerated. She knew he was right, but it didn't matter. When she looked at her own son, so loved and protected, it broke her heart to think of other mothers' children caught up in a nightmare.

She shook those thoughts from her head. This was no time for emotions. It was time for fact-gathering, information that could hopefully be used to help Frankie Bishop. "Tell us what you found."

"Before I focused in on Eldridge Academy, ML Juvenile Services had already closed another facility. At that one, a lawsuit had been brought on behalf of a fourteen-year-old boy who claimed he was sexually abused by a guard, who forced him to perform oral sex on him. Although the guard denied abusing the boy, the manager of the facility tacitly admitted that sexual acts occurred, but claimed they were consensual."

"Was the guard convicted of rape?"

"Nope. Case was settled, and the guard didn't even lose his job."

"How could that be? Even if the boy consented, he was underage, and the guard was in an authority position over him."

"That's juvenile prison. Although we're not supposed to call it a prison, but what else is it when you're locked up and can't leave?"

Dani felt like she would explode with anger.

"At that same facility, just two years later, the public defender's office became concerned with conditions there. They filed a petition with the court asking that it appoint an independent monitor to investigate allegations of rampant abuse. The residents claimed that they were routinely choked, had their heads slammed into concrete walls, or their arms and fingers bent and twisted by the staff, usually for minor infractions. Food quality was atrocious, and portions were minimal, with staff often withholding it.

"When the State finished its investigation, it claimed it found no improprieties. But three months later, the facility closed."

Dani wondered if the same result would occur if they investigated the circumstances that landed Frankie in the hospital. She suspected it would. She'd thought that her years as a federal prosecutor would have hardened her to the atrocities that some people inflicted on others. It hadn't. It was especially hard to accept that a government agency—or at least some of the people who worked for it—would close its eyes to such abominations. Especially when children were involved.

"The closing of that facility didn't stem the tide of complaints from others, although guards did everything they could to make it difficult to report abuses. Although the state has an abuse hotline, residents often have to make the call in the presence of the abusing guard. One resident reported that he was told by a guard that if the complaint wasn't proven to be true—something that regularly occurred because of lack of substantiation—he could be charged with filing a false report and have years added to his sentence. That threat was taken seriously by residents, who understood that when deciding who's telling the truth, juries will believe a guard over them.

"I knew of one case, a boy, sentenced to a detention center when he was thirteen. His time kept getting extended because of bad behavior. Shortly before he was due to be released, a guard claimed that the boy had attacked him. The boy claimed the reverse—that he'd been attacked by the guard. The jury believed the guard, even though a video later the same day caught a guard slamming the boy's head on the ground, leaving him alone and bleeding as he walked away. The boy was sentenced to five years in an adult prison.

"All of these things took place at ML Juvenile Services properties, so you can understand my skepticism over their reports, which, on the surface, made it seem like everything was fine. The private prison system in Florida operates on self-reports. So, often, complaints of abuse or violence go unreported. The State checks only to confirm that reports are filed in a timely manner, without checking their accuracy. I decided to pick one—Eldridge Academy—and started making unscheduled visits. And talking to some of the kids on those visits. A very different picture emerged."

He stopped and took a small notebook out of his pocket, then opened it up and read it. "I want to make sure I don't miss anything," he said after he looked up. "It quickly became clear that there wasn't enough staff, and those there were poorly trained. There were kids who weren't eating because the food was so bad, and even those who did eat weren't getting sufficient nutrition.

"But that was the least of the problems. Some residents were not only prevented from calling the state's abuse hotline but thrown in solitary if they tried to call. I had kids tell me they were forced to lie on their stomachs, on a concrete floor, for hours, while their hands and feet were shackled. The guards would bang kids against the wall, curse at them, punch them. Once, a kid complained that he couldn't breathe, and the guard covered his mouth with his hand. He thought he was going to die."

Dani's stomach, which had been tied in knots during the whole interview, now felt like it would burst. "Why didn't the State do anything about it?"

"Because even if, against the odds, a kid's complaint managed to get heard, it became a he-said-she-said situation, and the State more often than not ruled it inconclusive."

"But you must have reported your findings to the State."

"Sure. And that's what got me fired."

Dani looked at him quizzically.

"ML Juvenile Services spends more on lobbyists in Florida than any other industry—around a quarter million each year."

"How can they afford to spend so much?"

"Their contracts in Florida are worth over $40 million. Their CEO takes in a salary of $3.5 million annually."

Dani was stunned. She knew that guards in private prisons were paid poorly—it was one of the contributing factors for the problems inside. How could a corporation entrusted with children pay its staff so little and its top echelon so much? It infuriated her.

"Anyway, after I started documenting the problems, they got a meeting with my boss and complained about my unannounced visits. Two weeks later, I was fired. And in the years since then, ML has been awarded even more contracts in Florida. It's big business, and the goal is making money, not rehabilitating kids."

"It sounds like enlisting the State's help with Frankie Bishop's situation will be fruitless."

"Probably."

After he left, Dani was left with a feeling of despair. She understood why Frankie was afraid to return to Eldridge. His beating, the death he'd witnessed—and who knew what else he'd seen—were not rogue incidents. They were part of a culture of abuse. Still, he was a twelve-year-old boy, alone, without money or food. And she couldn't help but worry that he'd traded one danger for another.

—

The man pulled into a motel parking lot. When he turned toward Frankie, the boy saw a gun in his hand.

"We're going to go inside the office, and you're going to pretend you're my son. If you do as you're told, nothing will happen. Make any movement for help, and not only will I shoot you, but you'll be responsible for me shooting anyone else in the office. And I will do that."

Frankie could tell from the scowl on John's face—if that was even his name—that he wasn't bluffing. He felt his skin grow cold as his heart raced. He nodded at John, then slid out the driver's side of the car. John grabbed him by the collar and marched him toward the office. A woman, with skin as dark as his father's, arms as skinny as his own, was behind the counter.

"Can I help you?"

"Yes, we'd like a room for one night."

She looked the man over, then asked, "Two beds?"

"Of course."

"Eighty-five dollars a night. I need an ID and credit card."

"I'm paying cash." John took out his wallet and handed over his driver's license and two fifty-dollar bills.

The clerk eyed the money, then said, "Need a hundred-dollar deposit in case there's damage to the room."

John handed her another two fifties. She typed something into a keyboard, swiped a plastic card, then handed it to the man, along with his change. "Room 235. Drive around the back, and it's on the left side."

John thanked her, then steered Frankie out the door and back to the car. Frankie was too afraid to run, too afraid to speak. He got into the car, and when they parked near their room, he docilely preceded John up the stairs. He'd been warned about men like John, men who picked up young boys or girls and did terrible things to them. His body trembled, and when they entered the room, he began to cry.

"Too early for tears, kid. I'm not planning on doing anything to you. You're too valuable to me. I get good money for kids your age."

Frankie didn't know whether he should feel relieved or even more frightened. At least he had time. Maybe he'd think of something before it was too late.

—

Bobby Bishop paced back and forth in the PX, glancing at the watch on his wrist every few minutes. His mother had sounded hysterical on the phone, a sound that he'd never associated with her before. Through all of the trials he'd put her through during his high school years—missing curfews, coming home drunk, cutting classes—she'd never once seemed out of control. Jessica Bishop was the calmest person he knew. Even a rock can crumble, though, when the ground beneath it shifts and then opens up. And his mother's earth had shaken as much as a magnitude-seven quake. His father—missing in action. He still couldn't wrap his head around that. He wouldn't allow himself to, not as he was embarking on his own military career. Now Frankie. The most straight-arrow kid he'd ever known. And it was all his fault.

He thought he'd cleaned out his stash of drugs before he'd left for basic training. Not drugs, really. Just pot. He never was into anything else. But everyone smoked weed in high school, at least everyone he'd hung out with. Not Frankie, though. He was too smart to take that up. Then how could he have been so stupid as to bring it to school?

Bobby had left his mother's name at the gate so that she could drive straight through to the PX. Now that basic training was done, he'd been assigned to the weapons-training battalion at Camp Lejeune. It was a natural fit for him. He'd been around guns and rifles his whole life, and from the time he was twelve, his father had taught him to shoot and often had taken him to shooting ranges. He'd told his mother he'd be in the food court, tucked at the back of the massive store, with its aisles of discounted food and clothing—a Walmart for military personnel. The tables around him were filled with men and women, some Marines, some spouses.

Just as he was about to check his watch once more, he saw his mother walking toward him. As soon as she reached him, she threw her arms around him, pulling him close to her. After she finally let go and stepped back, he said, "You made good time."

"I only stopped twice—for lunch and then for gas. And I barely ate anything at lunch. Too nervous. Have you heard from him?"

Bobby shook his head. "Why don't you get something to eat? You must be hungry."

"I will. In a minute. Let me look at you." She stepped back and looked up and down at her son, dressed in his Marine fatigues. "You look so grown-up."

"I am grown-up."

Jessica nodded, then went to the Chinese-food stand to get some dinner. As she walked away, Bobby wrestled once more with whether he should tell his mother the truth, then realized he had to. As soon as she returned with her plate of food, he said, "It's my fault."

"What do you mean?"

"It was my weed. I thought I'd cleaned out my drawer, but I guess I left something behind."

Bobby saw the color drain from his mother's face. "You knew . . . you knew he was arrested. You knew before the trial—" Her voice had grown louder, and people sitting at nearby tables turned their heads toward them. "Why didn't you tell me? *Bobby*. How could you do this to Frankie?"

"I was afraid they'd kick me out of the Corps. And I never thought they'd send him away." He hung his head down. "I'm sorry, Mom. I'm sorry. I wish I could do it over. I'll never forgive myself if something's happened to Frankie. I already can't forgive myself for him going to Eldridge."

Jessica glared at him, silent for what seemed like the longest time. Finally she looked away. "It's done already. It can't be undone. Beating yourself up over it won't change anything."

"Do you hate me?"

Jessica picked up his hand. "You're my son. I'll always love you. Even when I'm angry at you."

Relief washed over Bobby. For months he'd been eaten up with guilt. As soon as the sentence was handed down, he'd wanted to tell his mother. Now that he had, he felt a weight leave his chest, even though he knew he'd carry the shame of his silence with him for the rest of his life.

"Do you think we should call the police?" Bobby asked.

"It's only been three days. As you pointed out, if he's going on foot, it'll take a lot longer. I'd hoped he would have called you, though."

"He has no money and no food. What if he's hitchhiking and someone picks him up who shouldn't? I think we need to get the police involved. Even if it means he goes back to Eldridge."

Jessica shook her head vehemently. "You don't know what it's like there."

"I know it's safer than out on his own."

—

An hour later, Jessica settled into her room. She'd driven into town after she left Bobby and checked into the first motel she found with a vacancy sign.

Despite her fright over Frankie, and now her anger at Bobby, she had to admit that it had felt comfortable being back again on a military base, back in a PX. Life in the military was structured, governed by rules that everyone knew and followed. It should have been the same way at Eldridge. Go to classes, do your work, follow the guards' instructions, and in four months you go home. But something had gone wrong, terribly wrong, and Frankie, her sweet, gentle boy, had landed in the hospital. It might be risky for him on his own, but she felt in the very marrow of her bones that it was more dangerous for him to go back to Eldridge.

She'd wait as long as it took for Frankie to either get to Bobby or call her. Unlike most army spouses, she'd never believed in prayer, but as she got ready for bed, she whispered, "Please, watch over him. Please, let him be okay."

D ani had been troubled ever since her meeting with Brian Bismark. She'd reported the conversation to Bruce, and he'd asked her to think about possible avenues to help Frankie once he was found. Now she wondered if she should take action before he was found. After all, the goal was to prevent his return to Eldridge. Maybe she could get a court order transferring him to another facility. That way, once they found him, he would go directly to that facility.

She decided to work on a petition for emergency relief, then realized this was new ground for her. She'd never represented a juvenile before—at least, not one adjudicated in juvenile court. Many times she'd had clients who'd been arrested and convicted of a violent crime when they were still in high school, but they'd been tried in an adult court. Even though the appeals process for adult cases varied from state to state, there were enough similarities that learning the differences was easy. But juvenile court was different. A finding of delinquency was not considered a criminal conviction. She put aside the petition and instead turned to Lexis and began researching the law. By the end of the day, she realized her options were limited. There was a very short window for an appeal, and the time had long passed.

She picked up the phone and buzzed Bruce. "How involved can we get in helping Frankie?"

"Don't ignore your current cases, but whatever you can do working around them, I'd really appreciate."

"And if it means going back to Florida?"

"Absolutely. As often as you or Tommy need to. I have more frequent-flyer miles than I know what to do with. And if I run out of them, I'll foot the bill."

Dani hung up, then walked over to Tommy's desk. Each time she saw him, she was reminded of Tom Selleck, who had the same thick, almost-black hair, and a big, bushy mustache. "I've been looking at our legal options for Frankie."

"Yeah?"

"It's difficult. We have to show either that the commitment order was illegal or that there was some mistake or fraud."

"How can we do that?"

"I'm not sure. I'll try to argue that the commitment to a residential facility was so out of proportion to the crime, especially when there hadn't been any previous problems, that it's illegal. But it's a stretch. What I'm really hoping is that by getting a motion in front of the judge, I'll be able to argue for his transfer to another facility."

"Okay. Is there something I can do to help?"

"Yeah. Frankie's classmate testified that Frankie claimed he could get as much pot as he wanted, and Jessica told me Frankie swore he'd lied. I think that must have swayed the judge into believing Frankie was involved with drugs, maybe even selling. I'd like you to go back to Florida and talk to the boy. See if he still sticks to the same story. It'll help me in court if he recants."

"I'll leave first thing tomorrow morning."

"He's just a kid himself. You can't strong-arm him."

"Hey, with five kids of my own, I learned a long time ago how to get the truth out of them."

Dani smiled. "You're the best, Tommy."

"You know it, doll."

~

Jessica paced back and forth in her motel room, twelve long steps from the door to the window. The lone bed and stark, white walls did nothing to relieve her apprehension. She'd brought her laptop with her and spent most of the day on a client's job, designing a new brochure for his business. She'd hoped it would distract her from the silence of her cell phone, but it hadn't. *Call, Frankie. Why don't you call?* And suddenly, it hit her. Although he knew her cell-phone number, what if he'd left a message on the home phone? What if he thought she hadn't returned his call because she was angry at him for running away?

Quickly, she called her voice mail for messages, and her heart beat faster when the machine announced she had one. She entered her PIN and prayed she'd hear Frankie's voice. Instead, she heard someone unfamiliar to her.

"I hope this is the right number. Frankie told me your name, and there's only one Jessica Bishop listed in the directory. But if you're Frankie's mother, I'm worried about him. My name is Bill, and me and my wife helped Frankie get to his brother, but he was supposed to call us when he made it safely, and we haven't heard from him. So, if this is the right person, would you call me back at 912-555-8320? Thanks."

Jessica stifled a sob. Something had happened to Frankie. She replayed the message and wrote down the number, then dialed. As soon as Bill answered, she said, "This is Frankie's mother. I got your message."

"Is he with you? We got concerned when he didn't call."

"No. I haven't heard from him. I'm worried sick. When did you see him last?"

"Almost two days ago. We put him on a train from Savannah to Raleigh. From there, he was supposed to get over to the airport and take a shuttle to Camp Lejeune."

Jessica sunk down on the bed. Frankie was in trouble. She asked Bill to tell her everything about his encounter with her son, then hung up and called Dani.

~

When Dani got off the phone with Jessica, she called Tommy.

"Frankie is missing."

"Yeah, we know that."

"No. I just heard from Jessica. Apparently, he made his way to the Ocala National Forest and found a couple there who helped him. They drove him to their home in Savannah, then put him on a train to Raleigh. No one's heard from him since."

"Oh, that's bad."

"After you interview Tony, can you stay and see what you can find out? He was on the one thirty a.m. train, two nights ago."

"Okay. They'll have security cameras, I'd think. I'll check it out."

Dani hung up and returned to Doug on their couch. Jonah was asleep, and the logs in the fireplace were burning.

"What was that about?"

Dani filled him in. She didn't know Frankie Bishop. She'd met his mother and seen his picture and heard about his life. Yet, even with never meeting him, she felt a strong connection. She thought of the possible things that could have happened to him: he'd changed plans and decided not to go to Bobby; his injuries from the beating slowed him down; he got hurt anew and went to a hospital, where he didn't give them his name; he was picked up by the police and again wouldn't give them his name. And the worst possibility, the one she hoped against hope wasn't the case: someone had taken him against his will, someone who did terrible things to children.

Doug was silent, a bleak expression on his face. "You've heard the stories—"

"I know. A young boy traveling alone, anyone could have grabbed him." She shuddered. "And he's small for his age. That would only make him more appealing to predators."

"His mother has to get the police involved. They need to find him before . . ." Doug just shook his head.

"I know you're right. It's just—it's the classic avoidance-avoidance conflict. Neither option is good. If Jessica calls the police and they find him, they'll send him back to Eldridge, where his life may be in danger. If she doesn't call the police, and Tommy can't find him, who knows what an abductor would do to him?"

"It isn't a hard choice, Dani. He has to be found. When he is, go into court and get him moved from Eldridge. But she can't waste time. She has to call the police now."

Dani wasn't so sure Doug was right. After all, the Florida police had arrested him for bringing two marijuana cigarettes to school. The Florida judge sent him to Eldridge. If Frankie had been eighteen and had no prior arrests, he would, at most, have gotten probation. She turned to face Doug. "Here's what I think. Let Tommy look at the security tapes. If he spots Frankie being taken by someone, he'll call the FBI. They would take up a potential child-trafficking case. If he spots Frankie by himself, then maybe it's just taking him longer than expected to get to the Marine base."

"Losing a day can make it harder to find him."

"I know. And it's really not my choice to make. I'll call Jessica back and give her the options." Dani left to make the phone call. When she returned, she said, "She wants to wait to call the police. Now we just hope for the best."

15

Frankie lay awake in the bed and watched John, still asleep in the second bed. His round stomach moved up and down like waves in the ocean, while soft snores emanated from his parted lips.

John had tied Frankie's hands and feet with rope and taped his mouth closed before he'd gone out for the night. It had been hard for Frankie to get comfortable enough to sleep, but he must have, because he'd awoken with a start, momentarily confused by his surroundings. It came back to him in a rush, and his body stiffened with the knowledge of what this man planned for him. He had to get away, somehow. John was bigger, stronger, and had a gun. Frankie had only his intelligence, and he needed to draw on that if there was any hope of escape. He knew that meant waiting for the opportunity, not attempting something too early, which would only land him in even deeper trouble if he failed.

He'd still been awake when John had returned. When John leaned over him to remove the tape from his mouth, Frankie could smell alcohol, not just from his breath. John reeked of it, as though someone had doused his clothes with whiskey. Maybe someone had. Frankie pictured John trying to pick up a girl and her laughing at his round, ugly face, his thinning hair, his droopy ears. He thought John would be the type to keep trying until the girl got so annoyed, she splashed his face with her drink. Or maybe instead, he'd gotten into a fight with another man. Frankie wondered if John was someone who'd start a fight. He thought it was possible.

He needed to go to the bathroom, but it was impossible with his hands and feet bound together. Suddenly, he was consumed with anger. Not at John, or Tony, or the boys at Eldridge who put him in the hospital, but once again, toward his father. Alex Bishop had moved his family from town to town, always causing his sons to start fresh in new schools. Frankie wanted to be like other boys, who became best friends with the boy on the block who'd started kindergarten with him and who remained friends as they moved from elementary school to middle school and maybe even high school. He wanted to be the boy who was sought after for the school's baseball and soccer teams from the first day, not someone who had to prove himself year after year, school after school.

Just as quickly as it came, his anger washed away, and he was left with the familiar pain in the center of his chest whenever he thought of his father, and his fear that he was dead. His father had taught both his sons the importance of service. He looked up to his father, to his belief in giving back. For his father, it was giving back to his country. But it didn't need to be military service, his father always said. He nourished Frankie's dream of becoming a doctor, and had spoken to him of the work done by Doctors Without Borders. Frankie had wanted to do that, after he'd finished his training. Now he had a record hanging over him. How would he get into a good college with that? A good medical school?

He shook his head. His problems were much more serious now. He'd heard about men like John, men who stole children. When that happened, they were almost never found. The anger returned, this time with John as its sole object. He wouldn't let this man steal his life. It wasn't fair. It wasn't right. He would get out of this somehow. He just had to.

An hour later, John awakened. He rubbed his eyes as he sat up, then looked at Frankie.

"What are you staring at?"

"I need to pee."

John grunted, then waved for Frankie to get out of bed. He untied the rope from his feet, then hands. "Don't dawdle."

Frankie rubbed his wrists where the rope had been, then grabbed his clothes and stepped into the bathroom. After he peed, he washed his hands, brushed his teeth, then got dressed.

"Hurry up in there. You better not be trying something funny."

Frankie stepped back into the bedroom. "I'm finished."

"Sit down on that chair."

Frankie did as instructed, and John once again bound his hands and feet, this time to the arms and legs of the chair. As he began to tape his mouth, Frankie begged him to stop.

John sighed. "All right," he said. "I'll just keep it on when I'm not around. I can't have you calling out to the maid when she knocks on the door. Or screaming your head off so the next room reports the noise."

"I'll be quiet. I promise."

John stared at him with his bloodshot eyes. "You're a payday for me. Nothing more. And I don't take chances with money. I'm going to take a shower, so on it goes." He bent over and placed the strip of duct tape over Frankie's mouth, then disappeared into the bathroom.

Frankie could hear the shower running, then the water from the sink. When John emerged, dressed and shaved, he said, "I'm going to get some breakfast. I'll bring you back food." Frankie watched him place the "Do Not Disturb" sign on the room door as he left.

Once alone, Frankie tried to squirm out of his restraints and got nowhere. Later, when he heard a cart roll past his door—the maid, he thought to himself—he thrashed wildly in the chair and tried to stomp his feet. But his ankles were taped to the chair's legs, and the chair was on carpet. Soon, the sound of the cart disappeared, leaving Frankie without hope for help.

Tommy reached the home of Tony Cuen shortly before two thirty.

Each time he came to Florida, he counted the number of days until he could retire. Even though he was already fifty-nine, he'd have to wait until his youngest was off to college—just six more years. He wouldn't leave during Amy's freshman year, though. He knew from experience that the newly found freedom that came with the transition from living at home to living in a dorm often led to problems. So they'd wait until her second year. Then, he and Patty would be Florida bound.

He parked his rental car two houses away and sat and waited. He'd already spoken to Jessica and gotten some information that would help with his interrogation. The home was in a middle-class neighborhood of mostly colonial houses, all well kept and lushly landscaped. It was his third time in Florida on a case for HIPP, and he enjoyed identifying the flowers and trees, so different from those in the Northeast. Tommy had taken over the gardening at his house when he was still in the FBI. He found that it relaxed him, that it helped relieve the stress from his job. Since then, he'd studied flowers, plants, and trees, and it always gave him pleasure when he spotted something he'd never seen before. Tommy was pretty certain the tree with bright-orange flowers in front of Tony's house was a geiger tree. That was a new one for him.

At ten after three, he spotted a boy with a backpack draped over his shoulders, who walked up to the Cuen house and went inside. Tommy climbed out of his car, stretched out the kinks in his back, and walked to the door. His knock was answered not by the boy but a pretty woman dressed in tight-fitting jeans that highlighted her curves. Her long, blonde hair fell in waves down to the middle of her back. *Bet she was the prom queen in high school and married the star quarterback.*

"Can I help you?"

"Are you Mrs. Cuen?"

"I am."

Tommy handed her his business card. "I'd like to talk to your son, Tony, if I may. It's about his testimony in Frankie Bishop's hearing."

"Why? Isn't that over and done with?"

"There've been some new developments, and it's going to be reopened. I just have a few questions for Tony. It won't take long."

"Okay, I guess. Come on in."

She led Tommy into the living room, then called upstairs. "Tony, there's someone here to see you."

A minute later, Tony entered the room. It was clear that he'd already started his growth spurt—he stood at least five eight and had the beginnings of a muscular body.

"Who are you?"

"My name is Tommy, and I'm here about Frankie Bishop."

Momentarily, Tony's face clouded, but it passed quickly. "The dweeb," he muttered.

Tommy looked at Mrs. Cuen. "Can we sit down?"

She took a seat, and Tony followed. As Tommy sat down, he said, "There's going to be a new hearing on his case. I wanted to go over with you what exactly Frankie said to you that day in the cafeteria."

"He showed me two joints. Said he could get all he wanted."

Tommy stared at him, a scowl on his face. "Do you understand what perjury is?"

"Hey!" Mrs. Cuen said. "What are you implying?"

Tommy turned to her. "I'm saying that Tony lied on the stand. His friend, Richie, was at the table with them, and he admitted Frankie never said that." This wasn't true. Tommy hadn't spoken to Richie. But Jessica had told him the names of others at the table with Tony that day, and Tommy had won more than his share of bluffs.

Mrs. Cuen turned toward her son. "Is that true? Did you lie at that hearing?"

Tony's eyes turned downward, and he began rubbing his arm. "Richie's the liar. He didn't hear anything."

"There. You have your answer," Mrs. Cuen said.

"Actually, no. He didn't answer my question. Tony, look at me."

Tony turned his eyes to Tommy.

"Do you understand what it means to lie under oath?"

Tony nodded. "It means I could go to jail if I lied."

"Not in this case. You wouldn't go to jail for it. You could say you were mistaken. You'd thought he'd said that, but you realized afterward he hadn't. Is that what happened?"

Tony's face reddened. With his voice weak, he said, "He shouldn't have brought drugs to school. Everyone knows that."

"You're right. He shouldn't have. But it makes a difference if it was one time, or he could keep getting more. Do you see that?"

"I suppose."

"So, which was it?"

Tony just sat silently on the couch, his eyes once again turned downward.

"Frankie is in real trouble. Some boys at the juvenile-detention center beat him so badly that he was taken to the hospital. If he goes back, they might kill him the next time. I know you don't like him, but do you want that to happen?"

Tony looked up and whispered, "No."

"Tell me what really happened."

"He showed me the joints, that's all. He never said he could get more."

Mrs. Cuen's hands flew to her chest. "Sweetie, how could you?"

"I didn't think they'd send him away. I just wanted to get him in trouble. He always rubbed it in our face how smart he was."

"Now's your chance to do the right thing," Tommy said. "I need you to sign a document admitting what you just told me. Will you do that?"

"He'll give you what you need," Mrs. Cuen said.

———

When Tommy left, he settled in for the drive up to Raleigh. He wouldn't get there until the middle of the night, but that suited him fine. With fewer people around, he hoped he could persuade the stationmaster to let him review the security tapes—that is, if they had any.

With just a quick stop for a bite to eat, and his foot on the pedal most of the way, he reached the Amtrak station in Raleigh at 2:30 a.m. He made his way inside and found the ticket booths. Only one was manned.

"Hi. I wonder if there's a security detail at this station?"

The man nodded, then pointed down a corridor. "Third door on the left."

"Someone there this time of night?"

"Someone's there twenty-four-seven."

Tommy thanked him, then found the office. He knocked first, then opened the door. Sitting at a desk inside was an elderly man who looked shrunken in his own skin. The few hairs that remained on his mostly bald head were white, and his hands were covered in age spots. Tommy figured it had been a long time since he had been able to handle any real emergency, but he supposed that's why he was on the graveyard shift.

He looked up when Tommy entered. "Can I help you?"

Tommy handed him his card. "A twelve-year-old boy took a train from Savannah to Raleigh two nights ago, and he hasn't been seen since. I'm here on behalf of his mother, who's worried sick. I was hoping you have surveillance cameras that might show if he got off here, and if anyone was with him."

The man leaned back in his chair and turned Tommy's card over and back. "Help Innocent Prisoners Project? This boy do something wrong?"

"My boss is his uncle. He's just trying to help."

"We do have cameras. Covers every track and the main terminal. But you're not police. Can't show it to you without a warrant."

"I appreciate those are the rules. I'm former FBI. Ten years with them. Worked out of the New York office—criminal-investigations division, then counterterrorism. This boy . . . we're worried that a predator has taken him." He pulled out his address book and flipped to the M's, then pointed out a name to the man. "This guy, he's on the FBI's Child Abduction Response Deployment team. If it looks like the boy's with someone, I'll bring him in. Can you help me out? It'd take a load of worry off his mother if she saw he was okay."

The man looked at the clock on the wall. "Well, can't say I'm real busy now. Since you're former law enforcement, I guess I can make an exception. But don't you go telling anyone I let you see them. If you spot someone squirrely, then bring in who you need to without telling them you already took a gander at the films. Deal?"

"Absolutely." Tommy smiled at the man. "What's your name?"

"Phillip. Former cop myself. Retired after thirty-one years, but it's too damn boring sitting at home."

Tommy wondered how it could be less boring than sitting in a mostly empty train station all night long.

Phillip walked over to a file cabinet and opened a drawer. "Two nights ago, you say?"

"He boarded the train in Savannah two nights ago. He would have arrived here the following morning."

He riffled through some folders, then took out three disks. "This one covers track three during the period from eight a.m. to eight p.m. that day. This covers the terminal, and the last covers the parking lot. You can watch them on that computer," Phillip said as he pointed to a second desk.

Tommy fought his fatigue as he sat down at the desk. He'd left his home early for a flight to Tampa, then waited hours to speak to Tony, then drove nine hours to Raleigh. He wanted to find a motel and crawl into bed, come back the next morning to screen the tapes. But, if Frankie had been abducted, then every minute counted. And, more important, the guard on the daytime shift might not be so accommodating. He put in the first disk and waited while it loaded, then double-clicked the lone file in the directory. Finally, a grainy picture of a train platform came up, with hordes of passengers. There was a time stamp at the top right-hand corner. The train from Savannah should have arrived shortly before nine a.m.

Tommy fast-forwarded to 8:50, then sat back and watched. At 8:53, a train pulled into the station. A handful of passengers disembarked from each car, and Tommy slowed down the tape to examine each one. Finally, he spotted a boy who looked like the picture Jessica had shown him of Frankie. It was hard to see the boy's face clearly on the video, but it seemed like him. A man stepped off the train right behind the boy, motioned for him to follow, and the boy did.

After a few steps, the boy tapped the man's shoulder to stop, then he bent down, opened up his backpack, and pulled out a jacket. As he stood up, he lifted his face for a clear shot on the camera. The boy was Frankie Bishop. Tommy watched as he walked away with a stranger.

T ommy waited until six a.m. to phone Clyde Metzger. He'd worked with him in the old days, before Tommy left the FBI and before Metzger transferred to the FBI's Child Abduction Response Deployment, or CARD, team at Quantico. "Better weather," he'd told him back then. "Can't take these New York winters anymore."

"Metzger," a drowsy voice said when the phone was answered.

"Clyde, it's Tommy. Tommy Noorland."

"What the hell time is it?"

"Early. And this isn't a social call."

Now the voice at the other end sounded wide awake. "Tell me."

"I think a twelve-year-old boy has been abducted." Tommy filled him in on the whole tale, from Frankie's arrest to his beating to his escape from the hospital, and finally, the surveillance video from the railway station. "Can you get a warrant for the video? Without letting on that I've seen it already? I don't want to get the old guy in trouble."

"Shouldn't be a problem. I'll call an agent in the Charlotte office. He'll bring their Division Counsel up to speed. We can get a warrant as soon as court opens. I have to tell you, though, two days is a long lead time."

"Yeah. I know."

"Where are you now?"

"Raleigh. In a motel near the railroad. Holiday Inn."

"Hold on a sec." The phone was quiet for a minute. "Just checked the schedules. There's a flight out at eight thirty, gets in at nine thirty-seven. Stay put. I'll put a team together, and we'll pick you up. I'll call you back when we're close."

Tommy had two more calls to make. First, to Dani, and then the harder call, to Jessica. He hadn't wanted to phone either of them before bringing in the FBI. He didn't want them, especially Jessica, to try to talk him out of notifying law enforcement. But what he'd seen on the tape convinced him that Frankie needed more help than HIPP could provide.

He waited another half hour before calling Dani. After he described what he saw on the video, she groaned. "You did the right thing, calling your friend first. I'll call Jessica and let her know what's happening."

After Tommy hung up, he lay down on the bed. He'd slept only a few hours. There was nothing more he could do until Clyde and his team arrived. Within minutes, he was asleep.

—

Dani turned to Doug, still half-asleep in their bed. "It's what we feared. He left the train station with some man."

"I'm sorry. It won't be easy to find him now."

She refused to believe that. With Tommy's ties to the FBI and his bulldog perseverance, she knew they wouldn't give up. Bruce wouldn't want them to. She didn't want to. She pushed away the voice in her head that cautioned her to be realistic, to not hold out false hope.

"I have to call Jessica, let her know." It was not a call she wanted to make, but she dialed the number anyway. When Jessica answered, she told her what Tommy had seen on the tape. Dani heard a low, guttural moan come from her, and waited until Jessica was ready to speak. Finally, after several minutes, Jessica asked, "What happens now?"

"Tommy has already brought in the FBI. They're on their way to Raleigh right now."

"And if they find him, they'll send him back to Eldridge."

Dani could hear soft cries on the other end of the phone.

"I thought returning to Eldridge would be the worst thing that could happen to Frankie," Jessica said. "Now I pray for that to happen."

———

With his thick, honey-blond hair and body sculpted by a daily gym regimen, Clyde Metzger, despite turning fifty-two months ago, still looked more like a movie star than a seasoned FBI agent. When Tommy opened his motel door to him, he shook his head and scowled. "What fountain of youth are you drinking from? You don't look a day older than the last time I saw you. And that was twelve years ago."

Metzger pointed to the few gray hairs at his temple. "Proof I'm still mortal," he said.

Tommy walked out with Clyde to his car, where another agent waited in the passenger seat.

"Tommy, meet Special Agent Henry Greco. He's out of the Charlotte field office."

They exchanged hellos, then Tommy got into the backseat for the drive to the Raleigh railroad station. Another man was in the security office, younger than Phillip by at least thirty years. Metzger handed him the warrant, explained what they were looking for, and when handed the disks, sat down at the same computer where Tommy had viewed them earlier. It didn't take long to cue up to the point where Frankie exited the train.

There was a clear shot of Frankie's face, but not of the man he was with. Metzger forwarded the disk frame by frame, and the best shot was a side view. "This may be enough," Metzger said. He took a screenshot, then forwarded it back to his office. "We'll run it through facial-recognition software. It'll probably take a few hours."

He slid in the disk from the parking lot, then fast-forwarded it to the time immediately after Frankie's train arrived. The three watched it silently, until Tommy, said, "There!" and pointed to Frankie and the man getting into a silver Mercedes sedan.

"Keep your fingers crossed," Metzger said as he slowed the tape down. As the car drove away, they caught a glimpse of the license plate, but it was too distant for them to make out the numbers and letters. Once again, Metzger took a screenshot of the plate and forwarded it to headquarters. "They should be able to enhance it."

Before leaving, Metzger made a copy of the disks for the security guard, then placed the originals in an evidence sleeve. "Okay. Let's go see the mother now."

Jessica hadn't stopped crying since the phone call from Dani. All day, she'd paced back and forth, blaming herself. She never should have moved to Florida, away from the familiarity of an army base. It was unfair to Frankie to make another move after so many. She should have paid more attention to his problems adjusting to the new school. She should have hired a better attorney, or not listened to him when he said it was pointless to appeal. She shouldn't have let her worry about Alex supplant her worry about Frankie.

Bobby's admission had stunned her. If he'd come forward before Frankie's hearing, wouldn't that have proven Frankie wasn't selling drugs? Wouldn't that have kept Frankie at home? Still, if Bobby had told her then, would she have insisted he testify? She didn't know the answer. Bobby's heart had been set on the Marines for so long, it would have been a terrible blow for him to be kicked out. And Frankie was just a child. His attorney had promised that he'd just get a slap on the wrist.

It was too much for her. She needed Alex. She needed him home, his strong arms around her, his reassurance that everything would work out, that they'd find Frankie, that he'd be okay.

She'd met Alex when they were still high school students, he the captain of the football team, she a flautist in the school's marching band. From the time they began dating in their junior year, they'd been inseparable, even when they attended different colleges four hours apart. She'd thought it would be her parents who objected to the interracial pair, but they welcomed him from the start. It was Alex's parents who'd been troubled by her, but they'd come around by the time they married.

She knew when she said yes to his marriage proposal that she'd be an army wife—Alex had always been clear about his goals. And her mother-in-law had helped her understand what it meant to be an army wife—the uprooting every few years, the stress when a loved one was engaged in a combat zone, the bulk of child care on her shoulders. It didn't matter. She loved Alex and would adapt. And she had. She'd built a career as a graphic artist that enabled her to find work wherever they lived. One that she could perform at home much of the time. As long as she had her laptop, she could work anywhere. But Alex had always been there for her, even when he was deployed. She'd never gone more than a week without Skyping with him, hearing his voice, and seeing his handsome face, with its big, brown eyes and lashes so thick, they didn't belong on a man. Bobby had the same eyes as Alex, the same dark skin and tall, muscled body. But Bobby was her son. She needed her husband, now more than she ever had. And he was gone.

She jumped from her chair when she heard the loud knock on the door, then opened it to see Tommy Noorland with two men.

"Jessica, how are you holding up?" he asked as he stepped in the room.

She immediately began crying again, and Tommy pulled her to him. One of the men retrieved a box of tissues from the nightstand and handed it to her. She took one and dried her tears.

"This is FBI Special Agent in Charge Clyde Metzger. He handles child abductions. And this is Special Agent Henry Greco, from the FBI's Charlotte office. They're going to find Frankie."

Metzger held out his hand. "We'll going to try our best to get him back, ma'am."

"Do you know who took him?"

"Not yet. But we're working on it." Metzger handed her the screenshot of the man. "Do you recognize him? Could it be someone Frankie knows?"

Jessica shook her head.

"We have the screenshot of Frankie, but we need a better picture. Do you have one with you?"

Jessica grabbed her purse and pulled out a school photo of her son. "This was taken six months ago."

"Perfect. We'll get this sent around to law-enforcement agencies right away. And speaking of law enforcement, we need to notify the folks at the Florida Department of Juvenile Justice. I expect they'll loop in the local police."

Jessica's heart sank. It kept getting worse and worse.

"Tell me about Frankie. What's he like? It'll help us if we know his strengths and weaknesses."

For the next half hour, Jessica talked about her son. It helped to talk about him, to get her mind off the heartache she felt when she thought about where he was now, whom he was with, what they might do to him.

They were interrupted by the ringing of Metzger's phone. He excused himself, stepped outside the room, then returned a few minutes later.

"We got an ID on the guy. Name is John Felder. He's been on our radar for a while as part of a ring, but we haven't been able to nail him. We don't think he's a pedophile himself, but he's part of a group that fills orders for particular requests from pedophiles."

"Damn," Tommy muttered.

"The good news is that they were able to make out the license plate. We're putting up an AMBER Alert with the description of his car and plate number on all the highway signs leading away from the train station."

"You're tracking his credit-card usage, right?"

Metzger nodded.

Tommy looked over at Jessica. She'd sunk down on the big-cushioned chair in the corner, and her face was deathly pale.

Yesterday, Dani had rushed off a petition for emergency relief, then filed it in the juvenile court located in Cypress County, where Frankie's delinquency hearing had been held. A copy had been faxed to Warren Camden, the assistant state attorney covering that court. When Dani entered the courtroom, Camden was already seated. She took in his wrinkled suit and hair combed over a bald spot, and wondered if he cultivated that look to make jurors sympathetic toward him.

After Judge Humphrey entered the courtroom, he asked, his voice tight, "What's this all about, Ms. Trumball?"

The judge looked down at her with eyes that seemed weary. His dull brown hair, devoid of any trace of gray, seemed inconsistent with the deep wrinkles on his face. *He dyes his hair, I bet.*

"Two months ago, you ruled that Francis Bishop was a delinquent and ordered him sent to a secure residential facility. He was placed at Eldridge Academy."

"I remember. He had a drug problem."

"That was your determination, although we continue to maintain he'd never used drugs."

"If his lawyer didn't like my finding, he should have appealed. It's too late for that now."

"I appreciate that. But, as you'll see in the filed papers, the boy who testified against him admitted in his sworn affidavit that he lied when he said that Frankie claimed he could get more drugs. Accordingly, we believe it's within your discretion to determine that he's spent sufficient time in a residential facility."

"Your Honor—"

Dani turned to the prosecutor. "I'm not finished, Mr. Camden. Your Honor, my esteemed adversary is no doubt about to tell you that Francis Bishop ran away from a hospital where he was being treated for very serious injuries sustained while at Eldridge Academy. It is our belief that he ran away because he was in fear of his life."

"Have you spoken to the boy?"

"No, Your Honor."

"Then how do you know what he was thinking?"

"I don't. What I do know is that he was rushed unconscious to a hospital, and in addition to several broken ribs, his spleen was so damaged that the doctors were unsure whether it could be saved. Most children would be afraid to return to a place where they had been beaten so badly."

Camden cleared his throat. "What Ms. Trumball leaves out is that the report filed by Eldridge with the Florida Department of Juvenile Justice indicates that Mr. Bishop instigated the fight, and that he had been a source of troublemaking since his arrival. Furthermore, the report of his counselor at the facility indicates that he admitted to smoking pot."

"Without Frankie's testimony, we've only heard one side. If Your Honor believes he should continue at a residential facility, then at least he shouldn't be returned to Eldridge until this court has heard his rendition of the attack."

"What efforts have been made to find the boy?" Humphrey asked.

"Francis was on his way to see his brother, who is stationed at Camp Lejeune. Unfortunately, the FBI believes he was abducted by a child predator in Raleigh. They're working on trying to find him.

Hopefully, they will, and in that event, we ask that Francis not be returned to Eldridge before a hearing."

"Okay," Humphrey said. "I understand both of your positions. Give me a few minutes."

Dani waited while the judge wrote on something in front of him. When he finished, he leaned forward in his chair. "Here's the way I see it. Francis Bishop was injured in a beating, during a fight he may have instigated. What we do know for certain is that he's a boy who admitted to drug use, was difficult to control, and who ran away. You say he was abducted, but for all we know, he could have hooked up with someone as part of his escape. This boy is a problem, and it confirms my judgment that he needed to be locked up. And still needs to be locked up.

"I've sent plenty of boys to Eldridge, and when they're released, I get letters from them thanking me for turning their lives around. Eldridge is a good facility, one of the best. I see no reason to change his placement."

"But Your Honor—"

"That's all. That's my ruling. Next case."

———

Each of the three nights they'd been at the motel, John left the room, leaving Frankie's hands and feet bound and his mouth taped shut. Each night he returned hours later, reeking of alcohol. It had been three nights without change. Now, as John readied to go out once again, Frankie asked, "What's going to happen to me?"

"You'll find out tomorrow. That's when I hand you off. I got lucky finding a kid too quickly. That's why we've been holed up here."

"But then what?"

"Kid, you ask too many questions. Better you don't know what's coming."

Frankie did know. If someone was coming to get him tomorrow, then he needed to get away before then. He'd been afraid to try. Afraid of what John would do to him if he were caught. It had taken all this time to work up his courage, to figure out a plan. He needed his hands and legs to be free. That happened only when he got washed up and dressed in the mornings, or, for his hands, when he ate meals. *Tomorrow morning. After I get dressed. That's when I take my chance.*

Bright sunshine streaming through the curtains woke him the next morning. It was the first sound sleep he'd had since John had taken him. When Frankie opened his eyes, John was already dressed and walking around.

"It's about time, kid. I was just about to wake you."

Frankie rolled onto his side, then pushed himself upright. After John untied the rope on his hands and feet, Frankie grabbed his clothes and shoes and went into the bathroom. *I can do this,* he kept saying to himself as he washed up. He wondered what his mother was thinking. She visited Eldridge every Saturday without fail. Did she know he'd been in the hospital? Did she know he escaped? He missed his mother. He missed his brother and his father. He missed his life.

He finished washing, then dressed himself. When he exited the bathroom, he walked toward John, who was standing by the desk. As he neared his captor, he didn't hold out his hands, as he had every other morning, ready to be bound up again. Instead, he walked up close, kept his eyes on John's, and when he reached him, swiftly brought his knee up and smashed his crotch. John howled in pain and, as he doubled over, Frankie ran to the door, unlatched it, and flew out of the room. He stopped briefly to look down the corridor for an exit sign, then sprinted toward it. When he reached the door to the stairs, he glanced back and saw John racing toward him. He thought about screaming, but that would slow him down.

As he rushed down the flight of stairs, he heard the door above him open, then footsteps behind him. He reached the first floor and flung open the door. He was in the back of the motel, with long rows of parked cars to both his right and his left. He paused as his fear tightened his stomach. Should he scream now? Hope someone in a first-floor room heard him? Run for his life and pray John didn't catch him? He was fast, had always been fast. But maybe John was, too. John's legs were longer; he could cover more ground with his stride.

Then Frankie remembered John's gun. If he'd grabbed it before he'd lit out after him, then even if Frankie was faster, John could shoot him. Frankie ran toward the fifth car in the row, then scooted down and slid underneath it. Hiding seemed like his only option. Hide and hope John figured he'd run around the building.

He heard the exit door open, then glimpsed John's feet planted outside the door. He was probably looking around, Frankie figured, trying to decide which way to go. He watched as John turned left, then sped toward the front of the motel. He stayed rooted in his spot, afraid to move. He hadn't taken his jacket with him, and the cool air pierced his chest, his arms, his legs.

Minutes passed, or maybe it was longer, much longer, he couldn't tell, but John was back, standing still in the parking lot. He moved, closer to Frankie's car. Frankie held his breath. *Make him go away. Please, make him go away.*

And then he was there, standing over the car Frankie hid under.

"Either you slide out on this side, or I'll shoot you right where you are."

Frankie wriggled out from under the car. When he stood up, John wrapped his beefy arm around his neck, put the cold barrel of the gun up to his head, and whispered in his ear. "Try that again, and I will shoot you. No second chances."

CHAPTER
18

"We got a hit off an ATM," Metzger told Tommy. "I guess he's been using cash for everything, because nothing's shown up. He's a pro—keeping the trail clean. But he must have run out of dough. Took four hundred from a machine in Greensboro around one a.m."

"You think he's still there?"

"Don't know. But the local police are bringing his picture around to motels and shops near the ATM. Maybe we'll get lucky."

"Still no hit on an address for him?"

"He moves around too much. Every time we follow up on a lead, by the time we get there, he's moved somewhere else."

Tommy had stayed in Jacksonville, more to give Jessica moral support than anything else. He'd taken a room in the same motel as Jessica, as had Metzger. The FBI were working the case, with help from local police when they needed it. There wasn't anything he could add. But Jessica was alone, her husband missing halfway around the world, maybe dead.

Tommy couldn't imagine Patty handling something like this on her own. Not because she was a woman, but because no parent should go through it alone. At times like this, spouses needed to lean on each other, get strength from each other. That's why he stayed. To give Jessica strength.

He walked over to Jessica's room and knocked on the door. When it opened, she asked, "Have you heard anything?"

Tommy stepped inside. "He was in Greensboro last night. They don't know if he's still there, but they're checking it out."

Jessica dropped down on a chair and buried her face in her hands. When she looked up, her cheeks were tear-splotched. "I keep thinking that this is a nightmare, that I'm going to wake up soon and realize it was just a dream. But nothing changes."

Tommy looked her over. She had dark circles under her eyes, and her skin was a pale, pasty color. He doubted she'd slept much the past few days. "This is a break, getting a location for him."

Jessica smiled wanly at him, then sank farther into the chair.

"Tell me about your husband," Tommy said, hoping to get her mind off Frankie. "How did you meet?"

"High school. Junior year. I knew I wanted to be with him from the first day I spotted him. He was brilliant. And gorgeous. And completely oblivious to me. I'm afraid I chased him shamelessly."

"It was the other way around with me and my wife. She barely noticed me. We hung out with the same group of kids, and she always thought of me just as a friend. Took me two years to convince her we belonged together."

"Do you have children?"

"Five. Two in college and three at home."

"Your wife must be a saint. It's hard enough with two."

"She's great—handles the kids like a drill sergeant when I'm on the road. They wouldn't dare get out of line with her. I'm the softy."

Jessica grew silent for a moment. "I thought I was doing a good job with Frankie. All the mistakes I made with Bobby, I thought I'd fixed for Frankie. And then this happened."

Tommy leaned over and took Jessica's hands in his. "This isn't your fault."

"Oh, the kidnapping isn't. But if Frankie hadn't been sent to Eldridge, it wouldn't have led to this. And it's my fault that he brought joints to school."

"No, it isn't."

"I should have seen how unhappy he was at the school. I should have spoken to him about it, tried to help him adjust."

"All kids hide things from their parents." Tommy understood the blame game. He'd seen it often in parents of kids who'd done something terribly wrong, or had something terribly wrong happen to them. All kids got in trouble sometimes. When it was minor trouble, the parents had no difficulty blaming the kids. When it was major trouble, they turned the blame onto themselves. If only they'd done things differently . . . except in most cases he'd seen, it wouldn't have made a difference. Sure, there were the neglectful parents, the abusive parents. Without a doubt, that behavior contributed to their child's actions, or to what happened to their child. But just as often, kids who ended up in trouble had very ordinary parents. Parents who tried their best to do the right thing for their children. The fact was, he knew, parents have never been able to protect their kids from all the dangers in the world. The best they can hope for was that luck would keep them out of harm's way.

There was a knock on the door, and Jessica stood up to answer it. Metzger entered the room. "We've gotten our first sighting. The bartender at a bar near the ATM said Felder has been there the past three nights. So he must have a room nearby. I'm feeling good about this. We're going to find your son, Mrs. Bishop."

———

It had been tense in the room ever since John caught Frankie. The ties around his hands and legs were tighter than ever, and even though John was in the room, he kept Frankie's mouth covered with tape. John paced back and forth, now and then hurling expletives at Frankie. After what seemed like hours, a faint knock was heard. John drew the curtain aside to see who was there, then opened the door.

A tall, thin man with bushy eyebrows and a goatee flecked with gray entered the room and glowered at Frankie.

"I didn't ask for a black kid."

"You didn't specify."

The man shook his head and scowled at John. "I didn't think I needed to. You should have known. When I want black, I tell you. Otherwise, it's white. Besides"—he looked Frankie up and down—"he don't look ten." The man ripped the tape off Frankie's mouth. "How old are you?"

"Twelve."

"I told you the order was for a ten-year-old. The most, eleven." His glare at John was so intense, it reminded Frankie of comic books he'd read, with drawn-in daggers flying out of someone's eyes.

"He's small. He can pass for eleven."

"Now, maybe, but it can change in a few months. This is a good client. I give him what he wants. I can't use this kid."

Sweat had begun to form on John's forehead. His hands were squeezed tightly together. "I've had expenses," he said. "This room. Food. Besides, what am I supposed to do with him? I can't just cut him loose."

The thin man looked back at Frankie, then pulled him up from the chair and eyed him top to bottom. "I'll give you half your fee for him. Maybe one of my other clients will take him."

"And if I get a ten-year-old for you?"

"Same deal. Full fee."

John smiled. "Okay. Take him."

19

As John packed up his toiletries, he heard a loud banging on the door, then shouts.

"FBI. Open up!"

Momentarily paralyzed with panic, he quickly calmed down when he realized Frankie had been gone for a good half hour. They couldn't have gotten him. And without Frankie, there was nothing to hold him on.

He opened the door and plastered on a big smile. "What's going on?"

The larger man pushed open the door and entered the room. The smaller man spun him around and slapped handcuffs on his wrists. "Where is he?" asked the larger man after he opened the bathroom and closet doors.

"Don't know who you're talking about. I think you got the wrong room, fellas."

"We have the right room, and you're under arrest for the kidnapping of Francis Bishop."

He read him his rights, then pushed him down on the bed. "I'll ask you again. Where is he?"

"Don't know why you think I'd know who you're talking about."

The bigger guy bent down and sneered in his face. "Because he was seen getting into your car, asshole."

John willed himself to remain calm. "You talking about the boy on the train? I gave him a lift to the airport. Haven't seen him since. That was four days ago."

"You're a bad liar, Felder. The motel clerk ID'd the boy." He pulled John up from the bed and toward the door. "Maybe your memory will return when you're in lockup. Get moving."

They had nothing on him, John told himself. Even with the ID. He'd been in worse spots before and gotten out of them. He'd get out of this one, too.

The men drove him to a police station twenty minutes away, and he was led into an interrogation room. Standard fare, he thought. One table with three chairs, and a one-way mirror, behind which no doubt others would be watching. Well, they could watch all they wanted. He had nothing to say.

After reading him his rights once more, they left him alone in the room for a half hour or so, with his hands still cuffed behind him. It was getting uncomfortable. He wished they'd start their questioning, get the whole thing over with. He knew he'd be leaving unscathed in a few hours.

Finally, a tall, well-built man took a seat in the room. "My name is Tom Noorland," he said, "and I'm your worst enemy."

John smirked. He was used to their tricks.

"You see, I'm not a policeman, and I'm not FBI. I'm just a private citizen who happened to wander in here while the law-enforcement folks were away. So, I couldn't care less about their rules." The man stood up and walked around the table, then stood behind John, with his hand on his neck. He bent down and spoke very softly in John's ear. "All I care about is one thing: getting Frankie Bishop back, alive and unharmed. I don't care about getting evidence that will stand up in court. I don't care if you walk away. If you want to walk away, tell me where he is."

"Fuck you."

Tom smacked the side of his head, then continued his soft talk in his ear. "See, that kind of attitude will make it hard for you to walk out of here. It'll make it hard for you to walk anywhere, because first, I'm going to break your legs. Then I'm going to break your arms. Then I'm going to grab your nuts and squeeze so hard, you'll wish you were dead. And finally, if you don't talk, I'll grant that wish."

"Bullshit."

In an instant, Tommy kicked the chair out from under John, pushed him facedown on the floor, then sat on top of him, locking John in place. In another instant, he wrapped one arm under John's foot, grabbed his ankle, lifted it up, then thrust it away from his body as he twisted it, stopping only when he heard it snap.

John let out a howl that could be heard blocks away, yet no one came into the room. "You broke my ankle! You broke my ankle!" he screamed.

"Yeah, I know. I'm sorry. I promised you a leg." Tommy hauled him up and placed him back in his seat. "I told you no one was watching, John. Shame about that nasty fall you took running away from the cops. I guess you broke your ankle then. Care to go for the other one?"

"You're out of your mind," John said, still moaning in pain.

Tommy smiled broadly. "Now you understand." He reached over to topple the chair once again.

"No, wait!" John screamed. "I'll give you what you want."

At that moment, the door to the interrogation room opened, and two men walked in. "I'm FBI Special Agent Metzger, and this is my colleague, Special Agent Greco. Sorry you had to wait. We got held up."

Metzger looked at Tommy, who held out his hand to shake. "I'm Tom Noorland. Friend of the family."

John began screaming. "He's crazy! He broke my ankle. I need a doctor."

Metzger's expressionless face had the barest hint of a smile. He looked at notes he held in his hand. "It says here that you fell while you were being chased. I suspect that's when you broke your ankle."

John understood now. It wasn't going to be business as usual. This whole dance had been choreographed. He had no doubt that if he wasn't forthcoming, he'd be left alone once more with the lunatic. "I want a deal."

"Lead us to Frankie Bishop, and then we'll consider it."

John moaned from the pain. His shirt was soaked with sweat, and he felt like he could pass out. But he still had cards to play. "You think I'm an idiot? No deal, no information. And I need a doctor!"

Metzger looked at his watch, then turned to Greco. "Didn't we have a conference call we needed to take now?"

"Yeah, I think we better go."

"Just a minute!" John screamed at them. "I know what they do inside to guys in for anything to do with kids. All I want is a promise that my sheet will say something different. Like embezzlement or something. And, look, if I wait 'til my attorney gets here, I'm sure he could get a knock-down on the charge. But you want the kid. And the longer it takes, the harder it'll be to find him."

"If we find Frankie Bishop based on what you tell us—and he's alive—we'll knock it down to criminal facilitation. Ten to fifteen."

John nodded. "Put it in writing, then I'll tell you what I know."

As soon as Dani returned to New York from the hearing, she placed a call to Joshua Cosgrove. The senior assistant US attorney for the Southern District of New York had helped her once before. She hoped he would again.

"How've you been, Dani?" Josh asked when he picked up the phone.

They chatted first, getting the usual pleasantries out of the way, before Dani said, "I need another favor."

"After what you landed us last year, you can have any favor you want."

"I'm not even sure how much you can do. It's outside your jurisdiction. And premature to boot."

"Go ahead. I'm already intrigued."

"There's a young boy in Florida, just twelve, who was sent to a secure juvenile facility because he brought two joints into school."

"Prior history?"

"None. Perfect grades, perfect behavior."

"That seems pretty harsh, but we have no sway over state juvenile proceedings."

"There's more. He was badly beaten while there and sent to a hospital. Before his discharge, he ran away."

"I gather they want to slap more time on his stay because of that."

"No. Well, probably, but they haven't found him yet. He was on his way to his brother, who's stationed at Camp Lejeune, when he was abducted by a child predator."

Dani heard a deep intake of breath on the other end. She knew Josh had worked child-pornography cases before and knew that he reviled those perpetrators above all others. More than murderers, more than drug dealers. They earned a special circle of hell, and he'd do anything he could to help them send them there.

"What can I do?"

"The FBI have a suspect they're hoping will lead to Frankie. They're questioning him right now. If they do get Frankie back, he'll be returned to Eldridge Academy, where he was beaten senseless. His mother believes that's why he ran away—because he's afraid of more of that when he returns."

"Have you gone into juvenile court to get him moved to another facility?"

"Yes. Yesterday. And the judge practically threw me out."

"I'll make a call to my counterpart in North Carolina. See if he'll agree to keep Frankie in protective custody as a material witness when he's found. Assuming he's found."

Dani felt a wave of relief wash over her. It was just what she'd hoped he would offer. It didn't get Frankie his freedom, but it gave them time. Time to look into the judge who sentenced him, the judge who wouldn't move him for his safety. Something was wrong there, and Dani needed time to find out what.

—

They drove for hours, the thin man silent the whole time. Frankie knew his name was Mark. At least, that's what John had called him. He could tell from the highway signs they were heading south, but he didn't know where. The sign where Mark exited the highway said

"Atlanta," and they drove on smaller roads for another half hour. By the time they pulled up to the small ranch home, it was already dark. Frankie hadn't had anything to eat since breakfast, and despite his fear, he was hungry.

"Out," Mark barked at him after he'd pulled into the garage.

He exited the car and stood there until Mark grabbed his hands and pulled them behind his back. He slapped cuffs on them, then ordered Frankie to move toward the door that led into the house. Once inside, Mark grabbed Frankie's collar, then marched him to the basement's door.

Mark opened it, then pushed Frankie in front of him. "Move. Downstairs."

Frankie did as he was told. There were three doors in the narrow hallway at the bottom of the stairs. Mark instructed him to open the door on the left. As soon as he opened the door, a nauseating odor filled his nostrils. He stepped inside and scanned the unfinished room, lit by a single bare bulb suspended from the low ceiling. Cement walls and floor, a dirty mattress in one corner, a bucket in another. He heard a whimpering sound and spun around. Shackled to the wall was a girl, maybe two or three years older than he was.

"Frankie, meet Daisy. But don't get too friendly with her. She belongs to me." Mark laughed, a sickening sound that turned Frankie's stomach. He pushed Frankie down on the mattress. "Might as well get comfortable," he said as he removed Frankie's handcuffs. "Could be a few days before I find a buyer for you."

Once Mark left, Frankie turned to the girl. She was painfully thin, with stringy blonde hair that looked like it hadn't been washed in weeks. Her pale-blue eyes had dark circles under them. "How long have you been here?" he said.

She shrugged, then with a hoarse voice said, "I don't know. Months, I think."

"Does he keep you like that? Chained up?"

"Not at first. But I tried to run away. Since then. Unless he's . . ." Her voice trailed off.

"What?"

She stared at Frankie. It seemed as though her eyes were hollow, devoid of all feeling. "Unless he's raping me. Then he unchains me and takes me into the other room. When he's finished, he brings me back in here and locks me up."

Frankie knew about rape. Bobby had showed him pictures of naked girls and told him about sex. And he'd cautioned him that anytime a girl said no, he had to back off. Not that any girl ever said yes to him. He'd never had a girlfriend, although there was a girl he liked at his last school. He couldn't imagine anyone doing to her what Mark must be doing to Daisy.

"How did . . . how did you get here? Did he grab you from the street?"

Daisy laughed, a hollow, bitter sound. "Grab me? No, I walked right into this. I caused this fucking nightmare."

Frankie didn't know what to say, so he remained silent. After a while, Daisy spoke again.

"I hated my home. My parents screamed at each other all the time, and treated me like I didn't exist. Just some stranger they were supposed to feed. Mark friended me on Facebook. At first, he said he was fifteen. We'd e-mail back and forth, and it was like he got me. Finally, someone understood what I was feeling." She gave an empty laugh. "After a few months, he admitted he was older, but by then, I didn't care. He promised to take me away from my family, give me gifts, whatever I wanted. So I said, hell, yeah, I'd meet him. I got in his car willingly, drove here willingly, happy to be with someone who cared about me. And then, we got to this house."

She grew silent again.

"Did he take you down here right away?"

Daisy nodded. "He told me he had something special to show me downstairs. As soon as he opened this door, he shoved me inside, then started punching me. When he finally stopped, he told me he wouldn't do that again as long as I did what I was told. He started raping me that night."

Listening to Daisy, the realization hit him hard: this is what he faced. He began to shake, his whole body in the grip of a terrifying fear. *My mom will find me,* he kept saying over and over to himself. *She'll rescue me.* Only he wasn't sure he really believed that.

"How did they get Felder to talk?" Dani asked Tommy when he called in.

"I had a little help in that."

Dani didn't want to ask what he meant. She loved working with Tommy, but she knew that sometimes he acted outside accepted rules, sometimes even outside the law. "What now?" Dani felt helpless back in New York, but she knew this was Tommy's bailiwick.

"He only had the first name of his contact. A man named Mark. He's part of an organized ring, all operated over the Internet. Mark gets a request for a child, giving the desired age, gender, anything else of importance to the requester, and Mark has a network of procurers—men who snatch a child fitting the desired description. Felder is one of them. A place and time is set up for the transfer to Mark, and the procurer gets paid $5,000. Felder doesn't know where he takes them, or if Mark works with anyone else."

Dani felt nauseated. It was repulsive. She wasn't naive. She knew such things occurred, but still—it broke her heart to think of a help-less child caught in such a sick web. "So, that's it? A dead end?"

"Not yet. Felder gets the request through a website. The feds turned over his laptop to their computer specialists, along with Felder's password. They're hoping to track down Mark's full name and location through the IP address."

Dani became aware that her hand had dropped protectively to her stomach. At times, she wondered if it was selfish to bring children into a world where such depravity existed.

—

Dani finished up her work in the office, then headed home, arriving in time to greet Jonah as he got off the school bus. They went into the kitchen, where Katie had left chocolate-chip muffins for Jonah.

After Jonah finished one, he pulled a single sheet of paper from his backpack. "Mommy, there was a man in school today. He wants to do a story about my musical endowment."

Dani had learned to hold back her smile when Jonah, like other Williams syndrome children, missed the mark on the words he chose, often substituting a synonym that didn't quite fit. "Really? Where's he from?"

"Mrs. Radler wants you to sign this paper so he can talk to me."

Dani took a look at the paper that Jonah handed her. A reporter from the *New York Times* was doing a story about the musical talent of some children with Williams syndrome. "Will he be talking to other students in your school?"

Jonah nodded. "Lucy and Eddie."

Dani knew that Lucy was a gifted singer and Eddie a piano prodigy. "How do you feel about it, Jonah? Do you want your story to be in the newspaper?"

"I think it would be superlative."

"Well, then, I'll talk to Dad, and if he's okay with it, I'll sign my permission."

Jonah beamed.

Dani had been so frightened when she and Doug first received Jonah's diagnosis. Afraid of what his future would hold. Afraid that they'd fail as his parents. Afraid to have another child. Time had allayed those fears. Jonah was doing well. They'd made mistakes, as all parents do, but Jonah had survived them, and they'd learned along the way how to do things better. Yes, horrible things happened in the world; evil people existed. But they would love this new child in spite of it. And, with luck, this child would never come face-to-face with those horrors, as Frankie Bishop had, wherever he was.

—

The door to the room opened, and Frankie saw Mark enter with two trays of food. The room's single overhead light gave Mark's face an eerie pallor.

"Here's the rules, boy. I feed you twice a day. An hour later, I'll take you out to the bathroom. If you need to relieve yourself in between, use the bucket. Light gets turned out at nine p.m. and turned on at nine a.m. Behave, and we'll get along fine. Give me any problems, and you'll end up like Daisy. Understand?"

Frankie nodded.

Mark placed a tray in front of him, and then released Daisy's right hand from the restraint, keeping the left one shackled. "Be back for you later, sweetie pie," he said to the girl, a leering grin on his face.

When he'd gone, Frankie looked at the food. It was a heated-up frozen dinner—some sort of pasta dish, maybe lasagna. He took a bite, and if he weren't so hungry would have spit it out. It was barely warm and tasted rancid. He ate it anyway.

He didn't understand how everything in his life had fallen apart. Sure, he didn't like moving around so much, but he'd gotten by. Eventually, he always made friends in his new school. His teachers always liked him. His mother and father loved him. His brother looked out for him. And then they got the news that his father had gone missing. What did that even mean? How could the army not find him? Would he ever come home? It was the stupid war. Not even a real war. That was the start of everything. They wouldn't have moved from the army base if his father hadn't been deployed. He missed his mother, but he missed his father more. It wasn't fair what happened to him. It wasn't fair that he might never come home. Home. That's where he wanted to be. Home with his mother and father.

He began crying, just silent tears at first, but then it caught in his throat, and he was sobbing and he couldn't stop. He hugged himself tightly and rocked back and forth, and Daisy didn't say anything until he'd cried himself out.

"I cried, too, at first. Every day. But it didn't change anything."

Later, Mark came back. He grabbed Frankie by his collar and pulled him to his feet. "Bathroom time," he said, and pushed Frankie toward the door. Mark waited outside the bathroom while Frankie peed, then shoved him back into the room. He turned to Daisy, unlocked her other hand. As she rubbed her wrists, he said, "Time for fun, my little darlin'." She turned back once to glance at Frankie, then walked out with Mark.

She was gone for more than an hour. When she returned, Mark snapped the handcuffs, attached to a chain on the wall, on her wrists, then shut out the one light in the room and left. It was pitch-black.

"Are you all right?" Frankie asked.

The only thing he heard in return were soft cries.

———

For two days, the pattern was the same. At nine the following morning, Mark returned with breakfast, another frozen-food meal of runny eggs and limp bacon. An hour later, he brought them to the bathroom. When it was Daisy's turn, she didn't come back for an hour, sometimes longer. Mark barely spoke to Frankie, barely took notice of his existence. Food and bathroom, food and bathroom. He didn't tell Frankie any more of what was in store for him, and Frankie was too frightened to ask.

The first night, after Daisy returned, Frankie pulled the mattress nearer to her so she'd at least have something soft to rest on. He remained upright on the end of it, giving Daisy most of the space so she could lie down.

"What did your parents do to you?" Frankie asked her that first night.

"What do you mean?"

"Did they hit you?"

"Hah. You think that's the worst thing parents can do?"

"No. I guess not. But it was bad enough that you wanted to run away from them. I just wondered if they'd hurt you." Frankie couldn't imagine parents so bad that you'd want to leave them. His mother always did nice things for him, like cook the foods he liked to eat, and drive him to places he wanted to go. Every night she still tucked him into bed, even though he wasn't a baby anymore, and told him she loved him. His father wasn't around as much, but when he was, he always played games with him and Bobby, like football or soccer or tennis. He always bragged about Frankie to his friends, even in front of Frankie, although that embarrassed him. He kept wishing over and over that his father was alive and able to find his way back. After all, his father was the strongest person he knew.

"From the time I was little, my parents told me how worthless I was," Daisy said. "Too stupid. Too ugly. Too skinny. Nothing I did was good enough for them. They never hit me, but they never loved me either. Sometimes, they'd disappear for a few days and leave me home alone, without any food in the house or money to buy some. I bet they're relieved that I'm gone."

Frankie felt sad for Daisy. She'd left one nightmare and marched right into a worse one. Whatever happened to him, Frankie was certain his mother would never stop looking for him.

CHAPTER

22

"How much longer?" Tommy asked. He and Jessica had been sitting idly by with Metzger at the Raleigh police station, where the FBI task force had borrowed a room and set up a temporary command center.

"They're working on it," Metzger answered. "Whoever set up the site did a good job of hiding himself."

Tommy had been trying to keep Jessica calm, but it hadn't been easy. He could understand her agitation. If one of his kids had been abducted, he doubted that he'd be able to sit by and wait for something to break. He'd want to bust down some walls, or go to a bar and pick a fight, or ram his car into a tree. Anything to provide some physical pain, so as to wipe away the psychic pain he'd be experiencing.

"Want a cup of coffee?" Tommy asked Jessica.

She shook her head.

"Candy from the machine?"

"I can't eat anything."

He wrapped an arm around her shoulder. "They're going to find Frankie. Their cyber experts are ace at cracking through encryptions."

She turned to look up at him. "My husband told me he'd be safe over in Afghanistan. That things had quieted down. And now he's missing. I know you're just trying to be helpful, but words won't bring either of them back to me."

Tommy understood her despair. Much as he wanted to soothe her, he knew his words were hollow. Frankie had been missing for five days. With stranger abductions, that was a lifetime. After twenty-four hours, the chance of finding the child became less and less likely.

They sat together in silence. Almost two hours later, Metzger entered their room sporting a wide grin. "They cracked it. Their e-mails had been encrypted using a public key, with a private key needed to decode it. They were routed through servers that bounced from India to Russia to Iceland, of all places. John gave us his private key, and with that our guys figured out Mark's private key. We've traced it to Mark Hollander, in Atlanta. We have a team headed over there now, but they'll sit on the house and watch first. We're leaving now to go there."

Tommy stood up. "I'd like to go with you."

Metzger shook his head. "This is a risky operation. You're a civilian now. Stay here, and I'll keep you updated."

"I won't get in your way. I'll sit in the car."

Metzger hesitated, then finally said, "No cowboy stunts. You do exactly what I say."

"Deal." Tommy turned to Jessica. "We're going to bring Frankie back to you. I promise."

Mark entered the darkened room and switched on the light bulb. "Rise and shine, my little ones."

Frankie had been awake for hours, barely able to catch any sleep on the corner of the mattress he'd taken for himself.

"Good news, boy. I found someone to take you. You'll be out of here by tonight."

Frankie shuddered. His time was running out.

When Mark left the room, Daisy said, "You have to try to escape. When he takes you out to the car."

"How am I supposed to do that?"

"You have to think of a way. If you see any chance at all, you gotta take it."

"He has a gun."

"I'd rather be dead than be his slave forever. You don't know what it's like."

Frankie was quiet. So far, no one had touched him. Still, his heart had been racing ever since he'd been thrown in this room. What would happen to him after he was turned over to this other man? He'd heard stories. Would he be chained up like Daisy? He'd hoped against hope that somehow his mother would rescue him. Or Bobby. But no one had come. Maybe Daisy was right. He had to rescue himself.

"You're my only hope." Daisy's voice was soft, her tone pleading. "If you don't get free, and tell people where I am, then I'll die here."

"Will you go home, then?"

Daisy took a while to answer. "Maybe. Maybe my parents will be glad I'm back. Maybe they'll realize they missed me. So you have to try. Please."

Frankie knew she was right. He had to get out. Somehow find a way.

Metzger's car pulled up down the block from the yellow ranch home just before eight p.m. Greco sat next to him in the front passenger seat, Tommy in the rear. As soon as they parked, a beefy man with a gray-flecked goatee walked up to the car. Metzger rolled down his window, and the man held out his hand.

"You Metzger?" he asked as they shook.

"I am."

"I'm Detective Paul Diamond. We've been staking out his house since you called. No one's gone in or out. And since no lights came on after it got dark, we suspect he's not there."

"Let's give it more time. He could be out picking up another kid. He drove to Greensboro to get Frankie Bishop."

Diamond returned to his car, while Tommy and the feds remained in theirs, chatting quietly. Almost two hours later, a car pulled into the driveway, the garage door opened, and the car drove in.

"Stay put," Metzger said to Tommy as he and Greco quietly exited the car. Several houses down, four more plainclothes police, Diamond among them, left another car. All had their guns drawn.

Two of Diamond's men soundlessly moved to the rear of the house, Diamond and another to each side. The FBI agents knocked loudly on the door and announced, "FBI. Open up!"

Metzger heard some rustling inside, but the door remained closed. He knocked once more, then turned to the men and nodded. As he reached out to check if the door was unlocked, it suddenly opened a crack. Two shots rang out, one of them catching Greco in the center of his chest. He fell to the ground. Metzger pulled him away as the door slammed shut again.

"You okay?"

Greco nodded, then stood up. "Just took the wind out of me."

"Don't ever complain to me again about wearing your vest."

Diamond rounded the corner. "I just called for backup."

"Good. But I'm not sure we can wait. If the boy is inside, I think we need to move quickly." Metzger called for one of the two men stationed in the back to come around front. "Is there a back door?"

The detective nodded.

"I'll draw him out here. You and your partner break in through the back."

As the two men ran around to the rear, Metzger walked up to the front door, staying on the hinged side. He banged on the door once more, and again, Hollander opened it slightly and began shooting wildly. Metzger returned fire.

When he stopped to reload, there was only silence inside. Moments later, the front door opened, and Sam Porter, one of Diamond's men, stood on the other side. "He's not on this level," the detective said. "Emilio's checking out upstairs."

Metzger and Greco entered the house, Diamond right behind. They heard the sound of footsteps above them, then a voice calling out, "Clear." Seconds later, the detective came downstairs, shaking his head. "He's not up there."

"There's a basement," Porter said, nodding toward an open hallway door.

Metzger switched on the light over the stairs, then led the way down, the others following. There were three closed doors along the tight hallway. He opened the first door, waited a beat, then with his gun in hand, swept his flashlight over the room. Only a double bed. No headboard, no carpeting, no other furniture in the room. Just a bed. A small casement window caked with dust looked like it hadn't been opened in years. He shook his head and backed out.

Greco stood by the second door, Diamond by the third. Metzger headed to Greco, then opened the door and once again waited a beat before sweeping his flashlight into the space. A small bathroom. Sink and toilet, with a stall shower. No window. Finally, Metzger opened the third door. A bare bulb hanging from the center of the room illuminated a man standing in the corner with a gun pointed at the head of a painfully thin girl. Her arms were handcuffed to a chain attached to the wall.

"Take one step inside, and she's dead," the man said.

Metzger stayed rooted in the doorway, giving him only a partial view inside the room. "You Hollander?" Metzger asked.

"You know I am."

Without looking away from him, Metzger hitched his shoulders slightly, a signal for Greco to call in a hostage-negotiation team. "Don't make this hard on yourself. You know there's no out for you."

Hollander laughed, the sound reverberating off the walls of the barren room. "Good try. You're not going to let me kill Daisy."

There was one casement window in the room. It, too, looked permanently shut. But if Metzger could get Hollander to move a few steps toward him, the marksmen would have a clear shot through the window. He needed to keep Hollander talking long enough for the hostage team, with their marksmen, to get to the house.

"Where's the boy?"

"What boy?"

"Don't play coy. We know you have Frankie Bishop."

"Not anymore. He's gone."

"Where?"

"Let me walk, and I'll tell you."

"That's not going to happen. Tell us where Frankie is, and it'll go easier on you."

"You don't let me walk, it ain't going to go easy for the boy." He pushed the gun right up against Daisy's head. "Or for her."

—

As Metzger kept Hollander talking, Greco slipped back up the stairs with Diamond and called for a hostage team. Fifteen minutes later, they arrived and immediately began their examination outside the premises. When they reached the window to the basement room where Hollander was holed up, they crouched down on their stomachs, ten feet away so as not to be observed.

"Are you certain you can do it through the glass? Without harming the girl?" Greco asked the sharpshooter.

"If Hollander moves into sight. I've done it before."

"Can you shoot the gun out of Hollander's hand without killing him?"

"I'm trained to shoot to kill."

"It's not just the Bishop boy. Hollander could lead us to others who've come through his system."

"I'll try. Just get him to move toward the window."

"Let your negotiator try to talk him down first." Greco turned to the negotiator, Sergeant Egton, and gave him Hollander's cell-phone number. Burke dialed it, and it was picked up four rings later.

"Yeah?"

"Is this Mark Hollander?"

"You the negotiator?"

"I am, Mr. Hollander. We'd like to get you out of there safely, with no one hurt."

"Get me a free pass, and the girl won't get hurt. I'll even tell you who has the boy."

"So, Frankie Bishop is alive?"

"For now."

As Egton spoke, the marksman lined up his shot through the window, ready to shoot if Hollander moved into his sight and the negotiator gave the go-ahead.

"How would I know you're telling the truth about the boy? If I let you go, you could tell me anything. Why don't you send the girl out as a show of good faith?"

"Hah. Soon as I do that, I'm dead. No, after I'm away from you goons, I'll phone the station and tell you where the kid is."

"Let me talk to some people, and I'll get back to you."

Egton hung up and turned to Greco. "I know you came here because of Bishop, but there's a child in there right now with a gun to her head. And a man who is probably very nervous. Are you willing to let him walk?"

Greco shook his head.

"Then we've got to take him out."

Greco slipped back down to the basement and motioned to Metzger that time was running out.

"They're trying to work something out for you," Metzger called in to Hollander. "But I need to speak to the girl first, make sure she's all right."

"Go ahead. Talk to her."

"I need to see her. Move her closer to me."

"No fucking way."

"This is your only chance to get out of here. They're working on it now. But you need to bring the girl closer to me, or let me come in the room. Otherwise, there's no deal."

Metzger heard some rustling, then Hollander stepped into view, one arm around the girl's neck, the other pointing a gun to her head. "Go ahead, ask your questions."

Metzger had just begun to say the girl's name when a loud bang and the sound of shattered glass broke the silence of the night.

As soon as Hollander dropped the gun and let out a howl of pain, Metzger rushed him and brought him down to the floor. Hollander's hand was too bloody to handcuff, but two other policeman rushed to his side and held him down. Metzger stood and looked at the girl, now awash in tears.

"Your name is Daisy?"

She whispered, "Yes."

"What's your last name, Daisy?"

"Malone."

"We're going to get you out of here." Metzger turned to Hollander, who was still groaning in pain. "Where's the key to unlock her?"

"Fuck you."

Metzger moved closer to him and positioned his foot right over the injured hand. "You have one chance to tell me where it is before I stomp on this."

Quickly, Hollander answered. "It's in my left pocket." One of the cops fished it out and handed it to Metzger. He unlocked Daisy's shackles.

"It's okay, dear. You're safe now."

The soft cries became sobs. Metzger dropped down next to her and wrapped his arms around her bony shoulders. When her cries subsided, he asked, "Do you know what happened to Frankie Bishop?"

Daisy nodded. "Mark took him away this afternoon."

The only thing on Frankie's mind as the car sped down the highway was that he needed to escape. He stole a glance at the heavyset man driving. He had a coarse, dark-brown beard, and his dark eyes were mere slits in his puffed-up face. Mark had headed northeast on Route 85, then about ten minutes after they passed the sign for Spartanburg, he had exited the highway, then driven down some country roads.

After several turns, he'd pulled onto a dirt road and stopped. The air was still and silent. Nothing was around them but acres of farmland. They waited what seemed like forever for this man to take Frankie away, and during that time, not one car passed them. As soon as the handoff car drove up and the man exited, Frankie knew he'd never escape. The man was huge—well over six feet. He had to weigh at least 250 pounds. Frankie's dad was six one and weighed 190 pounds, and this guy was bigger.

The man had walked over to Mark, looked Frankie up and down, then said, "He'll do." He'd bound Frankie's limbs in duct tape, then picked him up like he was a bag of cotton balls and plopped him in the passenger seat of his big SUV. Its tinted windows were so dark, no one could see inside. Frankie watched out the window as the man peeled money out of his billfold and into Mark's hands.

They'd been driving for hours—first continuing north on Route 85, then north on Route 77—and the man hadn't said a word to him, not even his name. The radio was turned on loud, and the man hummed along to the country-music songs. Frankie had started to drift off to sleep when a change of direction startled him awake. They were leaving the highway. At the end of the exit ramp, the man pulled into a brightly lit gas station, then turned to Frankie, put his finger to his lips, and said, "Not one word."

He got out of the car, punched some buttons, then began pumping gas. Frankie looked at the convenience store, fifty feet away from the car. Maybe he could tell the man he had to use the restroom? No, he realized. The man would stay right by his side.

He looked down at his hands once more, and the memory of a news show slowly returned to him. His mother had been watching, and he'd stopped as he'd passed by on his way to the kitchen for a snack. The woman was demonstrating how to get free when your hands were tightly wrapped with tape. Raise your hands high over your head, then swing them down hard onto your knee, she'd said. *Could it be that simple?*

He looked out the window. The man was on the other side of the car, facing the pump. Frankie lifted up his bound hands, then swung fast down to his legs and gasped when the tape broke. He bent down to unwrap his legs, but he couldn't free an edge to lift off. He tried lifting his legs up to his mouth, to bite into the tape, but couldn't get them high enough. He opened the glove box and felt around for something sharp, but found nothing. He opened the storage container between the front seats, and there he saw it: a screwdriver. Quickly, he took it out and began punching holes in the tape around his legs until he was able to get his small fingers in an opening, and then tear it apart. His legs were free.

The man was still at the pump. He had one chance. The man's legs were long, but Frankie was fast. With one swift movement, he opened the door, then sped toward the store. The man heard the noise, then bolted after him, but Frankie got to the door first.

"I've been kidnapped!" he screamed as he ran behind the counter and pointed to his abductor as he followed Frankie inside. "That man!"

The store clerk didn't look much older than Bobby, with the same dark skin and tall, muscled build. He reached under the counter and pulled out a pistol, then pointed it at the man. "Stop right there."

The man stopped, then smiled. "My son likes to make up stories. What's he told you?"

"Enough that you're not coming near him."

"Frankie just doesn't like being away from his mother. But we share custody, and this is my time with him."

"Tell that to the police."

The man took a step toward Frankie.

"I have no problem shooting you. Come any closer, and that's what I'll do. And by the way, I've already tripped my silent alarm."

With that, the big man turned and left the store, then got into his car and drove away. The distant sound of police sirens grew louder.

J essica was in her hotel room when her cell phone rang. Tommy had called her an hour earlier and given her the bad news: Frankie was already gone when they'd reached the predator's house. She'd spent the hour crying nonstop. She felt alone and helpless—incapable of coming up with any ideas to get Frankie back. She kept asking herself what Alex would do. Her husband was always calm in crises, always able to think clearly and come up with a plan. But he was gone now. And she had no plan. *I need you, Alex. I need you here,* she kept thinking as her tears ran down her cheeks. *Tell me what to do.*

She jumped off the bed at the first ring and grabbed the phone, expecting another update from Tommy, or maybe a call from Bobby.

"Mommy?" the soft voice on the other end said.

For a moment, Jessica thought she must have fallen asleep and was dreaming she'd answered the phone.

"Mommy, it's me."

"Frankie? Oh, Frankie, where are you?" she asked through her sobs.

"I'm okay, Mommy. I'm at a police station. Are you mad at me?"

"Oh, my sweet baby, of course not. Are you really okay? Nobody hurt you?"

"I'm really okay."

Jessica thought she might burst from happiness. Her son was safe. The knots that had tied up her body from head to toe instantly dissipated, and she realized she'd gone from tears to a great big grin. "Where's the police station?"

She heard Frankie turn from the phone and ask someone nearby a question.

"Beckley, West Virginia."

"I'm coming to get you, right now."

"I don't think you can. They said they're going to take me back to Eldridge."

Instantly, a ball of fury overtook Jessica. She wanted to scream at the phone, at the world, at anyone she could. Instead, she willed herself to calm down, to think like her husband would. "They're not going to bring you there, Frankie. I'm going to fix it so they don't." She got the address and phone number of the police station, then hung up and called Tommy.

—

As soon as Dani hung up the phone from Tommy, she called Josh Cosgrove's home. The assistant US attorney had given Dani his home number and told her to call if she had news. When he got on the line, she said, "They've found Frankie Bishop. He's safe."

"Thank goodness. He's lucky, you know. Most aren't."

Dani knew that was true. Although stranger abductions accounted for only a small percentage of the children missing in the United States, once twenty-four hours had passed, it became extremely difficult to find them.

"There's a problem now, though," Dani said. "He was found just south of Charleston, West Virginia, and taken to the police precinct in Beckley."

"That sounds fine. What's the problem?"

"There's a Florida warrant out for him because of his runaway status. They want to return him to Eldridge."

"Let me make a few calls. I think I can take care of this."

An hour later, Cosgrove called back. "I called an assistant US attorney in the Eastern District of North Carolina. His name is Noah Jacobs. He's spoken to the agent that headed up the search—Clyde Metzger—and everyone agrees Frankie is a key witness in an important case and should be in federal protective custody. Noah had a judge sign a temporary restraining order preventing the West Virginia police from returning Frankie to Eldridge. Instead, they'll transport him to Raleigh, and a judge there can determine whose claim has priority. I assume you'll want to be there for that."

"Josh, I can't thank you enough. Of course, I'll go."

Dani quickly phoned Bruce to give him the news, then returned to Doug in the living room to finish "honeymoon hour." She sat down on the worn couch and pulled a throw blanket over her. She loved their house, with its wide-plank wood floors and wainscoted walls, fireplace in the living room, and vintage stove in the kitchen. It was a home that reeked of family, of warmth, of security.

"Frankie's safe," she told her husband, a wide smile on her face.

"What a relief!"

She cherished this time with just her and Doug. Sometimes they'd talk about work, most times about anything else—what was happening in the world, what they'd been reading, what their friends were doing, and about Jonah. Always, they would talk about Jonah. How he was doing in school. How he was doing at home. What his life would be like when he was grown. That last one had always worried Dani—more than the threat of terrorist attacks or wars going on in the world. For so many years, she'd been terrified at the prospect that Jonah would be left adrift after she and Doug were gone. That his learning difficulties would deprive him of the ability to support himself. She no longer felt that way. Now she knew his incredible musical talent would open doors for him.

"I think it's time to tell Jonah," Dani said as she settled herself on the couch.

"I wonder how he'll take it. He's had us to himself for fourteen years."

"Probably the way most children do. Jealous at first, then it'll subside. Jonah is so social that he'll probably love having a sibling."

"There's such a big age difference."

"I think that's good. He won't be faced with a brother or sister close in age that can do so much more than him." She patted her stomach. "Assuming this one doesn't have special needs, too." Dani looked up at Doug and searched his face. He'd had reservations about this pregnancy. Would he be able to handle it if this baby had problems?

Doug seemed to read her mind. "And if he or she does, who'd be better qualified to deal with them? We're veterans now."

Dani breathed a sigh of relief, then wondered if they'd be able to continue "honeymoon hour" after the new child was born. She hoped so. Doug was usually so successful at wiping away her fears, her insecurities. And, despite her success at work, despite the remarkable gains made by Jonah, she still often felt apprehensive. Some events that triggered her old insecurities, she knew, were under her command—balancing motherhood with a career, making sure her clients got her very best. But some fears, such as those triggered by Frankie Bishop's ordeal, were outside her control. When terrible things happened, a sense of disquietude settled over her, and with it, the knowledge that no matter how good she and Doug were as parents, they could never protect their child from all the cruelty in the world.

—

Early the next morning, Dani flew to Raleigh, North Carolina. Tommy picked her up at the airport, and they began the drive to the safe house where Frankie was sequestered. Jessica was already with him.

"How's he doing?" Dani asked.

"Still frightened," Tommy said. "They didn't get here until past midnight. Then, he woke up screaming a few times during the night. And he's still hurting from his injuries at Eldridge."

Dani thought it would take a long time for those nightmares to subside. At least, for the moment, he was safe. It was her job to make sure he stayed that way.

"Have you spoken to him yet?"

"No. Just Jessica. She's been filling me in."

They reached the safe house forty minutes later. It was in a semi-rural community, with small houses set back from the road and spaced far apart. Two agents were stationed outside. Tommy nodded to them as they approached, and one of the men opened the front door for them. As Dani stepped inside, she glanced around the small clapboard house. It was spare but neat, with dark curtains covering each of the windows. Inside the living room was a small couch and two chairs. Straight ahead was the kitchen, where Jessica stood over the sink washing out some dishes. Frankie sat on a chair around the kitchen table, playing games on an iPad.

Jessica turned around when they entered the room, saw Dani, quickly dried her hands, then ran over and gave her a hug.

"Thank you for arranging this."

"Thank Josh Cosgrove. He's the one that pulled strings to get Frankie here."

Dani walked over to the kitchen table and sat down across from Frankie. He looked thinner than in the pictures she'd seen of him, and his expression was warier, as well it should be. "I'm Dani Trumball. I'm going to try to make sure you don't go back to Eldridge, but to do that, I need to ask you some questions. Is that okay?"

"Sure."

"Can you tell me how the fight started—the one that landed you in the hospital?"

Frankie looked directly at her. He had dark circles under his eyes, and his curls hung limply over his forehead. "It wasn't a fight. It was a message."

"What do you mean?"

"The warden had four guys ambush me because I told my mom about the boy who died."

"Frankie, it's important that you tell me the truth. Eldridge filed a report with the State about the incident and said you started a fight. That you'd been stirring up trouble ever since you arrived."

He shook his head vehemently. "That's a lie! Those boys attacked me. They said Big Joe was angry because I tattled."

"Who's Big Joe?"

"That's what everyone calls Warden Cummings."

"Is that why you ran away from the hospital?"

"I was afraid they'd kill me if I went back."

Dani leaned closer to the boy and placed her hand over his. "When we go to court tomorrow, I'm going to explain to the judge what happened to you there, so he won't send you back."

"No, no, you can't!" Frankie shouted as he bolted up from the chair and ran to his mother. He placed his arms around her waist and buried his head in her chest. "Tell her she can't tell anyone."

Dani stood up and walked over to him. "It'll be okay. Trust me."

"It won't. Big Joe will say I'm a liar, and they'll send me back. And then they'll kill me because I didn't keep quiet."

Jessica shrugged at Dani.

Dani wished she could promise both of them that he wouldn't be sent back to Eldridge. That he would be kept safe by the federal government. That's what should happen when they went to court tomorrow. And that's what probably would happen. But she'd been practicing long enough to know that sometimes the judge took everyone by surprise.

—

An hour later, Dani left Tommy behind and drove to the office of the US Attorney in Raleigh. The glass-and-concrete building on New Bern Avenue also housed the federal district court for the Eastern District of North Carolina. She passed through security and made her way to the eighth floor, where Noah Jacobs was waiting for her.

"Josh has high praise for you. It's good to finally meet," he said as he escorted her to his office.

Jacobs was a tall, lanky man with bushy eyebrows that framed huge, round eyes. It was his smile, though, that immediately drew her in. "I can't thank you enough for helping Frankie out."

Jacobs shook his head. "He's the one assisting us. We've been after this ring for a long time. Frankie's testimony will be instrumental in our—hopefully—putting them away."

"I meant, thanks for helping us keep Frankie out of Eldridge Academy."

He grew sober. "We've got jurisdiction over him so far. But tomorrow is another story. I can't promise you the judge won't turn him over to the State. I'm sure they'll argue that being locked up at Eldridge, in a secure facility, will ensure his safety to testify in our case."

"But that's just it. It's not safe for him there." Dani filled him in on everything Frankie had told her.

Jacobs sat back in his chair and twirled his pen in his fingers. "Well, that certainly puts a different spin on it."

"Just one problem. Frankie is terrified that if he testifies about it in court and is sent back to Eldridge anyway, they'll retaliate against him. Badly."

"I don't know what to tell you, Dani. Either Frankie testifies about what happened to him there, or he risks getting sent back. We pulled a decent judge for tomorrow, but still—I can't guarantee what she'll do."

Dani had expected this. She'd thought about the dilemma on the drive over from the safe house. After she'd parked, she'd pulled out her cell phone and made a call, then written down a name and phone number on the back of her business card. Now she handed that card over to Jacobs. "I think this man can help. I've already spoken to him, and he's prepared to fly down here tonight."

Jacobs turned over the card and looked at the handwritten name: Brian Bismark. "Who's this?"

"He used to be with the Florida Department of Juvenile Justice," she said. "He knows all about why it's not safe for Frankie to go back to Eldridge."

———

Later that evening, Dani met up with Tommy for dinner. They found an Italian restaurant a block from their Holiday Inn that looked inviting. Judging by the crowd inside, they guessed that the food likely would be good. Dani knew she was spoiled, working in Manhattan and living in one of its nearby suburbs. Sure, there were plenty of restaurants with mediocre fare, but there was also a plethora of restaurants with exceptional chefs. Unfortunately, they often had prices that exceeded her budget. Both Ivy League–trained lawyers, she and Doug could have taken the big-money route and been able to afford gourmet meals whenever they wanted. But they also would have worked eighty-hour weeks, with scarcely any time to spend with Jonah. They'd both chosen family first, and had never doubted that decision.

"Scotch and water," Tommy told the waitress when she came by for their drink order.

"Just water," Dani said, pointing to the already filled glass by her plate.

Tommy looked her over. "You on the wagon?"

Dani took a sip from her glass. "You know me, I don't like to drink before court."

"Is that all it is? Or are you pregnant?"

Dani practically spit out her water.

Tommy grinned broadly. "You forget. I have five kids. That means seeing Patty pregnant five times. I can always tell."

"I was going to wait to tell everyone, but yes." She leaned over and playfully tapped Tommy's arm. "I'm almost twelve weeks."

"I gather by the big smile on your face that you're happy about it."

"I am." She giggled. "I feel like I'm twenty-five again, and we're starting all over."

"In a way you are. Jonah's what? Fourteen already?"

Dani took another sip of water, then shook her head. "I never thought I'd be at retirement age when my kid finished college."

"Yeah, well, you know the saying: 'Man plans, and God laughs.'"

"This time I'm laughing with him—or her."

CHAPTER
24

Dani arrived early the next morning for the hearing on who got to keep Frankie Bishop—the FBI or Eldridge Academy. The federal courthouse in Raleigh was like most throughout the United States. Some were housed in more ornate buildings than this one, but inside, the stately courtrooms reflected the importance of the cases that came before the justices. She made her way to Room 203, where Judge Rachel Gottlieb presided. Jacobs was already seated, and Dani joined him.

"That's Warren Camden, the Florida prosecutor," Jacobs whispered to her as he pointed to the man sitting at the opposite table.

"Yes, I've met him before. Have you spoken to him yet?"

"Just to say hello."

They waited only ten minutes before the bailiff announced the entrance of Judge Gottlieb. Dani figured her to be about her age, mid-forties, with long, chestnut-brown hair and graceful features. Despite her pretty looks, her expression was all business. *It's where I would have hoped to be now if I'd stayed at the US Attorney's Office—sitting as a federal court judge, working my way up to higher courts.* Dani shook her head. She was right where she should be.

The bailiff called their case. Jacobs and Camden both stood and gave their appearances.

"Okay, now," the judge said. "This is the petition of the Florida Department of Juvenile Justice. So go ahead, Mr. Camden. Tell me why I should grant its request."

Camden stood. "Your Honor, Francis Bishop was adjudicated a delinquent and sentenced to a secure facility—Eldridge Academy—where he was receiving counseling for a drug-abuse problem. While there, he instigated a fight, during which he received injuries that required hospitalization. From there, he escaped. We now believe he instigated that fight for the very purpose of enabling his escape. He should not now be rewarded by permitting him to avoid completing his sentence."

Camden sat down, and the judge turned to Jacobs. "Sounds reasonable. Why shouldn't the boy be returned?"

Jacobs raised himself slowly from his chair. "Even if everything Mr. Camden said were true, the federal government's interest in keeping Francis in protective custody is greater than that of the State of Florida. It is true that the child fled the hospital, where he was recovering from potentially life-threatening injuries. Once on his own, he was abducted by a man involved in a ring of child predators that has operated for years, forcing children into sexual slavery. Until now, the FBI has been unable to crack their enterprise. Francis's testimony is crucial to getting a conviction against two of its operatives. Facing life in prison will, we hope, serve to convince them to give up the remaining members of their group, and lead to the rescue of potentially hundreds of children."

"I appreciate the importance of his testimony," Judge Gottlieb said. "But why isn't Eldridge Academy sufficiently secure to protect anyone from getting in and harming him?"

"Because, once again, assuming everything the State says is true—and, for the record, we don't believe that's the case—he almost died while under their care. We simply can't afford to take that risk. Too many innocent children's lives are at stake."

The judge entwined her fingers and remained silent. Dani held her breath as she waited for Gottlieb to speak. She hoped no hearing would be necessary, that Jacobs's arguments were persuasive. Frankie was terrified of returning to Eldridge, but more frightened of having to testify against the authority there.

Finally, the judge sighed deeply. "I'm going to need to hear testimony. Nine thirty a.m. tomorrow. Have your witnesses here." She banged the gavel, and the bailiff called the next case.

—

Dani met Jacobs at the courthouse the next morning, Jessica Bishop at her side. "Bismark's all set," Dani said to him as she sat down next to him at the attorneys' table.

"Good."

Jessica took a seat behind Dani, in the first row of the gallery, and they all waited quietly for the proceedings to begin. Promptly at nine thirty, the bailiff entered the courtroom, and everyone stood. Seconds later, Judge Gottlieb took the bench.

"There are no jurors here, counselors, so don't waste my time with theatrics. And don't pile on witnesses where one will do. Understand?"

The attorneys nodded.

"Okay. Call your first witness, Mr. Camden."

"I call Fred Williamson."

Dani turned her head toward the back and saw a tall, muscular man with a shaved head enter the room and walk confidently to the witness chair.

After he was sworn in, Camden said, "Please state your occupation."

"I'm the assistant warden at Eldridge Academy."

Naturally, Dani thought. The warden wouldn't allow himself to be subjected to cross-examination. He'd sent his underling.

"And what are your duties there?" Camden continued.

"I oversee the guards, make sure discipline is being maintained."

"Okay. Now, in the course of your duties, do the guards report to you problems with any of the children?"

"Yeah. They write up a report, I review it, then pass it over to the warden."

"What happens if a child repeatedly gets written up?"

"Then he gets privileges taken away."

"Such as?"

"No time in the TV room, that kind of thing."

"Let's talk now about Francis Bishop. Was he ever written up?"

Williamson nodded. "More times than I can count."

"For what?"

"That kid had a chip on his shoulder from the day he walked in. Kept talking back to his teachers, kept picking fights with the other boys."

"Physical fights?"

"Not at first. At the beginning, he just taunted them. Then, one of the bigger kids shoved him, and Francis punched back. For a small kid, he was pretty strong."

Camden walked back to his table and picked up some papers, then stepped back to the witness stand. As he did so, Dani turned around for a quick glance at Jessica. Her hands were clasped tightly together, and she was biting her lip. Dani knew this had to be hard for her—listening to a man lie under oath about her son.

"Let's turn to the afternoon of March 26," Camden said when he continued. "Did an altercation occur between Francis and any other boys?"

"Yes. Francis followed a boy out of the lunchroom and began hitting him. A few other boys tried to intervene, and it seemed like Francis just went crazy. That drew more boys who tried to stop him, and in their efforts, Francis was hurt, badly enough to need hospitalization."

As Camden started to ask another question, Jacobs stood. "I don't know where this is going. There's no dispute that Francis was injured in a fight and hospitalized as a result."

"I agree, Mr. Camden," the judge said. "If anything, this seems to support Mr. Jacobs's contention that it's not safe for the boy there."

"On the contrary. It's to demonstrate that this is a troubled boy who shouldn't be stashed away in some safe house. He needs help, and Eldridge can provide it—it has been providing it. But more time with him is needed."

The judge sighed deeply. "I'll let you continue, but keep it tight."

Camden stepped closer to Williamson and handed him the papers. "Is this the report that was filed with the State concerning the incident?"

Williamson looked it over, then answered, "Yes."

"Did you prepare this report?"

"I did."

"And does it accurately describe the incident on March 26 of this year?"

"It does."

"I ask that this be marked as petitioner's Exhibit 1."

Camden handed a copy to the judge and to Jacobs.

"So marked."

"Your Honor, I had planned to ask this witness more questions, but in light of your admonition to not be repetitive, I'll have my next witness cover the treatment Francis has been receiving at Eldridge Academy. I have no further questions for Mr. Williamson."

Judge Gottlieb nodded at Jacobs, who then stood and walked over to the witness.

"Mr. Williamson, is it your responsibility to prepare all reports?"

"Well, the employee observing the problem prepares a report for me, then I collate all the reports into one report that goes to the warden."

"But you prepared Exhibit 1, the report that went to the State?"

"Yes, I prepare all those reports, subject to any changes the warden may have."

"Now, you said that Francis Bishop was a disciplinary problem from the outset, is that correct?"

"Yes."

"So, I assume there are other reports to the State to confirm that."

"Well, we only file a report with the State when there's a serious incident. Other than our regular quarterly reports, that is."

"And you prepare those quarterly reports?"

"As I said, I do them for the warden's approval. He signs them."

"But you see them, right?"

"Sure."

"So, in those quarterly reports, is Francis Bishop mentioned?"

"Uh, well—see, those reports don't name names unless something extraordinary happened."

"How about the reports you get from the staff, the ones you use to prepare your report to the warden. Exactly how often was Francis Bishop mentioned?"

Williamson squirmed in his seat, all the while twirling his thumbs. "I don't remember. Like I said before, a lot."

"Would it surprise you if I told you we got copies of those reports, and his name wasn't mentioned once in any of them?"

Dani knew Jacobs was bluffing. He'd thought about serving a subpoena for those records but decided against it. If the warden manufactured a report to the State describing Frankie as the instigator of the fight that landed him in the hospital, she had no doubt he'd easily manufacture internal reports.

"Not really," Williamson answered. "We got lots of acting-out kids. The staff can't write up every incident. But they told me about his acting out, plenty of times."

"So, just to be clear. The only written evidence of Francis Bishop misbehaving is a report prepared by you, correct?"

Williamson squirmed even more in his seat. "Yeah. I suppose that's true."

"And this report was prepared after he was hospitalized, right?"

"Yes."

"Let's assume that your rendition of that incident is accurate. You supposedly knew that Francis was a troublemaker, that he'd been starting fights, that this had been going on since he arrived two months earlier. Yet the staff was incapable of preventing a group of boys from pummeling him, isn't that true?"

"We can't be everywhere at once."

"So, tell me, Mr. Williamson, how can you prevent it from happening again, next time with perhaps a fatal outcome?"

"We'll have people watching out for him. The boys who did it to him—they lost privileges. They won't be doing it again."

"I doubt your word is very reassuring to Frankie or his mother. I have no further questions for you."

Jacobs returned to his seat, and Camden called Amanda Rays to the stand. As she walked to the front of the courtroom, Dani thought she looked like a college student with her trim figure, freshly scrubbed face, and shoulder-length, silky blonde hair.

After she was sworn in, Camden asked, "What is your occupation?"

"I'm a counselor at Eldridge Academy."

Dani suspected that half the boys there must have a crush on her.

"Do you know Francis Bishop?"

"Yes, he's in one of my drug-counseling groups."

"Would you describe his progress?"

"Slow at first. Like many of the boys, he was reluctant to acknowledge his dependence on drugs. But finally he opened up. I think, in his case, drugs helped him deal with his father's disappearance in Afghanistan."

"And do you think he's now in an emotionally healthy place?"

"Oh, no. Far from it. He has a long way to go. But we're making progress."

"Are you familiar with what happened to Francis after he fled the hospital?"

The counselor hung her head down momentarily, then looked up. "Yes. It must have been awful for him."

"Given what has occurred, in your professional opinion, what placement would be in Francis's best interest?"

"Oh, without a doubt, Eldridge Academy."

"Why is that?"

"Because he's gone through a traumatic event. And past experience has shown that when he's upset, he turns to drugs. We've certainly made progress toward him finding better outlets for his stress, but he's not there yet."

"Thank you. No further questions."

Jacobs stood at his seat. "What are your professional qualifications, Ms. Rays?"

"I have a bachelor's degree in counseling from Florida State University."

"And when did you receive that degree?"

Softly, she answered, "Two years ago."

Jacobs walked over to the witness stand. "Is this your first job as a counselor?"

"Yes."

"So, just to be clear. You're not a licensed psychologist, are you?"

"No."

"And you're not a psychiatrist either, right?"

"No. But my degree has prepared me for counseling adolescents."

"No doubt. Tell me, how do you determine when someone is telling the truth in your group sessions?"

"Well, I—I can just tell."

"By reading their minds?"

"Spare us the flippancy, Mr. Jacobs," admonished the judge.

"Sorry, Your Honor." He turned back to the witness. "Isn't it true that when a court has determined a juvenile needs drug counseling, if the child doesn't acknowledge his drug use, you report him as being resistant to being helped and recommend further counseling?"

"Admitting the problem is an important step in treatment."

"So, if Frankie didn't admit he had a drug problem, if he insisted he'd never used drugs, you'd recommend his incarceration be extended, right?"

"But he had marijuana."

"Which he claimed he found in the street. How do you know with certainty that isn't the truth? That he lied about using drugs so he could finish counseling and get home?"

The young woman shook her head, then slowly answered, "I guess I don't."

"Thank you. I have no more questions." Jacobs started to walk away, then suddenly spun around. "I'm sorry, I do have a few more questions. Have you ever seen Francis act aggressively around the other boys?"

"No. He's usually rather quiet."

"Ever see him pick on other boys?"

"No."

"Ever see other boys pick on him?"

"No."

"Ever told by any of the guards or the warden that he was aggressive toward other boys?"

"No."

Jacobs returned to his table and picked up Exhibit 1, then handed it to Rays. "Take a look at this report, please."

Rays read through it, then looked up.

"Does the description of Francis in that report surprise you?"

"Well, I only see him in counseling three times a week. I don't see him interacting with the boys at other times."

"But based on your knowledge of Francis in his counseling sessions, does this report of his behavior surprise you?"

"I . . ." She glanced over at Camden, then her eyes locked on Jessica Bishop. She sat up straighter in her seat, and with her voice strong said, "Yes. It does surprise me."

"Thank you, Ms. Rays. Thank you for your honesty. I have no more questions."

"Anyone else?" Judge Gottlieb asked Camden. Dani saw him slumped over in his seat, twirling his pen in his fingers.

"No, Your Honor."

"Do you have any witnesses, Mr. Jacobs?"

"Yes. I call Clyde Metzger."

Metzger made his way to the stand with a confident swagger. Once seated and sworn in, Jacobs asked his occupation.

"I'm a senior FBI agent assigned to the Child Abduction Response Deployment team."

"How long have you been in that position?"

"Seven years."

"And during that time, have you been monitoring the activities of a group of men, operating mostly in the southeastern United States, that traffic in the child-sex trade?"

"Yes. We've tracked their Internet activities, but until now, haven't had any success identifying the men in charge."

"Tell me how this group operates."

"For the most part, they're brokers. They get orders for a particular type of child, say, a female between ten and twelve, and fulfill that order."

"How do they do that?"

"Most often they take runaways and entrap them with the promise of a better life. Sometimes, they'll ensnare kids by starting an Internet chat, claiming to be a teenager themselves. When a meet is finally arranged, they grab them. Less frequently, it's an abduction, maybe from a mall or a kid walking home from school. Or, like Francis Bishop, by lucking into a child traveling alone."

"What do they do with these kids once they have them?"

"Most go to commercial sex traffickers. They keep them locked up and pimp them out. Sometimes they get them hooked on drugs to keep them in line. A pimp can take in up to $200,000 a year for each child they have working. And it's not unusual for them to have five or six at any one time. It's big business. A United Nations study found that human trafficking generates $9.5 billion a year in the US alone."

"And the ones that don't go to commercial traffickers?"

"Once in a while, they'll take an order from an individual who wants to keep a child for his personal use."

"Aren't most of these children brought to the US from other countries?"

Metzger shook his head. "Plenty are from within the United States. It's hard to quantify the number, because we can only count the ones that are rescued, or escape and seek help. Those number in the hundreds each year. But we calculate that at least 300,000 American children are at risk of sexual exploitation."

Camden stood up. "Your Honor, what's the relevance of this testimony? It sounds like a treatise on human trafficking rather than testimony about the particular men whom Francis will testify against."

Jacobs turned to the judge. "Those men operate within the context of a larger industry, and taking them down can impact that industry. It's important for Your Honor to understand the big picture."

"I'll allow you some leeway, but wrap it up soon."

"Thank you. I have just a few more questions." He turned back to Metzger. "What happens to the children forced into sexual slavery?"

"Most live only a short time—maybe seven years at the outside. They die from a variety of causes—attacks, abuse, drug overdoses, illness. Some take their own lives to escape what they've been forced to endure."

"Now, let's turn to the enterprise in question. How long do you think they've been operating?"

"We've been following them for three years."

"During that time, how many children do you estimate they've ensnared?"

"Probably in the hundreds."

"What is the importance of Francis Bishop's testimony in relation to this operation?"

"He can testify as to his abduction by John Felder, and he can show through his own experience that both Felder and Mark Hollander, the man he was sold to, were child sexual brokers. With Francis's testimony against these men, we hope it will lead to unraveling the whole operation, and perhaps rescuing children still imprisoned."

"If he's placed in a safe house, what provisions can you make for his continued schooling and counseling for his alleged drug problem?"

"His mother has agreed to homeschool him, and our office will arrange for a psychologist to evaluate him. If he or she determines he needs counseling, it'll be provided for him in the safe house."

"Thank you. No further questions."

Camden stood up and walked to the podium.

"Isn't it true that a girl was rescued along with Francis Bishop?"

"Yes."

"Can't you make the same case against the man Francis was sold to with the girl's testimony?"

"Actually, no. Unlike Frankie, the girl went willingly with Hollander and remained with him. Twice, Frankie was passed on to someone else, and both times, he observed the parties exchanging money for him. Francis's testimony is crucial to demonstrate the men's roles as brokers."

Camden fumbled through some notes in his hands, then changed gears. "Where do you propose to keep Francis if he's not returned to Eldridge?"

"We'll place him in an FBI safe house. We've used it successfully in the past to house key witnesses."

"Wouldn't it be easier for someone who wanted to silence him to reach him at your so-called safe house than at a lockup facility with armed guards?"

"We're not worried about our targets getting to him at Eldridge. We're worried about the population inside harming him. We can't take that chance. He's too important to us."

"Have you ever had a witness in protective custody—stashed in one of your safe houses—killed before he was able to testify?"

Metzger paused, then looked toward Dani and Jacobs before answering. "It's happened—on rare occasions."

Camden smiled. "That's what I thought. No further questions."

Jacobs squeezed Dani's hand under the table, then stood. "I have just one more witness, Your Honor. I call Brian Bismark to the stand."

Bismark entered the courtroom and took his seat in the witness box. He was dressed in a suit and tie, and still had the same sad expression as when Dani had first met him.

"What is your current occupation?" Jacobs asked after the witness was sworn in and spelled his name for the record.

"I currently review applications by private companies to operate for-profit prisons in the State of New York."

"And are you an employee of the State of New York or a private consultant?"

"Private consultant."

"Was there a time when you worked for the Florida Department of Juvenile Justice?"

"Yes. From 2001 through 2010."

"And what were your duties there?"

"I monitored the performance of juvenile for-profit prisons in that state."

"In that capacity, did you become familiar with Eldridge Academy?"

"I did."

"Was Warden Cummings in charge during those years?"

"Yes."

"How were you supposed to evaluate Eldridge Academy?"

"I was supposed to make one scheduled site visit annually, and review the reports they filed."

"Is that what you did?"

"At first. But I became suspicious of the reports and began to make some unscheduled visits."

"What did you find on those visits?"

"Conditions were unsanitary, staffing was insufficient, and those there were poorly trained. Especially troubling was the discovery that grievances by the boys were dismissed internally and not reported to the State."

"What kinds of grievances?"

"Bugs in the food. Portions too small. Repeated physical abuse by the guards. Lack of responsiveness to medical issues. I tracked some of the complaints reported to me by the boys against the reports filed with the State. The majority never showed up in a report."

"In your opinion, do you think Francis Bishop would be safe from harm—whether by other youth or the guards—if he were returned to Eldridge Academy?"

"I do not."

"Thank you. No further questions."

As Jacobs sat down, Dani flashed a quick smile at him. Bismark's testimony had been strong. She hoped it was strong enough for the judge.

Camden stood up and walked slowly toward the witness box, a serious expression on his face.

"What happened when you reported your findings to your superiors at the Department of Juvenile Justice?"

"I was let go."

Camden did a stagey double take. "How could that be?"

"Because the Department only wants to know if its policies are in place, not whether they're being enforced."

"Isn't it true that you were let go because of complaints that you were intimidating the staff at Eldridge?"

"If expecting answers to tough questions is intimidating, then I suppose I was."

"And isn't it also true you were accused of undermining the management of the facility, thereby creating a dangerous situation?"

"Look, I got too close to the truth, and Roger Wilcox, the owner of ML Juvenile Services, complained. He's a big fish, and I was easily expendable. I wasn't surprised they did cartwheels for him."

"When was the last time you were at Eldridge Academy?"

"Four years ago."

"So, even if everything you claim you observed there were true, you'd have no way of knowing whether those conditions had changed since then, would you?"

"A leopard can't change its spots. Warden Cummings headed it up then, and he still does now."

"Mr. Bismark, I'm not asking for your opinion. I'm asking what you know to be factually true. Can you state with certainty that Francis Bishop would be in danger of harm if he were returned to Eldridge Academy?"

Bismark looked toward Dani and Jacobs, then back at Camden. He sighed deeply, then answered, "No, not with certainty."

"That's what I thought. I have no more questions for you."

Jacobs stood up. "I have no more witnesses, Your Honor." He picked up a large packet of documents from his table. "This is the transcript of Francis's hearing. I'd like it marked as respondent's Exhibit 1."

"I object," Camden said. "It bears no relevance to whether Eldridge will be a safe place for Francis."

"I believe it will help give Your Honor a fuller picture of Francis, and eliminate the need to call the people who testified as to his character at this hearing."

Judge Gottlieb nodded. "I'll allow it. Now, gentlemen, this isn't a jury trial. I understand each of your positions, and I don't need a summing up. I'm inclined to forgo closing arguments unless one of you strongly objects."

Hah! Dani thought. It was a foolish attorney who went against the wishes of a judge deciding their client's fate. As she expected, neither Jacobs nor Camden objected.

"Okay. Be here tomorrow at ten o'clock. I'll have my decision for you then."

———

Tommy joined Dani and Jacobs for dinner that evening. "How do you think it went today?" Dani asked Jacobs.

"Got a coin to toss?"

"You think it's that close?"

"I wish you would have let me put Frankie on the stand. If Gottlieb heard the truth about his beating, it would be a slam dunk."

Dani picked up her glass of water and took a sip. "I couldn't convince Frankie that he'd be safe if he testified. And he's gone through so much already, I didn't have the heart to push him."

"I hope that decision doesn't come back to haunt you."

Dani smiled weakly. "I hope not."

"You did the right thing," Tommy said as he patted Dani's shoulder. "I've spent a fair amount of time with Frankie. He'd rather take his chances at Eldridge than go on record ratting them out."

What a terrible choice for a twelve-year-old to have to make, Dani thought. He was a child, prepubescent. He should be out shooting hoops with his friends, or playing baseball in a Little League game. He should be back in school, worrying about upcoming tests. Not worrying about whether he would be killed for testifying truthfully about an abusive and corrupt juvenile prison.

"How's it going with Hollander?" Dani asked Jacobs. "Has the FBI gotten anything from him?"

"Nope. He clammed up right away and asked for his lawyer."

"What about his computer? Have they been able to track down any kids from that?"

"Not yet. Everything was done in code. They've been trying to crack it, but no luck so far."

Dani knew Frankie could make all the difference. With his testimony, Hollander faced life in prison. If he were sent to a maximum-security facility, and it leaked that he'd been engaged in child trafficking, the prison population would exact its own version of justice. That would be a strong incentive for Hollander to make a deal. He wouldn't be able to avoid a lengthy jail term, but his testimony could change where he was sent, and what was made known about him.

She took another sip of her water and wished that it were wine. She wanted the alcohol to erase her knowledge of the ugliness in the world. She wanted the heat it would spread through her body to remind her of the warmth she felt when she lay entwined in Doug's arms, the orange glow from the logs in their fireplace mesmerizing, washing away all thought of despicable men who robbed children of their innocence along with their liberty. And, most important, she wanted the numbness it provided to strip away the tension she felt about tomorrow's decision.

—

At ten o'clock the next morning, the bailiff announced, "All rise." As Judge Gottlieb took the bench, Dani looked back at Jessica. Frankie's mother sat stiffly in her seat, her face held tightly in a mask, as though to release it would cause her entire body to collapse.

"I'm going to read my decision from the bench," Gottlieb said. "This is not a clear-cut case. Both sides have compelling arguments as to where Francis Bishop should be held. The Florida DJJ rightly points out that Francis was adjudicated a delinquent and sentenced to a secure residential facility. There's no dispute that his sentence has not been completed, and on top of that, he escaped while in the custody of the hospital. In ordinary circumstances, there would be no question that young Mr. Bishop should be returned to Eldridge Academy. On the other hand, there is also no dispute that Francis is a crucial witness in an important child-trafficking case. The US attorney claims that because Francis was badly injured previously at Eldridge, it is too risky for him to be returned there.

"In such a situation, I must weigh the competing claims. In doing so, I have reviewed the underlying adjudication hearing that found Francis to be a delinquent. Although it is not my place to second-guess a state court judge's ruling, I have found nothing in the record of that hearing that makes me believe that Francis will be a high risk of danger to others if he is not returned to Eldridge. If the authorities at Eldridge are, despite their assurances, unable to protect Francis from further harm, his loss as a witness can lead to the continued enslavement of innocent children, and potential future enslavement of other children. It is an outcome that far outweighs the need for one boy to complete his sentence. I hereby order that Francis Bishop be placed in the custody of the FBI, to reside in one of their safe houses. He shall not be permitted to leave said house except for court appearances or medical attention, the latter with the advance approval of this court. Toward that end, he is to be fitted with an ankle bracelet that shall monitor his movements. His time in the safe house shall count toward the completion of his sentence at Eldridge. So ordered."

When Dani turned around, she found Jessica had slumped down against the bench, and tears were running down her cheeks. She smiled at Dani and mouthed, "Thank you."

Thank goodness was the only thought in Dani's head. Thank goodness for the levelheadedness of the judge. Thank goodness Noah Jacobs had been willing to fight for Frankie. And most of all, thank goodness that the nightmare Frankie had endured, first at Eldridge, then caught in the web of those despicable men, was finally over.

Joe Cummings picked up the phone on its first ring. He didn't wait for his assistant to answer it—he saw from the caller ID it was Williamson. "What's the verdict?"

"Judge is letting the feds keep him."

"But he didn't say anything about us, right?"

"Not a word. Kid didn't testify."

"Still, Wilcox doesn't like him being out there. He may feel safe enough to start talking now."

"I know."

"I've got a call to make. It's not over yet."

25

For once, Dani's plane landed on time, and she made it home for dinner. On the thirty-minute drive north from LaGuardia, she encountered another rarity—there wasn't stop-and-go traffic on the highway. She hated to spend even one extra night without tucking Jonah into bed and kissing him good night. Soon, she knew, he would be too old to allow it.

Katie had left a meat loaf in the oven for the family. Jonah chattered throughout dinner, filling Dani in on school happenings while she'd been away. When he finally paused for a break, Dani said, "There's something Dad and I want to tell you."

He looked at her expectantly.

"We're going to have a baby. You'll have a brother or a sister."

"I think I'll take a brother."

Dani suppressed a laugh, then quickly glanced at Doug and saw the amused twinkle in his eyes. She reached over and touched Jonah's hand. "I'm afraid we don't get to choose."

"Oh."

His relative silence surprised Dani. Jonah was so naturally effervescent about everything. She'd wanted him to be excited about the baby, too. Was it possible that jealousy had set in so quickly? She hoped not. She was an only child herself and had longed for siblings. She'd often wondered whether Jonah had as well, although he'd never asked about it.

"So, what do you think about that?" Doug asked.

"I think you've tarried long enough. I was getting haggard waiting."

Dani knew she'd miss Jonah's special way of speaking when he was living elsewhere—if not independently, at least in a group home. "I didn't know you felt that way."

"Well, Timmy has a brother and so does Harris. And David has a sister. I can teach him how to play video games. I'm really commendable at them."

"You could teach a sister, too."

Jonah smiled brightly. "Yes. I think I will."

—

When Dani arrived at HIPP the next day and stopped in the doorway of Bruce's office to say good morning, he beamed up at her.

"Dani, I can't thank you enough—you and Tommy."

"It was our pleasure. Frankie's a brave boy. I'm glad it worked out for him."

"Jessica said she's all set up now. Frankie's school provided her with the materials she needs to homeschool him, and her boss has agreed that she can work off-site as long as necessary."

"That's terrific, Bruce." She nodded toward her own office. "And now, reentry. I've already seen how many e-mails have stacked up. Here's hoping I can push the door open for all of the mail and phone messages waiting for me."

As it happened, it didn't take her all that long to perform triage on the messages awaiting her attention. In less than an hour she got up from her desk and walked into Melanie Stanton's office. She had trained Melanie in litigation when the young lawyer, fresh off of two years in a Wall Street firm and anxious to work at a job she found more meaningful, began at HIPP. She was Melanie Quinn then. Now, newly married, she carried her husband's name. Melanie handled her own caseload now, but she and Dani were still close.

"Hey, Melanie."

"You're back. I heard it went well. Thank goodness it's over. That poor boy."

"Well, it's over for me. Frankie will still have to testify against the men who grabbed him. I suspect that'll be hard for him, dredging it back up again."

Melanie nodded her agreement.

Dani motioned to her. "Would you mind coming with me into Bruce's office?"

"Sure. What's up?"

"Just something I want to tell both of you."

Melanie rose and followed Dani into Bruce's office. He looked up from his desk with an expression of surprise on his face. "What'd you forget?"

"Didn't forget anything. I have some news I'd like to share with you."

Bruce blanched. "Please, don't tell me you're leaving HIPP."

"No. But in about six months, I'm going to need some time off. I'm pregnant."

Melanie squealed a joyous "Congratulations," then hugged Dani tightly. "How exciting!"

Dani stole a glance at Bruce. His brows were furrowed, and he twirled a pencil in his fingers. "Don't worry," she told him. "I'm only planning on taking three months off."

"And when you come back, will you still handle cases from inception?"

This was the issue. When she'd started at HIPP, she handled only appeals, not wanting to be away from home as much as was needed if she picked up matters from the investigation stage.

"I've given this a lot of thought. I think for the first year, I want to minimize my travel. So yes, just appeals. But Melanie is handling cases on her own now, so I think HIPP will be okay."

"Not death-penalty cases."

Dani looked up at Melanie. She had seemed like a coed when she first started at HIPP, a beautiful, fresh-faced, wide-eyed ingénue. Now she was a seasoned pro. "Melanie can handle them. She has the skills for it."

"That true?" Bruce asked Melanie.

"I can."

A smile broke out on Bruce's face. He stood up and walked over to Dani and pulled her into his arms. "Well, then, I'm thrilled for you."

Relieved, Dani made her way back to her office, stopping at Tommy's desk to let him know she'd told Bruce and Melanie her news. With Frankie Bishop's case finished, she took out her folder of letters from inmates. It was time to pick a new case to handle.

She picked up the top letter. It was from Julio Rodriguez, a man who'd been sentenced to ninety-nine years for the kidnapping and rape of a woman. He was eighteen at the time of his conviction and had been in jail for twenty-two years. Like the authors of all the letters HIPP received, he insisted he was innocent. Dani did a quick Lexis search for his case and read the recitation of facts from his first appeal. A woman had been standing outside her apartment when two men grabbed her and threw her into their car, which she described as a late-model SUV with tinted windows. They drove to a nearby abandoned lot and raped her. When the police arrived a few hours later at the woman's apartment, they spotted a vehicle that matched her description leaving the complex. They wrote down the license number and subsequently brought Rodriquez in for questioning.

The SUV belonged to Rodriguez's father, who'd been working when the rape occurred. Rodriguez admitted he'd driven the car that night to visit a friend in the same complex where the victim lived, but he didn't match the description of the rapists the victim had given to the police. He was noticeably shorter than the woman, not considerably taller, as she'd said, and had a bushy mustache, which she'd failed to mention. Nevertheless, several days later, the woman, who was white, identified Rodriguez in a lineup.

Dani looked up from the computer. Eyewitness identifications were always tricky, and cross-racial identifications were the most suspect. Studies repeatedly showed that most people had difficulty distinguishing facial characteristics in people of a different race.

She continued reading about the case. Rodriguez was interrogated for hours. He spoke little English at the time and had no criminal history. The officers typed out a confession for him in English, supposedly read a translation of it for him, then ordered him to sign it, which he did.

At the trial, the two friends Rodriguez had visited the night in question confirmed he was with them. Despite the only evidence against Rodriguez being his car and a questionable victim identification, he was convicted. Throughout his years of incarceration, he'd continued to maintain his innocence.

Dani finished going through the stack of letters, then returned to the first one. She prepared a letter to send to Rodriguez, saying she would take his case. Hopefully, the evidence kit still remained in police custody and contained DNA from the attackers. If so, it was the kind of case that HIPP, and other Innocence Projects throughout the country, were especially adept at handling. She'd long ago given up the hope that with the advent of DNA testing, fewer men and women would end up wrongfully convicted. Although it was true to some extent, she'd seen firsthand, through her work at HIPP, through the thousands of letters they received, that sadly, mistakes were still made. And because of those mistakes, some innocent people spent their most productive years locked away. Over time, Dani accepted that she couldn't change the system, only chip away at the mistakes, one person at a time. Today, that person would be Julio Rodriguez.

⸺

Jessica Bishop had no idea where she and Frankie were. They had been driven to a small house tucked away in a rural area, an hour from Raleigh. A mile of dirt road led to the one-story cottage, with beige siding and burgundy shutters framing the windows. Inside, the living room was comfortably furnished with a deep-cushioned sofa and two club chairs flanking a wood-burning fireplace. There were two bedrooms, a snug kitchen, and a bathroom. If one of the FBI agents hadn't followed with Jessica's car, she would have been frightened of the isolation. Instead, she felt safe. She felt Frankie was safe, especially with the agent sitting on the porch overseeing the house.

She'd just finished Frankie's math lesson and left him with worksheets to do when she realized it had been days since she'd checked her home telephone's voice mail. Once Frankie was back with her, she'd forgotten all about it, something that never would have happened had she not been so worried about Frankie returning to Eldridge. Most anyone who called her used her cell-phone number. She didn't know why she held on to a landline—a relic of an earlier time, it seemed to her—but she had, and it was the number she listed on all her official records. She dialed her home number, pressed the asterisk key when she heard her voice, then tapped out her PIN. "You have two new messages and five saved messages." The first message was from her pharmacy, letting her know her prescription allergy medication was ready to be picked up. She erased it, then listened for the second message.

"Mrs. Bishop, this is Major Stillman. Please call me back at 800-555-2962. We have some news about your husband."

Jessica's breath caught. The message had come in three days ago. She walked into her bedroom, away from Frankie's ears, then quickly dialed the number. She paced back and forth in the room while the phone rang, too nervous to sit down.

"Major Stillman," a man's voice said upon answering the phone.

"This is Jessica Bishop, Alex Bishop's wife. You left a message for me a few days ago about my husband."

"Yes. We've located him. He's in a Taliban prison camp."

"He's alive?" Jessica asked, her voice choked.

"We believe he is."

Jessica sank down on the bed. Relief washed over her.

"He was captured with another soldier from his platoon," the major continued. "As part of our withdrawal from the country, there will be a prisoner exchange."

"When? How soon?"

"I can't answer that. It could be a month, a year at the outside."

"But . . . but . . . he's okay? They're not mistreating him?"

There was a pause on the line. "I'm sorry. We just don't know."

Jessica thanked him, hung up, then buried her face in her pillow, smothering her sobs so that Frankie wouldn't hear them. Finally knowing where Alex was had burst the dam she'd built around her heart, closing in all her fears, enabling her to be strong for her sons. *Alex is alive! He's going to come home!* She pushed away thoughts of what he was enduring. She couldn't let herself think that they might torture him. No. Her husband would survive. Frankie would get through the next few months. Everything would return to normal.

O nly six weeks had passed since Dani had taken on the case of Julio Rodriguez. She was lucky. The police kit contained DNA from two males, neither of which matched Rodriguez's DNA. If only all cases were this easy. Even with cases that could turn on DNA, it was often a struggle to get the police to release items for testing, or even find any. Even if items containing DNA were still in the evidence kit, and police tested it, or turned it over to HIPP's lab, and it cleared HIPP's client, prosecutors many times fought her request for a new trial. She had just hung up from a phone call with the prosecutor in Rodriguez's case, in which he'd agreed to jointly file to have the conviction set aside, when her assistant buzzed her.

"Noah Jacobs is on line two."

Dani's heart sank. She hadn't heard from Noah since the court had ordered Frankie to remain in federal custody. She hoped something hadn't happened to him.

"Noah, how are you?" she said when she picked up his call.

"Good. I'm calling about Frankie."

"Is something wrong?"

"He's doing fine. It's just—since he's in FBI custody, they got served on his behalf. With a summons in a new criminal matter against him. For running away."

"I don't understand. The federal court ruled in your favor. They can't get him back."

"Not right away. But once we have a deal, or Frankie's testimony in their trial is complete, if there's any time remaining on his sentence, he'll go back to Eldridge. I think they're trying to tack on this new violation in order to make sure that happens. And as long as the threat of that hangs over Frankie, I'm guessing they think he won't talk."

Dani felt sick. Since her pregnancy, any unwelcome news always made her nauseous. And this was certainly unwelcome. That poor family, she thought. They've been through so much. "So, logistically, what happens next?"

"We'll have to bring him to an arraignment. If you're going to represent him, I assume you'll plead him not guilty. He'll come back with us until his hearing, and then we'll bring him back for that. If he's found guilty, then we'll still take him back to the safe house until the sex-trafficking trial is over. But when it is, he'll be returned to Eldridge."

Dani's nausea intensified. She couldn't stop the negative images that flooded through her mind. This wasn't HIPP's case. She'd stepped in to do a favor for Bruce—that was all. Her desk was filled with pleas from inmates swearing they were innocent. Frankie had a Florida attorney, the one who'd represented him at his initial hearing. He could handle this new matter. He should handle the new matter. And yet . . . she remembered the frightened boy—still a child—clinging to his mother, terrified of returning to Eldridge.

"When's the arraignment?" Dani asked. "I'll be there to represent him."

Dani lay on the examining table as her doctor lathered her baby bump with gel. Doug stood at her side, holding her hand. Dr. Kaplan moved the wand over her stomach, up and down, side to side, while watching the images on a screen. She turned the screen toward Dani and said, "There's your baby. Everything looks good. Do you want to know the sex?"

Dani looked toward Doug. They had discussed it for hours. Dani wanted to know; Doug wanted to be surprised. Eventually, they'd reached a compromise. "Would you mind writing it down on a piece of paper and putting it into a sealed envelope for us?"

"No problem."

Dani stared at the image of her baby. Seeing the picture made it all so real. At times, she'd wondered if she were crazy, having another child at her age. She'd be collecting Social Security while still paying college tuition. But now, looking at the perfectly formed hands and round head, she knew how much she wanted this child, how much she would cherish him or her.

They left the office, with the doctor's envelope tucked away safely in Dani's purse, then headed back home, stopping first at their local bakery with a special request.

—

The next day, Dani returned home from work, cake box in hand.

"Who's that for?" Jonah asked. "Is it someone's birthday?"

"It's a special cake. You'll see after dinner."

Katie had been invited to join them. After all, by now, she was part of their family. At seven o'clock, the doorbell rang, and Dani opened the door to Doug's parents. Her own parents were gone, her mother to breast cancer and her father to a heart attack two years later. Right behind them were Fran and Duncan, Dani and Doug's closest friends.

"Gammy, Pop-Pop," Jonah squealed as he gave his grandparents a hug. "I was incognizant you were coming."

Dani ushered everyone into the kitchen, where Katie had placed the cake in the center of the table. It was covered with white frosting and decorated with blue and pink flowers. She turned to Jonah.

"Remember we told you that you were going to have a brother or sister?"

Jonah nodded.

"Well, we don't know which it'll be. But this cake is going to tell us." When she and Doug had stopped by the bakery the previous evening, they'd handed the baker the sealed envelope Dr. Kaplan had given them. They'd asked him to open the envelope after they'd left and then prepare a cake where the inside filling was blue if they were having a boy, pink if it was a girl. Dani explained this to Jonah, then handed Doug the cake knife.

"Go ahead, Dad."

Doug held the knife over the cake, then cut out a piece, and held it up for everyone to see the pink filling. Hugs and cheers rang out as Dani's eyes teared up. She hadn't thought it mattered whether it was a boy or a girl—and it really hadn't. Yet images of dolls and frilly dresses and tea parties flashed through her mind. *I'm having a daughter. I'm having a daughter!*

Two days later, Dani was back in juvenile court in Cypress County. Frankie sat by her side, with Patrick Collins, the FBI agent who'd escorted him from the safe house to Florida. Today was a formality—Frankie would enter his plea of not guilty to the charge of escape.

Once Judge Humphrey entered the courtroom, the whole proceeding took less than five minutes.

"How do you plead?" Humphrey asked after reading the charge.

"Not guilty," Frankie answered.

"Hearing set for three weeks from today. Any problems with that, counselors?"

"No, sir," Dani answered.

"I'm okay, too," Warren Camden said.

The judge banged his gavel. "So ordered."

They exited the courtroom, and Dani pulled Frankie and Jessica over to a bench, where they sat down. Agent Collins waited five feet away, giving them space for a quiet conversation.

"You're going to need to explain your reason for running away," Dani said to Frankie. "It's your only defense."

"I can't. I won't." Frankie's arms were locked over his chest.

Dani didn't know how to convince Frankie that it would be worse for him if he didn't testify. Speak out, and there was a good chance he'd never go back there. Remain silent, and the judge would have no choice but to extend his sentence. On their way outside, she took Jessica aside. "We have a few weeks before the hearing. You need to persuade him to talk. If he tells them who was behind his beating, even if he's found at fault for running away, we can convince the judge to send him to a different facility."

"But will that matter? What if it's all like some big fraternity where they each have the others' backs?"

Dani sighed. "I don't think that's the case. Please, keep working on Frankie."

On the flight back to New York, Dani realized she'd never been in this position before—a client who wouldn't testify. She'd represented men and women who eagerly took the stand to assert their innocence. She needed to figure out something, or without a doubt, he would be sent back to that hellhole.

The next day Dani sat in Bruce's office. "Is there any chance you can get Frankie to testify?"

Bruce shook his head slowly. "I doubt it. If Jessica can't persuade him, I have no chance of it."

"There's got to be something I can do—but for the life of me, I can't think of what."

"I've been trying to figure it out myself. But, if anyone can come up with an idea, it's you. Somehow, you always pull one out of the hat just when it's needed."

Dani wished she shared Bruce's confidence in her. She'd racked her brain all last night and come up empty. But as she walked back to her office, a thought began to swirl around her mind. *Maybe I shouldn't try to fight the escape charge. Maybe I should fight the original sentence.* If Frankie shouldn't have been sent to a lockup in the first place, then he wouldn't have needed to escape.

She sat down at her desk and began drafting a subpoena for records from the Florida Department of Juvenile Justice. *Maybe, just maybe, this will work.*

—

Joe Cummings hadn't stopped gnashing his teeth since yesterday's arraignment of Frankie Bishop. He'd expected the boy would be held in county lockup until his case was called, which would've given Williamson a chance to pay him a visit, reinforce the original message that snitches don't last in his prison. But that damn FBI agent had stayed glued to his side.

It was a risk, pushing for the new charges against the kid, but Wilcox insisted on it. Another hearing just gave the kid another opportunity to squeal. Cummings believed in toughness, but it'd gone too far in the case of the boy the Bishop kid had told his mother about. He'd told the guards to ignore the boy's pleas to see the doctor. Doctors cost the company money, and he got rewarded for keeping expenses down. Make him tough it out, he'd told them. He'll be stronger for it. How was he to know that the boy had pneumonia? He supposed it didn't help when the guard made him do those push-ups. And then kicked him. That wasn't on him—it was on the guard. It didn't matter, though. He was in charge.

Wilcox had made himself clear—he couldn't take a chance on anyone finding out about the boy who died. Big money was on the line. So was Cummings's job. "Make this go away," Wilcox had told him. Maybe it had. Maybe the Bishop boy had learned his lesson. But he couldn't know for sure until he was face-to-face with the kid. He could always tell when he looked into a boy's eyes if he'd stay quiet.

He took a deep breath, then picked up the phone to call Wilcox.

Spread before Dani were piles of documents from the Florida Department of Juvenile Justice. They'd tried stonewalling her at first. After all, juvenile records were confidential. She didn't care about the names. They could black out anything that was personally identifiable. She wanted a record of the violations charged and the sentences meted out. She'd had a hunch that other boys and girls with records as spotless as Frankie's, caught with a small amount of marijuana, weren't sentenced as harshly as he was. Maybe there was even evidence of a racial bias in the sentencing. If she could show that Frankie received a harsher sentence because he was black, she could use that to overturn his original sentence. And if that sentence were improper, if he shouldn't have been locked up in the first place, then running away from it shouldn't matter. At least, that's what she would argue if she could find the proof to back up her theory.

Only, that's not what she found. What she discovered was far more disturbing. Once more, she read through the chart she'd made from the DJJ documents. It was true that the standard sentence for a first offense of possession of marijuana rarely resulted in incarceration. But there were many times when it did. And the affected youngsters ran the gamut of all races and ages. What had startled her was that those sentences all emanated from one judge: Judge Humphrey. It wasn't just drugs. She read of a high school student who posted on her Facebook page negative comments about her principal. Despite being an A student, on a track for college, she was charged with harassment and sentenced to a juvenile-detention center. A boy in middle school was arrested for egging a house on Halloween. He, too, had never been in trouble before. Yet, instead of a stern warning or probation, he was sent to a juvenile prison. Case after case, Dani read of children as young as nine being sent away for seemingly minor offenses—what in her day would have been considered "kids being kids." In all, almost half of the youngsters who came before Humphrey were locked up.

At first, she assumed he might just be an exceptionally tough judge. But, as she looked over the dates, she found they all had occurred during the past three years—shortly after ML Juvenile Services had been awarded the contract to run three more juvenile prisons in Florida. Before that, Humphrey's sentencing was in line with juvenile-court justices throughout the state. Driving down further into the numbers, she realized that the only institutions to which Humphrey sent the juveniles were all owned by ML Juvenile Services.

Was it possible? Could Humphrey be getting kickbacks from ML Juvenile Services? The thought was repugnant to her, but it had never made sense for Frankie to have been sent to Eldridge, and this would explain it. Dani shuddered. Frankie was going back before the same judge in just over a week. She had nothing but data suggesting the possibility that Humphrey was corrupt. Without proof, she couldn't level an accusation against him. And that left Frankie Bishop defenseless.

—

"What should I do?" Dani asked Doug as she lay entwined in his arms that evening.

"Find the evidence."

"Hah! Just wave my magic wand and poof—it'll appear?" Dani thought it must be so easy to be a law professor. Everything was clean and simple. Read a case, and dissect the decision. The people involved weren't real to them; they were names on a page. Not so in her world, where uncovering evidence was messy and often elusive. Still, if her fears were correct, there would be money somewhere, probably hidden, but still more than any judge would be expected to have—at least, a judge without family money or a wealthy spouse. As a plan started to rumble around in her mind, she suddenly let out a squeal.

"What's wrong?" Doug asked.

Dani laughed, then took Doug's hand and placed it on her stomach. "She kicked me. Her first strong kick. A real wallop!"

"She's going to be a fighter. Just like her mother."

———

As soon as Dani arrived at work the next morning, she stopped at Tommy's office. "I'd like you to find out everything you can about Judge Humphrey. About his wife, too, and children, if he has any. Also, whatever you can dig up on Roger Wilcox."

"Sure. What gives?"

"I could be all wet on this, but I've started to wonder if Humphrey is getting paid by Wilcox to send kids to the prisons he operates."

"That's quite an accusation."

"Just a theory at this point. But there were two judges in Pennsylvania a few years back that got busted doing just that. They're in prison now."

"If that's the case, why would another judge try the same scheme?"

"Greed can make people think they're smarter than those who got caught. So, if my hunch is right, he'll have hidden the money more carefully."

"What did the other two do?"

"Put everything in their wives' names. I think you should start by seeing if Humphrey is living a more lavish lifestyle than would be expected."

"Okay. I'll check him out."

"But, Tommy . . ." Dani stopped and waved her finger at him. "Nothing illegal. No unauthorized searches, understood?"

Tommy gave her a mock salute. "Aye, aye, captain."

Although Dani loved working with Tommy—he was her go-to investigator—she knew he had a tendency to be a cowboy. If she was right about Humphrey, this was going to be a tricky situation, and she needed to be sure everything Tommy did was completely legit. She returned to her office and, as soon as she got settled in, called Jessica Bishop.

"The FBI agent will escort Frankie to the courthouse for the hearing," Dani told Jessica. "I'll try not to call him at all, but if I need to, I'll only ask him about the beating, not what they said to him."

"I'm afraid, Dani. What if this is a setup?"

"You mean, what if the whole purpose is to get Frankie back in Florida and then try to keep him there?"

"Exactly."

"Don't worry about it. I'm going to make sure Frankie stays with you. I promise."

In a Florida courtroom, the bailiffs took their orders from the judge, not an FBI agent. If they lost the hearing, and Humphrey ordered Frankie to begin his sentence immediately, she'd be unable to stop them. And if they got their hands on Frankie, Dani shared Jessica's fear that he wouldn't survive another attack.

After she said good-bye to Jessica, Dani placed a call to Noah Jacobs. As soon as he got on the line, she said, "I need your help."

29

Dani ran into the courthouse in a futile attempt to avoid getting soaked from the downpour. As soon as she had awakened that morning in her Florida hotel, she'd regretted not packing an umbrella. She'd checked the forecast before heading south, and the probability of rain had maxed out at 20 percent. She always packed light on her trips, ensuring that even with all the documents she carried with her, she wouldn't need to check a bag on the flight. So no umbrella. And pouring rain.

She entered the building and shook herself out, then went through security. Once past the guards, she found a bathroom and tried to dry herself off. She retrieved a comb from her purse and ran it through her soft, brunette waves. She'd let her hair grow longer since cutting it the previous year, so it now reached her collarbone. Wet from the rain, it looked like an overgrown bush. She did her best to tamp it down, then gathered her belongings and made her way to Judge Humphrey's courtroom. Jessica was waiting for her inside, along with Frankie and his FBI escort.

Dani briefly chatted with them, then took Frankie with her to the defendant's table. Moments later, the bailiff announced the judge. Everyone stood, and Judge Humphrey entered the courtroom.

"Everyone ready?" he asked the attorneys.

"Actually, Your Honor, may we approach?" Dani asked.

The judge nodded, and Dani and Warren Camden, once again representing the State, walked up to the podium.

"I believe you should recuse yourself, Your Honor."

The judge's eyes narrowed, and his lips turned into a frown. "And why would I do that?"

"One of the defendant's defenses is that the underlying sentence was improper, and therefore, he can't be charged with escape from an improper sentence. Since you imposed that sentence, it would be a conflict for you to decide whether it was improper."

"I remember you, missy. You were before me trying to do an end run around the clock on appeals. If the sentence was wrong, it should have been appealed. The time for that passed. Step back. We're going to get this started."

Dani held her ground. "It has since come to light that you sentence a much higher percentage of juveniles who come before you to incarceration, and every one is placed in a facility operated by ML Juvenile Services. At the very least, that creates the perception of a relationship between yourself and ML. Whether or not there is, you shouldn't be the one to pass on it."

Humphrey's face reddened. "You are dangerously close to being held in contempt, Ms. Trumball. Now, either you start this trial, or I will hold you in contempt."

Dani turned and took her seat. She knew it was a long shot that Humphrey would turn the trial over to another judge, but she also knew that Frankie had almost no chance of being acquitted of the charge against him with Humphrey presiding. She felt she had nothing to lose.

Camden stood. "I call Fred Williamson."

Williamson took the stand, was sworn in, and gave his name and address to the court reporter.

"What is your occupation?"

"I'm the assistant warden at Eldridge Academy."

"Are you familiar with Francis Bishop?"

"I am."

"Did there come a time when Francis was transferred to Crescent Hills Regional Hospital?"

"Yes. He instigated a fight with a boy but was overpowered and got injured too badly for us to treat him inside."

"Did his doctor inform you that he'd suffered any injury to his brain?"

"No."

"Did he tell you that he'd suffered any damage to his mental processes?"

"No."

"Were you advised at any time that he was well enough to return to Eldridge Academy?"

"Yes. I spoke to the hospital and was told that he could be picked up the next afternoon. That except for his ribs, he had healed and was ready to participate in our program."

"And was he picked up?"

"No. He must have known he was coming back, so he ran away during the night."

"Did you conduct a search for him?"

"We tried to find him, unsuccessfully."

"Had you or anyone else informed Francis that he didn't have to return to Eldridge?"

"No. Of course not. He knew he was required to return."

Dani called out an objection. "Mr. Williamson can't testify as to Francis's state of mind."

"There's no jury here, just me, and I know what to consider and what not to consider, Ms. Trumball." The judge looked at Camden. "Continue."

"Thank you. I have no further questions."

Dani stood and walked up close to Williamson.

"Mr. Williamson, did you post a guard outside Frankie's hospital room?"

"We don't normally do that with younger juveniles, not unless they have a history of violence. And despite Frankie's behavior at Eldridge, he wasn't considered a threat to others outside the institution. Given his age and injuries, we didn't think a guard was warranted. But he wasn't allowed any visitors or phone calls. And I checked in every day to monitor his treatment."

"Was he handcuffed to his bed?"

"No."

"Was he confined in any other way?"

"Not physically. But he knew he was going back to Eldridge."

"If Francis had returned to Eldridge, could you have guaranteed that he wouldn't be injured again?"

"We'd make sure he was safe."

"Really? How?"

"Well, we'd put the word out not to touch him."

"Oh, I see. So you can control the other residents. They do what you tell them, is that it?"

"I maintain good control."

Dani wanted so much to ask the next logical question: "So, you could tell them to beat up a twelve-year-old boy to send a message to him, couldn't you?" But she'd promised Frankie she wouldn't go there. Instead, she asked, "Would it surprise you that a boy who'd been beaten as severely as Frankie would be afraid that would happen again?"

"I suppose not."

"Thank you. You can step down."

Camden called a few more witnesses, mostly to fill time. When he rested, and it was Dani's turn, the judge glared at her. "You may begin your case, Ms. Trumball, but I warn you, I won't look kindly on you impugning my integrity. I suggest you tread lightly."

"Duly noted, Your Honor. I call Oscar Martinez."

A pasty-faced man who looked to be in his midforties with a receding hairline and expanding waist entered the courtroom and took the stand.

"What is your occupation, Mr. Martinez?"

"I'm an analyst with the Florida Department of Juvenile Justice."

"And how long have you worked there?"

"Fifteen years."

Dani picked up a packet of papers from the defendant's table and handed them to Martinez. "Are these records from the DJJ?"

He leafed through the pages, then looked up at Dani. "They are."

Dani retrieved two more packets and handed one each to Camden and the judge. "I'd like these marked as defendant's Exhibit A."

Judge Humphrey glanced at the report. "I warned you, Ms. Trumball—"

"This has nothing to do with your integrity. It merely addresses the standard of sentencing in juvenile courts throughout the State of Florida. If Francis's sentence varied from that standard, it could have been the result of a variety of reasons, some of which may have made his sentence improper. I have every right to pursue this line of questioning."

"You're in my court, and I'm the only one who decides what a proper line of questioning is. And this isn't. You may not mark this into evidence, and if you have no other purpose for questioning this witness, then he's excused."

"Note my objection for the record." Dani needed to do this for an appeal. "You can step down, Mr. Martinez."

Although she hadn't wanted to, Dani had no choice but to call Frankie to the stand. She would steer clear of implicating the warden and his crew, though. She watched as he walked slowly to the witness box. His face was pale, and he kept biting his lip as he sat down.

"Francis, would you describe the beating that landed you in the hospital?" Dani could see Frankie's hands shaking.

"I'd just left the dining room and was walking back to my room when four older guys jumped me and started punching and kicking me."

"The warden's report said that you started a fight first."

"That's probably what they told the warden. But I've never started a fight with anyone in my life."

"Tell me what happened after they stopped hitting you."

"I don't really know. Everything got dark, and I kind of passed out, I guess. Next thing I remember, I was in the hospital, and doctors were talking over me. I think I fell asleep maybe, because when I woke up, I was in a hospital room. The doctor told me I had a lot of injuries. And I hurt. A lot."

"You knew you were supposed to return to Eldridge when you were better, right?"

"Yes."

"Tell the court why you didn't."

"I was afraid those boys would beat me up again, and I thought the next time, they'd kill me."

"Why didn't you go back and tell the warden what really happened?"

"Because he might not have believed me. And even if he did, those boys would be put in isolation for a while, and then they'd be out and even angrier at me."

"Why didn't you tell your mother?"

"What could she do?"

"So, let's be clear. The only reason you didn't go back to Eldridge was because you were afraid for your life, correct?"

"Yes. That's the only reason."

"Thank you, Francis. I have no more questions."

Camden stood up. "Again, just to be clear, you knew that you were required to return to Eldridge Academy?"

"Yes, sir."

"When you left the hospital, did you call your mother?"

"No."

"Did you try to return to your mother?"

"No."

"Why is that?"

"Because that's the first place they'd look."

"So, you knew it was wrong to leave the hospital."

Frankie looked down at his hands, now shaking even more. "Yes, sir."

Camden smiled the smile of a prosecutor who knew he'd won his case. "No further questions."

"Anyone else, Ms. Trumball?"

"No, Your Honor."

"I'm going to rule from the bench. I find that Francis Bishop knowingly and purposefully escaped from Crescent Hills Regional Hospital to avoid completing his sentence. He is hereby guilty of escape, and I sentence him to twelve months at Eldridge Academy."

Dani had prepared Jessica and Frankie for this verdict—it was inevitable—but Jessica nonetheless ran to the defendant's table and hugged Frankie.

Judge Humphrey banged his gavel. "I hereby order the sentence to begin immediately. Bailiff, escort Francis to the holding cells."

Dani jumped up. "Your Honor, pursuant to a federal court order, Francis is in protective custody of the FBI until the case in which he's an essential witness is completed."

"A federal court in North Carolina doesn't control here." The judge motioned to the bailiff to take Frankie.

Interesting, Dani thought. He knows the order came from North Carolina.

Before the bailiff could move, three men in the gallery stood. One of them walked to the front.

"Your Honor, my name is Noah Jacobs. I'm an assistant US attorney, and I have an order from the US District Court, Middle District of Florida, continuing the authority of the FBI to keep Francis in protective custody. I believe that court order does, in fact, supersede your order to return him immediately to Eldridge Academy."

"Did you know about this, Mr. Camden?" Humphrey asked.

"No. I received no notice of it."

"We went in on an ex parte motion late yesterday afternoon," Noah said. "There wasn't sufficient time to notify the state attorney's office. They, of course, can ask for a rehearing, but in the meantime, Francis is returning with us."

The other two men, both big and burly, moved closer to the front.

"Sir," Noah told the judge, "these men are with the US Marshals Service, and they are tasked with bringing Francis back to his safe house."

Humphrey was silent. Dani could see the muscles of his jaw tightening. *He's dirty.* After several moments, he looked at Jacobs with a cold, hard stare. "Take him," he said, and then turned to the bailiff. "Call the next case."

⸺

Frankie wasn't out of the woods yet. Dani knew all she'd done was buy him time. Time for Tommy to try to uncover a connection between Humphrey and ML Juvenile Services. After Frankie and Jessica left the courthouse, she called Tommy. Each day, he'd reported the results of his efforts to locate a connection between the judge and the prison operator. Each day, he'd come up empty.

"What's the verdict?" he asked as soon as he answered her call.

"Just as we expected. Judge found him guilty and tried to order him to Eldridge immediately. Noah stopped him."

"Bastards. I bet they were just waiting to get their hands on him."

"Have you found anything yet?"

"Zilch."

"Do you think you can track down Humphrey's home address?"

"Don't need to. Already have that."

"Great. Check with Bruce to make sure it's okay, but I'd like you to fly down here and stake out his house. I rattled him pretty badly in court today. Maybe he'll try to get rid of something incriminating in his house."

"I'm sure Bruce will be fine with it. I'll get the next flight out."

"Thanks, Tommy."

"Don't thank me. Frankie's a good kid, and he's gotten a raw deal. Even if he weren't Bruce's nephew, I'd want to help him as much as you."

"Let's hope we can. Because if we can't find something, then as soon as the feds' case against Felder and Hollander is finished, he's going back to Eldridge."

⸺

Judge Humphrey took off his robe, hung it on the back of the door to his chambers, and told his assistant not to disturb him. He settled himself into the high-backed leather chair behind his desk, then took a cell phone from his jacket pocket and dialed a number.

"Wilcox here."

"Roger, I tried, but the feds still have the boy."

"What the fuck?!" came the explosion on the other end.

"Look, he hasn't said anything yet, and he had ample opportunity on the stand today. If his lawyer knew, she would have asked him about it to strengthen his case—but she didn't. I think you're okay."

"No, *you* look. Three of my contracts are up for renewal over the next three months. If the State knew the real reason that boy with pneumonia died, that would be it. They're already paying too damn much attention to our operations. Plus, the kid knows Cummings ordered his beating. If Cummings gets called on the carpet, he won't hesitate a second to point the finger at me. Any of that gets out, I can kiss the renewals good-bye. Too much money is on the line."

"Why would they believe him? He's a juvenile delinquent. You're a respected businessman."

Wilcox laughed. "Respected? The other states I was in threw me out. Florida's all I have left. No—I can't take a chance."

"I'm sorry. It couldn't be helped."

"I suppose he's on his way back to North Carolina."

"That'd be my guess."

"Flying or driving?"

"I'd think flying."

"There's one evening flight to Raleigh from Gainesville and one from Orlando. I can cover the arrivals."

"What makes you think he's returning to Raleigh?"

"That's where the court was that signed the order. They probably didn't take him too far away."

"Roger, he's a twelve-year-old boy. Haven't you put him through enough already? He's not going to talk."

"It's my business now. Stay out of it."

Humphrey hung up the phone and hung his head. This was a terrible mess that just kept getting messier. He walked over to his credenza and poured himself a scotch, downed it in one gulp, then poured a second.

30

The tall man in the baseball cap recognized the boy and his mother immediately. They were flanked by three men as they came past the security gates into the terminal. Looking over the lip of his coffee cup as he sipped, he saw that the kid looked just like the picture in the text he'd received. Scrawny. Pretty mom. Good chance she'd go down, too. Too bad, he thought.

When he followed them out to the curb, he saw one man split from the group and stand in the taxi line while the others headed into the parking garage. He stayed far enough behind not to attract attention, coffee cup still in one hand and his head bent over what would appear to be his cell phone in the other. When they slowed at a car, he quickened his steps and headed straight toward them. He reached their car as they were getting inside, then pretended to stumble, spilling the cup of coffee onto the car's trunk. He bent down to pick up the cup, then in a flash, placed a GPS tracker on the underside of the car. He stood up, wiped the spilled coffee from the trunk, mouthed "Sorry," and continued on his way.

Fifteen minutes later, he was on the highway, following a quarter mile behind them. When they exited, he did as well. They'd traveled almost an hour when they pulled onto a private dirt road. He went past the turnoff, then did a U-turn and waited. There was no need to rush. Another ten minutes and the car driving the boy and his mother came out of the dirt road and turned back in the direction from where they'd come. He could see the two men inside. The boy and his mother were gone.

He assumed they had someone watching the house. Probably an FBI agent who wasn't expecting trouble. After so many weeks of watching, the agent would have gotten careless by now, the man figured. Still, he wouldn't take chances. He pulled his car to a stop about ten yards down the dirt road—just enough so it wouldn't attract attention from the roadway, but not enough to draw attention from the boy's guard—and waited, making sure no one was returning.

The sun had already set, and darkness enveloped the thickly treed road. He stayed inside the car for an hour. In his line of work, patience was necessary. When no one entered the dirt road, he got out of the car, grabbed the cheap, black case resting on the passenger seat, and quietly made his way forward. Within ten minutes, he spotted the cabin. Its lights were on, and he could see shadows through the curtained window.

A lone agent sat underneath a light on the front porch, reading a book. The man moved closer to the house, and when he was about eighty yards away, stopped and opened his case. Inside was a Remington 700 ADL, with a twenty-four-inch barrel rather than the standard twenty-inch. He'd found it at a gun show, one of the many that didn't ask for IDs and didn't do background checks. He'd replaced the Leupold scope on it with a FSI Sniper 6-24 x 50mm scope, and knew that even at a hundred yards, he'd land a bullet within a quarter inch of his target. He pulled out the rifle, attached the bipod to it, then loaded four cartridges, one by one, into the internal magazine. When he was finished, he dropped down to his knees, aimed his rifle at the window, and waited for the boy to come into view.

"Freeze," a loud voice boomed behind him. He spun around with his gun, then stopped. Facing him were the two men from the airport, with assault rifles pointed at his chest.

"Set the rifle on the ground, and step away from it."

He did as instructed.

"We made you at the parking garage, ass-wipe. Saw you place the tracker. You saw that coffee move on TV, I'll bet. Who sent you?"

The man said nothing. Even if he'd wanted to help—and he didn't—he never knew who'd ordered a hit. He'd get a call from his handler with instructions, and he'd deliver in exchange for $10,000. Sometimes more, if the target was high profile. This was a rush job— always a mistake. This time, he'd pay for the mistake.

Clyde Metzger sat opposite "Java Joe." That's what they called him, since his fingerprints weren't in any database, and he hadn't said a word since they'd brought him in. Not even to say he wanted his attorney. Just a cold, hard stare, as though looking right through them.

"This will go a lot easier for you if you give us the person who hired you," Metzger said once more.

Java Joe sat still, his back erect, and said nothing.

"Was it Mark Hollander? John Felder?"

"We're wasting our time with him," Henry Greco said. "Let him rot in jail for twenty years."

"See, I think you're wrong, Henry. I think our friend here really wants to give us a name, but doesn't appreciate what it'll mean for him." Metzger turned back to the prisoner. "Right now, you're looking at a minimum of twenty. Maximum security. Now, I understand you have some sort of code of silence and all that. But help us a little bit, and we can knock ten years off that."

There was no reaction. Just the same silent stare.

"Tell you what I'm going to do. I'm going to leave three pieces of paper: Hollander's name on one, Felder's name on the other, and the third will say, 'Someone else from their network.' We'll leave the room. Turn over the page of the one who hired you. That way, you won't have said a word to us, but you'll still get a deal. Got it?"

Not even a nod from the man.

Metzger and Greco stood up and left the room. They watched through the one-way glass, but Java Joe didn't move a muscle. Ten minutes later, they walked back in and gathered up the sheets of paper. "It's your funeral," Metzger said as they walked out.

Silent or not, Metzger felt pretty sure Hollander was behind the assassin. Felder had already struck a deal; it was Hollander who'd been holding out. Maybe now, with the attempt on Frankie a failure, he'd finally crack. Metzger hoped so. Hundreds of kids were out there, waiting to be rescued. It's time that they were.

———

Tommy pulled into the block of Humphrey's home, then slowly drove past the house. He'd caught a break. On the flight down, he'd worried that the home would be in a gated community, so common in Florida. Then, it would be difficult for him to get in, but not impossible. Instead, the home was on a quiet public street, about three-quarters of a mile from the Gulf. It was nice enough, but not ostentatious. It had a small, manicured lawn with attractive landscaping—something he always noted—but fully in keeping with what he guessed the judge's income to be. If he was on the take, he wasn't spending the money on his home. In the past two weeks, Tommy had scoured records for any other real property owned by the judge, his wife, or his children—two sons who had children of their own. He'd come up empty. They had no boats registered in their names, and the cars driven by the judge and his wife were lower-end luxury cars.

None of the homes on the street had garbage pails out by the curb. He figured that meant no pickup the next day. He drove around a bit more, familiarized himself with the streets, then left for his motel.

He'd return the next night, after midnight, when the homes were dark and the streets silent. And each night after that until he could pick up the judge's trash.

—

Tommy was back on the judge's street just before midnight the next evening and found a trash bin at the end of the judge's driveway. Next to it were two clear plastic bags containing papers and plastics. He checked up and down the street, saw no lights on in the homes nearby, and quietly lifted out two plastic bags filled with garbage, then placed them in the trunk of his rental car. He left the bag containing plastics but grabbed the bag with papers. He drove to his motel and brought the trash bags into his room. In the recyclable bag, he hoped he'd find bank or credit-card statements mixed in with the old newspapers. He'd grabbed the bags with garbage in case the judge mixed papers in with scraped-off food to better hide incriminating evidence.

He quickly looked through the bags with garbage and saw they didn't contain any papers. He then started on the recycled papers, pouring the contents of the bag onto one of the two double beds in the room. No shredded papers, which might've suggested something to hide that he could've pieced together to reconstruct. He sorted through the pile, placing newspapers and magazines on one side, everything else on the other, and then shoved the newspapers and magazines back into the recycling bag. With the remaining pile, he quickly pulled out what looked like financial statements and credit-card bills and brought those over to the desk.

Tommy settled back in his chair and began with a bank statement. One by one, he scrutinized each document, looking for large deposits, unusual withdrawals, evidence of payments to utility companies for other properties—anything that suggested hidden assets. When he was finished, he'd found nothing. That was bad news for Frankie Bishop.

Frankie and Jessica had been moved to a new safe house a few days ago, this one a small ranch in a row of identical ranches. She'd questioned Patrick Collins, the agent assigned to watch over them, but he dismissed her concerns. "Just a routine move," he'd said. "We do it all the time. Not to worry."

And so she hadn't. She'd been ecstatic ever since leaving the courthouse with Frankie by her side instead of turning him over to the courthouse officers. She'd been terrified in the weeks leading up to the hearing that Frankie would once again be in danger. Now, at least, there was time on his side.

She'd been homeschooling him each day with books provided by his school. It quickly became clear to her that Frankie was more advanced than the materials she'd been given. She could barely figure out the problems in the math workbook herself, yet Frankie answered each one easily. The books recommended by his English teacher also seemed too basic for him. With no one to play with, he went through three or four novels a week. She'd begun downloading some of the classics usually recommended for high-school students onto his iPad.

She left Frankie with a history assignment and turned to her computer. Although her employer had been supportive of her situation, allowing her to work fully from home, she'd fallen a few days behind because of Frankie's hearing. She wished her husband was back home with her, helping distribute the stress from Frankie's situation between both of them, instead of it all being on her. The news that Alex was alive helped reduce some of the stress—but it was still a far cry from him being home, telling her everything would work out.

Her work was interrupted by the ringing of her cell phone.

"Hello?"

"Jessica, this is Noah Jacobs. I wanted to update you on our case against Felder and Hollander."

Please, don't tell me you're plea bargaining with them. Please, take it to trial. A plea could wrap it up in days. A trial would take months, maybe six or more.

"We're making progress. Felder cooperated from the start, but we really want to track down other kids they've taken, as well as other procurers, and Hollander is the key to getting that information. He now seems inclined to reach a deal—we're stuck at the moment on the length of time he'll have to serve. We want twenty minimum; he's pushing for ten. If he gives us enough information about other players, and we can rescue the kids, we'll probably go down to fifteen. If that happens, we won't need Frankie's testimony anymore. I thought you should have a heads-up, given his new sentence."

Jessica's stomach had twisted into knots. If a deal happened soon, Frankie would go back to the lion's den. Take your time, she wanted to scream. *Don't settle!* Instead, she thanked Jacobs, hung up the phone, and slumped down over the computer.

Before Dani had left for work, Tommy had called with the results of his search the night before. As soon as she arrived at the office, she placed a call to Josh Cosgrove.

"What do you need?" Josh asked as soon as he got on the line. "If you're calling me, you must need a favor."

"Ooh . . . am I that transparent?"

"'Fraid so."

Dani wondered at times if she'd taken advantage of their friendship. She didn't like being the kind of person who took without reciprocating. She assuaged her conscience by reminding herself that each time she'd called on Josh to use the resources of his office, it had led to a win for the US Attorney's Office as well.

"It's still about Frankie Bishop."

"I thought it went well in court. Isn't he back in the safe house?"

"For now. But when the case against Felder and Hollander is over, he goes back into the system."

"I'm sorry about that. But you knew we could only hold him temporarily."

"I think something fishy is going on with the juvenile-court judge."

"Why's that?"

"I've matched up sentencing by juvenile-court judges in Florida for the past five years, and his sentences are way out of whack."

"So, he's a tough judge. That happens."

"Only he wasn't five years ago. Something changed around three years ago. That's when he started sending kids to juvie for pretty minor offenses. And he only sends them to ML Juvenile Services facilities."

"You think he's taking money from them?"

"I think it's a real possibility."

Dani heard a deep sigh on the other end.

"There has to be a basis for us to investigate him. Let me think about it, okay?"

"You remember those two judges in Pennsylvania a few years ago, right?"

"Yeah."

"It was the Justice Department that took them down."

"I'll see what I can do. Promise."

—

Two hours later, Josh called Dani back. "Turns out the federal DJJ has an open investigation of ML. So I have the go-ahead to look into potential fishy dealings with your judge."

"Oh, Josh, that's great." Dani felt a rush of relief. The Justice Department had the resources to check into bank accounts both in the US and, in many cases, overseas. If Humphrey or any of his family had suspicious deposits, there was a good chance they'd find them. They'd also have a better shot of finding other assets that Tommy couldn't locate on his own. "Can you tell me what they're investigating?"

"I shouldn't, but you're dealing with some of this yourself. They're looking into widespread abuses in the facilities he runs."

"Did Noah tell you? Frankie knows of a boy in Eldridge who died because the guards not only denied him medical care, but continued to physically abuse him."

"He did tell me about it. He told the folks leading the investigation into Wilcox, too. It's just the kind of information that would help them. But he also said that Frankie wouldn't testify to it."

"He's too afraid."

"I suspect our investigation will go on for a while. Maybe when it's all over for Frankie, when he's back home and away from Eldridge, he'll give us a statement."

"I'm sure I could convince him of that. After all, you and your team have done so much for him."

"I'll let our people know. And I'll call you if I come up with something on Humphrey."

As soon as Dani got off the phone, she called Tommy back to tell him the news.

"I'm going to keep checking on my own," Tommy said.

"Good. I don't want you to stop. But maybe with both of you on it, we'll turn up something."

"We need to do it fast. I just got off the phone with Metzger. They're close to a deal. Which means Frankie doesn't have much time."

～

Howard Humphrey sat down at the desk in his study and pulled out a stack of bills from the top drawer. He opened his checkbook, then one by one pulled out a statement from each envelope. He always paid the mortgage and utilities first, saving the cable bill and credit cards for last. With those, he always checked each item listed to ensure it was an item he'd charged. Too much theft going on nowadays. Too easy to steal someone's account number or, even worse, their identity.

He stopped cold as he eyed a charge on his Visa bill for Verizon. Seven hundred and twenty-nine dollars. Quickly, he turned to his computer, logged on to his credit card's website, and opened his recent bill. He remembered Doris saying she was buying an iPhone for their grandson, but this amount was too high, even with a phone case. He left his study and called out to his wife.

"I'm in the kitchen."

Humphrey walked toward her, the bill in his hand. "Doris, when you bought Eric's iPhone, did you charge anything else at Verizon?"

She turned around. "Let me think. Yes, I believe I did. A prepaid phone for you."

Humphrey willed himself to stay calm. "You know I've asked you to pay cash for those phones."

"Well, I always have. But it just seemed easier, since I was charging the iPhone, to put it all on one bill."

Humphrey nodded, then walked back to his study. He couldn't get angry at Doris. It was his own fault for entrusting her with the task of buying his prepaid phones—a new one every two months, used to call only one person: Roger Wilcox. It was the timing of her mistake that had him worried. That New York attorney had rattled him with her accusations. She seemed like the type who wouldn't let go.

He patted his pocket to make sure his phone was on him, then told Doris he had to go out briefly.

"But dinner's almost ready," she said.

"I won't be long. Twenty minutes at the most."

"What's so important it can't wait?"

"Judicial business, sweetheart."

His wife sighed. "Just make it quick."

Humphrey got into his car, then drove to a diner ten minutes from his home. He pulled into the parking lot, got out, then threw the phone into one of its dumpsters in the back. Tomorrow, he'd buy a new burner phone himself.

—

It's not fair, it's not fair, it's not fair, Jessica kept thinking as she muffled a scream in her pillow. *We've been through too much. How much more can we take?* She'd faithfully called her landline's voice mail each day to retrieve her messages, hoping there would be one saying Alex was on his way home. Her heart had done flip-flops when she'd heard the message this morning from Major Stillman, asking her to call him. She dialed his number eagerly, but when he got on the phone, his first words were, "I'm sorry, Mrs. Bishop, I've got some bad news." Their source had told them Alex was no longer at the Taliban prisoner camp. The source didn't know if he'd been moved, or he'd died, or they'd killed him. The major would keep her informed if they learned anything further. *I can't go on. I can't.* But she knew she had to, for Frankie, for Bobby. And for Alex—because that's what he'd want her to do.

Dani jumped out of bed as soon as she awakened, even though she normally liked to sleep in Sunday mornings. She threw on her robe and slipped into her slippers, then padded out the front door. She smiled when she saw the *New York Times* in her driveway, quickly retrieved it, and brought it upstairs to her bedroom, where Doug was just rousing himself from sleep.

"You have it already?" he asked.

"Yep." Dani tore off the plastic wrap around the newspaper, then thumbed through it to find the Science section. There it was, on the front page. She began to read it aloud to Doug. "Westchester special-needs school teaches children with extra-special talents." She showed Doug the picture of Jonah that accompanied the story, then read quietly to herself. When she finished, she read the section about Jonah to Doug.

"At the age of thirteen, Jonah Trumball was the youngest composer to have a symphony performed by the Westchester Philharmonic. The conductor of that orchestra hailed the young Mr. Trumball as a 'musical genius,' who has created a 'lush, evocative piece that will stand the test of time.' Now fourteen, Jonah continues to compose sophisticated music despite having difficulty performing the most basic mathematical functions learned by elementary-school children.

"Jonah is one of several musically talented students at the Carlton School. Another—" Dani stopped reading and looked up. "That's it about Jonah. It goes on to describe Lucy's operatic voice and Eddie's piano playing."

"I think it's a fine article. Jonah will be pleased."

"I suppose I can be forgiven if I violate the copyright laws by making dozens of copies of the article."

Doug laughed. "Yes. I think for once you can be a proud mother instead of a crusading lawyer."

―

Back at work on Monday, Dani felt nothing like a crusading lawyer. Sitting on her desk when she arrived at the office were the results of a DNA test run on one of her clients. It matched the DNA of the victim. It happened once in a while. A client who'd convinced Dani of his innocence turned out to be guilty. She knew she should take it in stride. No one in the office had a perfect record of predicting innocence. Her record, in fact, was the best. Still, it always rankled her when her judgment was found to be wrong. A guilty person had taken up the time she could have spent working to free an innocent person. She prepared a letter to send to the guilty client, advising him of the DNA results, then took out her folder of inmate letters and began the search for her next client.

As she reread each file, her thoughts kept turning back to Frankie Bishop. He wasn't even an official client of HIPP, yet even if he hadn't been Bruce's nephew, she'd have felt she had to see his case through to the end. She'd never helped a child before. Although there were young men and even some women who'd entered prison while still in their teens, by the time HIPP became involved in trying to overturn their convictions, they were long past childhood. Frankie was still a boy, a young boy, and it broke her heart whenever she thought of the ordeal he'd been through. Dani wondered if it was her maternal instinct in play, made more acute because of the baby growing inside her.

She pushed aside the folders on her desk and called Noah Jacobs. "I'm just checking in for a status report on your pedophile case," she said when he answered the phone.

"Good news for us, bad news for you. I think we'll have it wrapped up in a week."

"Oh." Dani felt a heaviness throughout her body. As she chewed at her lips, all she could think was that it wasn't enough time. Not nearly enough.

"Hollander's given us a wealth of information," Jacobs continued. "We've already rescued more than sixty kids, and arrested nine more procurers and twelve pimps. And there's more to come. This is the biggest child-trafficking case the office has handled since I've been here."

"So you won't need Frankie's testimony?"

"Looks like it. It could all fall apart next week when the paperwork is signed, but I doubt it. Everything Hollander's told us so far has panned out, so he'll get his deal."

"And what is the deal for him?"

"You're not going to like it."

"Probably not, but tell me, anyway."

"Twelve years in a minimum-security prison."

No, Dani didn't like that at all. This scum of the earth who had destroyed the childhoods of so many, who'd taken their souls if not their lives, didn't deserve to ever come out of prison. Still, she understood that sometimes a bad deal for the prosecution was the lesser evil. As reprehensible as it was to her, saving so many children—if they weren't already too damaged to be saved—was more important than one man.

"If you can, would you give me two days' notice before Frankie is cut loose as a witness?"

"Sure."

After ending the call, Dani found Tommy at his desk. "Anything on the judge?"

Tommy shook his head. "I'm keeping my search legit—just like you want—and I can't find any money trail."

Dani's legs felt like weights were attached as she walked back to her office. *Maybe it won't be terrible for Frankie if he's sent back to Eldridge. As far as they know, he's kept quiet about what goes on inside. Maybe that's good enough for them.* Somehow, thinking it might be okay didn't make her feel any better.

She placed the inmate folders back on the center of her desk. *Focus on work. Don't think about Frankie.* She managed to get a few productive hours in before her assistant buzzed and told her Josh Cosgrove was on the phone.

"Please, tell me you found something," Dani said.

"Maybe. We need to dig further to find the source, but we turned up a deposit of $545,000 in a brokerage account held jointly by the judge and his wife, from two and a half years ago."

The heaviness that had weighted Dani's body down all morning and into the afternoon began to lift. "That must be it! He started sending all the kids before him to ML Juvenile Services just shy of three years ago. It has to be a payment from Wilcox."

"Well, we don't know that for sure yet. But it's out of character with all his other accounts, so I thought you'd want to know."

"Keep digging, Josh. I bet that's just the first. Maybe he got smarter after that one and figured out better places to hide the money."

"Don't worry, Dani. We'll keep going on this."

"Frankie only has a week."

There was silence on the line for a moment, then Dani heard a deep sigh. "I expect we'll need more time. I'm sorry."

As Josh hung up, Dani could feel the heaviness return to her body.

"I have a new number," Howard Humphrey told Roger Wilcox. "Same area code. 555-4732."

"Why? You just got the last burner three weeks ago."

"It got wet. Stopped working." Humphrey had no intention of telling Wilcox the real reason. No point in getting him more agitated over the Bishop boy. He was already over the edge, as far as Humphrey was concerned.

"I'm glad you called," Wilcox said. "You're down on referrals this month."

"Can't be helped. I won't send you a kid without evidence of wrongdoing."

"We have a deal."

"I'm not a magician."

"Magician or not, it's up to you to get me the kids. I don't care how—just do it."

Humphrey hung up and sat back in his chair. He looked around his study, the walls covered with plaques he'd received for good works. He'd dedicated his life to public service, choosing that path instead of the more lucrative route of a private law practice. But, along the way he'd made a deal with a devil, and like all such deals, it could only end in ruin for him.

⁓

Roger Wilcox marched into the front doors of Eldridge Academy and barked to the guard at the reception desk, "Tell Cummings that Wilcox is here."

Almost immediately, another guard appeared to bring him to the warden's office. Cummings was standing at his desk when Wilcox strode in.

"Roger, I wasn't expecting you. Can I get you a drink?"

"I'm not here on a social visit. I've gotten word that the Bishop kid won't be needed as a witness soon. That means he'll be coming back here. I want to make sure we're on the same page."

"As soon as he arrives, he'll be brought into my office. I'll reinforce the message already given him. I don't think he'll be a problem."

"You're not being paid to think. I do that. Your job is to carry out my instructions."

"He's been gone months and hasn't said a word."

"You don't know that."

"If he had, wouldn't it have come out already?"

That was the easy answer, Wilcox knew. Assume silence meant everything was good. But too often he'd seen nonchalance bite him in the back. Maybe the kid was just waiting for the right time. Maybe once the threat of returning to Eldridge was gone, when he'd finished his sentence, he'd start squealing. He'd seen just that happen before, and it had cost him dearly in lost contracts, lost money. Now even more was at stake. He'd gotten word from a well-paid source that the Justice Department was investigating him for abuses within his prisons. If they learned of that boy's death at the hands of his guard, it could be the final straw to shut him down completely. He wouldn't let that happen.

"I want an example made of him," Wilcox said.

"We've already done that."

"A stronger example than just beating him up."

"What are you suggesting?"

Wilcox stared into Cummings's eyes, then leaned forward. "You like this job?"

"Sure."

"You damn well know what I want."

Cummings nodded. "I'll take care of it."

"Hah! You really think I'd leave this to you? So far, you've botched everything. If you hadn't let the other boy die, we wouldn't have this problem. No, you're going to sit here with me, and we're going to figure out how to get to this boy."

Thirty minutes later, a plan in place, Wilcox stood up and turned to leave. As he reached the door, he turned back to Cummings. "Always nice to see you, Joe. Have a good day."

—

Frankie's nightmares had finally begun to subside. At first, he'd awakened screaming several times each night. Images of Mark and Daisy filled his head. Not John. He'd been frightened when John had him in the motel, but not the way he'd been with Mark. Mark oozed malevolence. Maybe it was because of what he knew Mark did to Daisy, maybe because of what he feared the man Mark sold him to would do to him. It hadn't mattered that he was safe now. That Mark was locked up and couldn't reach him.

The psychologist sent by the feds had helped him. With her guidance, he began to recognize when he was dreaming and quiet his fear. Now he only occasionally saw Mark's face during the deepest part of the night. He still dreamed of Daisy, though. In his dreams, she was always crying, her frail arms locked around her chest. He hoped her parents were helping her, like his mother was helping him, although he worried that wasn't the case. He knew she was in a safe house, also, and had asked the FBI agent guarding his house if he could call her, but had been told no.

He knew he'd be going back to Eldridge. Dani had told him that he wouldn't need to testify against Mark and John at a trial. He was relieved he wouldn't see them again, but scared of what he'd find when he was locked up again. She said she'd know two days before it happened, and that she would fly once more to Florida and speak to the warden. Warn him against Frankie getting hurt again. She said she could do that without letting Big Joe know Frankie had told her the truth. She said he'd be safe. He hoped she was right.

———

Three days later, Dani got the phone call she'd dreaded.

"It's your two-day warning," Cosgrove said.

"Any luck with a money trail?"

"Just the opposite. The large deposit in the brokerage account? It came from an inheritance from his wife's mother."

"Damn."

"We did uncover something interesting, though. Right after the hearing on returning Frankie to Eldridge ended, Humphrey made a phone call to Wilcox."

"That is interesting. Although Humphrey could probably come up with a reason why he needed to speak to him that's legit. After all, he sends a lot of kids to his detention centers."

"True. Except he called Wilcox on a burner phone, and we were able to get a trace on the number assigned to it. A judge doesn't need to use that kind of phone to conduct legitimate business, especially when the call was made while he was still in the courthouse, and when he has a regular phone."

"How'd you discover it if it's a burner?"

"We saw from his credit-card history that his wife made a large purchase at a particular Verizon store, so we checked with that store. She charged an iPhone and a prepaid cell phone. But here's the thing: the store said that every other month she comes in and pays cash for a prepaid phone. So my guess is she slipped up this month."

"They have a scheme going on. I just know it. Humphrey has to be getting money from Wilcox."

"There's one other thing. With the case near the finish line, Jacobs wanted to tie up any loose ends. Someone had ordered an attempted assassination of Frankie."

"*What?*"

"Our agents apprehended a hit man near the safe house the night Frankie and Jessica returned from the hearing. They subdued him before he had a chance to do any harm, but he already had a rifle in his hand and was in a position to shoot."

Dani was gripping the phone so tightly, it seemed possible she would crush it. The baby had begun kicking, as though she could feel her mother's anger. "How could you not tell me this?"

"At first, the agents thought Hollander had sent him. The would-be assassin wouldn't talk, but it just made sense that Hollander would try to shut Frankie up. We moved Frankie and Jessica to a new house as a precaution, in case he sent someone new. A few days after the assassin was apprehended, Hollander finally broke down and started spilling. That made sense, too—he'd gotten word that the assassin had failed, so realized his best option was to cut a deal."

"It sounds like there's a 'but' coming."

"Yeah. A big one. Right before finalizing the agreement with Hollander, Jacobs offered to take a full year off the sentence if he admitted to hiring the assassin. Hollander swore up and down it wasn't him. And Jacobs now believes him."

"But, if not Hollander, then . . . oh, my God!"

"Yeah. We're now thinking it might have been Wilcox. Or Humphrey. Or both."

Dani felt like her heart was going to stop. "That must be what Humphrey's phone call to Wilcox was about. Frankie can't go back there. They're going to kill him!"

"I don't know what to tell you. We can't keep him. We have no proof Wilcox was involved."

"Just one extra day. Can you do that?"

"Yes. If you think it'll help."

"It will." Dani didn't know what she'd do with that time, but hoped that she'd think of something to help Frankie. She just had to. But first, she needed to alert Jessica. As much as she dreaded telling her, Dani knew she must. She placed a call to Jessica's cell phone, and when it was answered, Dani said, "I have bad news."

———

Jessica's hands were shaking when she got off the phone. Would their nightmare never end? If Frankie were sent back to Eldridge, she was certain he wouldn't leave alive. And if Dani was successful in keeping him at home? Then no safe house. No FBI guard. No one to watch over him.

She needed Alex. He would thwart an attacker. He was fearless. *What would he do? What would he want me to do?* And then it hit her. "You're never alone," he'd told her each time he was deployed in a combat zone. "My fellow officers, the men in my battalion, they're my family, and they'll treat you and the boys like their own family." Maybe Alex hadn't come home, but many of his friends had. She picked up the phone and called Peter Burke, a captain who'd served under Alex and the only one she knew who lived in Florida. By the time she finished the call, her hands had stopped shaking. Now she prayed silently, let Dani be successful.

CHAPTER 35

Two days later, Dani was back at the circuit court in Cypress County, sitting in Judge Humphrey's antechamber. She'd gotten there promptly at nine a.m. and was waiting for him to arrive. The room's decor was spartan—just his assistant's desk and four chairs against one wall. The large, round clock on the wall opposite Dani read 9:12. The judge still hadn't arrived.

Five minutes later, he opened the door with a cheery "Good morning" to his assistant. His smile immediately dimmed when he saw Dani.

"Did we have an appointment, Ms. Trumball?"

"No, but I'm hoping you can spare me five minutes."

"I have a very busy calendar."

"I promise it'll be quick. It's important."

Humphrey nodded to her, and she followed him into his chambers. Like most judge's chambers, it was furnished with fine wood furniture and plush seating. Humphrey settled himself behind his desk, then pointed to a chair for Dani to sit. Dani sat, then opened up her briefcase and removed a petition.

"I'm planning to file this in the appeals court today. I'm hoping we can avoid this."

"Ms. Trumball, attorneys appeal my decisions all the time. That's what the appellate courts are for."

"This appeal is personal. Personal to you."

Humphrey leaned over his desk. His eyes narrowed. "What are you saying?"

"I'm alleging that you have a personal relationship with Roger Wilcox, and that's why you send a disproportionate number of children to the residential facilities he operates."

Humphrey's face reddened as he shouted at Dani. "How dare you! You file that piece of crap, and I'll slam a libel suit against you so fast, your head will spin."

"I won't file it if you send Frankie back to a prison that Wilcox doesn't own."

Dani knew she was treading in dangerous waters. Her demand could be viewed as a threat, even as extortion. She didn't care. After Noah told her about the man sent to kill Frankie, she would do what was necessary to protect him.

The silence in the room seemed to last forever, but it was probably less than a minute before Humphrey broke his glare at Dani and sat back in his seat.

"Why is it so important to you that he go somewhere else?"

"Because I think his life is in danger at Eldridge."

"You're being overly dramatic. He got beat up there. It's unfortunate, but it happens. It's probably toughened him up."

Before flying to Florida, she'd thought hard about how much she would reveal to Humphrey. Was he part of the plot to silence Frankie? He might be, but her gut said no. The judge might be in cahoots with Wilcox for the money, but she hoped he thought murder crossed a solid red line. "Someone tried to murder him at the safe house. The FBI apprehended him before he got off a shot."

"I assume your client was in a federal safe house precisely because they thought the people he was to testify against might try to silence him. It seems they were right. This has nothing to do with Eldridge Academy."

"Yes, that's possible. But those men have cooperated with the FBI. And the timing of the attempted attack is suspicious."

"And why is that?"

"Because it was the night his hearing before you ended, when it became clear he wasn't being returned to Eldridge. The same night you made a call to Roger Wilcox from a burner phone."

Humphrey's face paled, and he licked his lips. He picked up the petition that Dani had laid on the desk and looked it over, then handed it back to her. "I don't make my placement decisions based on attorney threats, Ms. Trumball. And if someone tried to hurt your client, I can't imagine it had anything to do with Eldridge Academy. Go ahead and file your petition."

—

Dani couldn't claim to be surprised her bluff hadn't worked. Both she and Judge Humphrey knew she couldn't go into court with only speculation to back up her allegations against him. That's why she'd prepared a second petition—one that appealed Humphrey's sentence of a year for escape and requested emergency relief, asking that Frankie be allowed to remain at home pending the argument on the appeal and the court's ruling. She left the courthouse and drove to the Second District Court of Appeal in Lakeland, filed the petition with the clerk, and asked to be put on the calendar for a hearing the next day. She then called her assistant and had her fax a copy of the petition to Warren Camden. When finished, she returned to her hotel to prepare for the next day's argument.

—

Howard Humphrey seethed. Surely, the woman had been grasping at straws. Roger wouldn't have gone that far. No amount of money could justify killing a young boy. Probably an innocent one, too, even though he'd found him guilty. Two joints—that was nothing. He felt disgusted—with Roger, with himself, with the trap he was in. He pulled out his new burner phone and dialed Wilcox.

"What now?" Wilcox said. "You just phoned me yesterday."

"Tell me you didn't hire someone to kill the Bishop boy."

He was met with silence on the other end.

"You did, you son of a bitch."

"Stop it. I didn't hire anyone. The boy's alive, isn't he?"

"Someone tried to kill him."

"It wasn't me."

Could he believe him? Humphrey wondered. With a deep sense of sadness, he realized he wasn't sure. "It's over. I'm out."

"No, you're not. You're just panicking."

"I mean it. I don't want to have anything to do with you."

Humphrey heard a low chuckle over the phone. "It's not that easy. You're in as long as I say you are."

"Go ahead. Turn me in. Then we can be cellmates, because you'd go to jail right alongside me."

"Don't be a fool."

"I can't do this any longer."

"You love your wife? Your kids? Think of their humiliation if you're exposed. They'll be ostracized wherever they go. Some will probably think your wife knew all about it and approved. Even benefited financially from it."

Much as it pained him, Humphrey knew Wilcox was right. He couldn't extricate himself from this mess, much as he'd like to. He should never have started in the first place. Now it was too late to stop.

———

Dani arrived at the Second District Court of Appeal in Lakeland shortly after nine a.m. The one-story concrete building looked more like an insurance office than a courthouse.

It was rare that she was alone when arguing an appeal. Usually she had a junior associate by her side, sometimes Tommy as well.

But this wasn't an official HIPP case, so it was staffed leanly. Warren Camden was already seated when she entered the courtroom. Her case was an add-on to the calendar—a petition for emergency relief—and so it might be called first, before the regularly scheduled cases, or last. Either way, she had to be present when court opened and just wait.

Thirty minutes later, she was in luck. Frankie's case was the first to be called. Three justices sat on the bench, each one a man, each one looking well past retirement age.

Dani stepped up to the podium. "Your Honors, I have asked for the unusual emergency relief in the petition before you to preserve the safety and mental health of my client pending an appeal of his conviction of escape on statutory grounds. First, some background." Dani took them through Frankie's saga point by point, from his initial poor decision to take the joints to school to his beating at Eldridge, his escape from the hospital, and his subsequent kidnapping and second hair-raising escape.

"Until now," she went on, "he has been kept in a safe house by the FBI as an essential prosecution witness. That is about to end, as a plea agreement has been reached in those cases. After his rescue, the State filed charges against Francis for escape, and he was sentenced to an additional year at Eldridge. Were it not for this additional charge, he would have satisfied his original commitment to that detention facility, and he'd be free to return home.

"As I'll demonstrate in my argument on the merits of the appeal, Francis Bishop should not have been convicted of escape, as he wasn't under confinement when at the hospital, nor being transferred to or from confinement, and his purpose for leaving wasn't to avoid confinement. Of importance today, though, is that the very reason he didn't return to Eldridge Academy is still present—the same boys who almost killed him continue to reside there. To put him back in that environment presents too grave a risk to his safety.

"I believe that we will prevail on the merits. In the meantime, we ask that this boy be permitted to return home pending the outcome of his appeal. He has served the time for his original sentence and, needless to say, has gone through an ordeal that shouldn't happen to any child. Attached to my papers is an affidavit from a highly credentialed psychologist stating that, in his opinion, Francis is not at risk for abusing drugs, and that his best hope of recovering emotionally from the recent traumatic events is to return to his home with his mother and continue to receive counseling. If the court deems it necessary, he can continue to wear an ankle monitor and be homeschooled until a decision is reached on his appeal. Thank you."

Dani wasn't surprised that none of the justices had interrupted her argument. Since the papers had been filed only yesterday, they'd had little time to peruse them and so were a "cold" bench. That worked against her. Since she was asking for unusual relief, the better informed the judges were about Frankie's situation, the better her chance of prevailing.

Camden now walked up to the lectern. "Your Honors, the State appreciates that Francis has gone through an ordeal. But it's one that wouldn't have happened to him if he had not escaped from the hospital in the first place, and therefore it should not affect your decision on his placement. I believe when you hear the argument on the merits, you'll conclude that the trial-court judge was correct in finding Francis violated Section 985.721 of the Florida Statutes and that his sentence was appropriate. He can receive counseling at Eldridge Academy, as well as continue his studies. The warden has assured me that steps will be taken to ensure those responsible for Francis's beating will not engage with him again. For these reasons, there is no basis to forestall his immediate return to Eldridge Academy. Thank you."

"We understand the arguments," the chief judge said. "We'll have a decision for you by the end of the day. You can pick it up at the clerk's office."

Was it enough? Dani wondered. Had she done as much as she could to stave off Frankie's return to Eldridge? It was a coin toss. And if it came up wrong, she had nothing left in her bag of tricks. She called the HIPP office and spoke to Bruce about how the morning had gone, then transferred to Tommy.

"We'll know by the end of the day," Dani said to him. "Even if we're lucky today, don't stop looking for something on Humphrey. If it's not money, maybe it's something else. There's something wrong there."

"I think so, too. But whatever it is with the two of them, they've hidden it well."

"Keep looking."

There was nothing more Dani could do until the court's decision was in. After she hung up, she thought about heading to the beach, grabbing some lunch at a restaurant overlooking the Gulf, biding her time until it was late enough to return to the court. Instead, she headed in the other direction. She was less than an hour from Walt Disney World, and she thought strolling through Epcot or the Magic Kingdom would be a perfect way to stop her worrying over Frankie Bishop.

—

At four p.m., Dani returned to the courthouse. She popped into the clerk's office to see if the decision had arrived.

"Not yet," the clerk said. "I'll let you know as soon as it's here."

Dani made herself as comfortable as she could on the wooden bench outside the office. Forty minutes later, the clerk stuck her head outside the door. "It's here," she said, as she handed Dani a one-page document. The decision contained two sentences. "Although it is highly unusual to override a trial court's placement of a juvenile found to be delinquent, based on the unique circumstances of this case, we order that Francis Bishop be confined to his home, with ankle monitoring, pending resolution of his appeal. So ordered."

Try as she might, Dani couldn't stop the tears from rolling down her cheeks. "Hormones," she muttered to herself, but she knew that wasn't all. It was her overwhelming relief that, at least for a little while, Frankie Bishop was still safe.

36

Tommy realized Dani was right. It was time to shift tactics. Both he and the feds had hit dead ends trying to find a money trail, which could only mean it was hidden too deep. Probably learned from his crooked brethren before him who'd gotten caught, Tommy figured. He'd start with the present and work backward. Piece by piece, he'd build a picture of Humphrey's life, and somewhere along the line he'd figure out why he'd sent so many children to ML Juvenile Services.

The circuit court where Humphrey presided over juvenile cases covered an area served by three school districts. Tommy began making phone calls, starting with a call to the principal of the high school in Frankie's district. Although Frankie had only been in middle school, Tommy figured most of the kids who ended up before Humphrey were older.

"This is Principal Harding," the woman said when she came on the line.

"My name is Sam Bolton, and I'm a reporter with the *New York Times*. We're doing a story about juvenile courts throughout the country, and judges who are taking a harder line with kids." Tommy had thought about giving this woman his real information but decided she'd be more forthcoming to a reporter. "We understand that Judge Humphrey is a no-nonsense judge."

"Oh, my, that's an understatement. He doesn't let kids slide on anything."

"As a principal, how do you feel about that?"

"I'm thrilled. There are clear consequences now. The students know that if they cross the line, they'll go before him and stand a good chance of being sent away. I'm convinced it's really curbed a lot of bad behavior in the school."

"In talking to some parents, it seems like that began around three years ago."

"Well, I don't know the time frame, but it does seem like he's gotten harder on kids who come before him."

"Do you know if anything prompted that change?"

"I'm not sure what you're referring to."

Tommy could sense a wariness in her tone. "Well, perhaps some groups got together and urged him to take a tougher stance."

"If that's so, I'm unaware of it."

"Thank you, Ms. Harding. I'll send you a copy of the article when it's published."

Almost each principal Tommy spoke to reiterated the same sentiment. They were happy with Judge Humphrey's toughness but were unaware of what brought about the change. The one holdout was a middle-school principal.

"I've seen some disturbing rulings from him," Principal Gareth Toler said. "He sent away an eleven-year-old for shoplifting a candy bar. First time. Good kid. He returned three months later and was completely different. Used to be an A student, friendly and outgoing. Came back a loner, never smiled. His grades plummeted. Another student got into an altercation with a kid and pushed him. No one was hurt, but the second kid's parents reported it to the police, and the judge locked him up. It's insanity—that's what I think."

"Has Humphrey always been that tough?" Tommy asked.

"Something changed a few years ago. Before, he sent away the kids that deserved it, put the others on probation. I don't know why he's doing this now, but it's wrong. Just plain wrong."

So far, all Tommy had established was something he already knew. Humphrey's tough-on-kids stance had changed three years ago. He still wasn't closer to finding out why.

—

Roger Wilcox paced around the four walls of his office, cursing under his breath. That damn kid had lucked out once again. He tried telling himself that it didn't matter. The boy had been away from Eldridge for almost two months, and nothing had come out about the kid who'd died of pneumonia, or who had really orchestrated the Bishop boy's beating. So maybe he shouldn't be worried. Still, the three contracts that were up for renewal were worth $30 million in profits. Not all to him, of course. He had shareholders. But he'd walk away with a tidy sum from that—more than $10 million. He'd lined enough pockets in Tallahassee to ensure the renewals, but politicians were weaselly sorts—give them an excuse to back away, and many would. And now he had the Justice Department on his back.

He'd worked out a plan with Cummings to take care of the boy without raising suspicions once they got him back at Eldridge. Now that damn attorney with her sneaky legal maneuvering had messed it up. Still, maybe it wasn't bad that Frankie would be returning home, without any FBI agents stationed outside his house. He could get at him more easily now. But was that the smart move? Humphrey was already antsy over the first attempt. If he sent someone out again, Humphrey would know for sure it wasn't the child traffickers. Would he tell the authorities? Even though his own involvement would come out? Wilcox didn't know the answer. Better to leave the kid alone. For now, at least.

—

Jessica was overjoyed when she heard the news from Dani. They could go home—no more Eldridge, no more safe house. Peter Burke had come through, just as Alex had promised his friends would. He'd contacted a dozen other men, and they'd set up a rotating schedule to move in with Jessica and Frankie and watch over them. Sure, she'd have to continue to homeschool Frankie, although school was almost out for the summer. But he was so smart, maybe that was better, anyway. She'd been able to go at his pace for learning, not the pace of his teachers, who had to consider all the children in their classes.

She couldn't get too excited, though. Dani had warned her that if their appeal was lost, he'd still have to go back. That was months away, though. Maybe once they were home and Frankie was in his own bedroom, his own bed, his nightmares would completely stop. He was still waking up once or twice a week, screaming in terror. The psychiatrist provided by the FBI had helped somewhat. During the daytime hours, Frankie seemed more relaxed. At night, though, in his sleep, terror flooded over him. He would be allowed to leave the house for medical appointments, and Peter or one of the other men would always accompany them. She'd make sure she found someone good so that he could continue with counseling.

Frankie kept asking about Daisy. She'd asked Metzger for her phone number, so Frankie could speak to her. Daisy, too, had been kept in a safe house, cloistered to ensure she could testify against Hollander. She'd returned home yesterday, Hollander's deal in place, and Metzger gave Jessica her parents' phone number.

Thankfully, she'd called before giving the number to Frankie. Daisy had been home less than a day when her parents found her hanging from a rope in her room.

Yes, Jessica knew she would keep Frankie in counseling, as long as it took for his nightmares to go away.

As Dani worked on her brief to the Florida appellate court on Frankie's behalf, she became more confident that she'd prevail. It was a uniform rule in most states that statutes should be strictly construed, especially criminal statutes; and in Florida, to be guilty of escape, the escapee had to have been confined at an institution, or in the process of being transported to or from the place of confinement, or working on a public road. The irrefutable fact was that Frankie hadn't been confined at the hospital. Just like any other patient there, he'd had no one to stop him from getting up and leaving.

With the escape conviction gone, Frankie would be allowed to return to school at the end of the summer break and start living like a teenager again. He'd be able to play soccer in the fall and baseball in the spring. He'd be able to hang out with a friend after school or on weekends. Except . . . there was still someone out there who wanted Frankie dead. It had to be Wilcox. Or Humphrey. Or both. If only something could be found tying Humphrey to Wilcox, they could be locked up, Dani thought. If that happened, they'd have nothing to gain by silencing Frankie. He would finally be truly free. Alex's army buddies could return to their own families, and Frankie would go back to being just a typical boy.

Only Frankie wasn't typical. He was intellectually gifted and for years had nourished a dream of using those gifts to become a doctor. What would his chances be with an adjudication of delinquency on his record? Under Florida law, Frankie wouldn't be eligible to have his record sealed or, even better, expunged, because of that ruling. That meant that on any college application that asked about previous arrests, Frankie would have to answer yes. With admission to the top colleges already competitive, it could be enough to deny him entrance. And the same was true for medical schools. It infuriated Dani that he'd been deemed delinquent. It was simply unfair that he'd be marked for life. She realized she and Tommy couldn't stop even if she won Frankie's appeal. She'd keep searching until she found out why Humphrey had treated him so harshly. And then, just maybe, she'd be able to get his record wiped clean.

She finished up the brief, then handed it off to her assistant to make copies and serve on the court and the state attorney. After giving her instructions, Dani wandered over to Tommy's desk.

"Hey, gorgeous."

"Hey, yourself."

"How's Frankie's appeal going?"

"Just finished. I think we're pretty solid on it."

Tommy nodded. "But you're here to tell me it's not enough, right?"

Tommy knew her so well, Dani realized. They'd worked together for many years now, always having each other's back. Although there were other investigators in the office, ever since Dani had started handling cases from the investigation phase, she'd worked only with Tommy. They made a good team. She'd even gotten to the point where his sexist banter just slid off her back.

"I don't want you to give up looking for a connection between Humphrey and Wilcox."

"I haven't stopped. Just keep coming up empty, though."

"Perhaps we're coming at it from the wrong angle. We know the change in his rulings began about three years ago. Let's delve into his life and see what was going on then. Maybe that will lead us to the answer."

"I'll get right on it."

Tommy had always been her miracle worker, coming up with the answer whenever they'd hit a dead end. Frankie Bishop needed one more miracle from him.

———

Dani lay wrapped in Doug's arms during "honeymoon hour" that night. The windows were open, letting in a gentle breeze and the sweet smell of forsythia, the first blooms of the season.

As Doug ran his hand over Dani's expanded belly, he said, "We should start thinking about names."

"Do you have any in mind?"

"How about Emma?"

"It's a nice name. I don't hate it."

"That means you already know what you want."

Dani sat up and looked at Doug. "I know it's an old-fashioned name, but I was thinking of Ruth, after my mother." From a young age, Dani had realized her mother was special. She'd used her keen intellect to fight for causes she believed in, never backing down in the face of bullies. She'd taught Dani to stand up for herself first, and then stand up for those who couldn't. Dani missed her terribly.

"I think that would be lovely," Doug said. "And we can give her Emma as a middle name."

"Perfect."

After Doug went up to bed, Dani lingered downstairs a little longer. She padded into the kitchen to make herself a cup of decaf tea, and as she waited for the water to boil, wished everything could be as simple as naming a child. She remembered when Jonah was an infant, how she worried over every little thing. Was he getting enough nourishment? Was he growing as he should? Was he crying because he was in pain? Nothing was easy then, especially when he failed to develop as expected. They'd taken him from doctor to doctor until one finally diagnosed him with Williams syndrome. Then the worrying intensified. Would it be the same with Ruth Emma? Or had she learned that worrying didn't change much? That the only thing that mattered was loving her children and letting them know they were loved? Whatever Frankie Bishop had gone through, whatever was yet to come, he had parents who loved him and let him know they did. And because of that, she believed that even if she failed at unmasking Humphrey, Frankie would succeed in the end.

—

A few days later, Tommy had reached another dead end. He'd discreetly checked around with some of Humphrey's neighbors, as well as the country club Humphrey belonged to and the bar association for Cypress Country. Nothing. Nobody could point to any connection between the judge and Wilcox. He picked up his phone and buzzed Dani's intercom.

"I got nothing on Humphrey," he told her. "If I were still an FBI agent, there are things I could do, but you want me to stay on the up-and-up with this. I can't think of where else to go with it."

"What would you do differently if you were an agent?"

"Well, then, I could make up some story that it was official federal business. Get people to open up that way. But I can't tell people I'm a fed when I'm not. That's a jailable offense."

"Maybe I can make it work. I'll get back to you."

—

As far as Dani knew, ML Juvenile Services was still the target of a Justice Department investigation. She picked up the phone and called Josh Cosgrove.

"He's in court this morning," his assistant said. "I'll leave him a message you called."

Two hours later, Josh returned her call. "What's up?"

"Is the Justice Department still looking for dirty dealings between Humphrey and Wilcox?"

"Of course, especially now with the concern that one of them hired a hit man. We'd love to find something, but so far nothing's come up."

"Would you be willing to send an agent down there? Tommy has some ideas."

"I think we could do that."

"And let Tommy and me tag along?"

"Sure. As long as you don't get in the way."

"Once again, thanks."

"Hey, if Wilcox was willing to resort to murder, we've got to nail him. And if this judge is dirty, we want to catch him."

"He is. I know it."

One week later, Dani and Tommy were back in Florida, this time with Clyde Metzger. Bruce still hadn't run out of frequent-flyer miles and had encouraged them to go. It was mid-May and the temperature hovered near ninety-five degrees. With the humidity, it felt like over a hundred. They were on Judge Humphrey's block, ready to speak to his neighbors.

"Remember," warned Metzger. "I do the talking. You're both just here to observe."

"Aye, aye, captain," said Tommy.

They walked up to the home next door to Humphrey's and rang the bell. No answer. They moved on to the next one, did the same thing. After a minute, the door opened, and a woman who appeared to be in her sixties stood in front of them.

Metzger whipped out his badge. "Ma'am, my name is Clyde Metzger, with the FBI. We're doing a background check on your neighbor, Howard Humphrey. I'd like to ask you a few questions."

The woman held her hand over her eyes to block the sun. "Has he done something wrong?"

"No, ma'am. He's being considered for a federal position, and a background check is routine."

"What position is that?"

"I'm afraid I'm not permitted to say. And before we go forward, I must advise you that you cannot talk to Judge Humphrey or his wife about our visit. Doing so would violate federal law. Do you understand?"

The woman nodded. "Would you like to come in?"

"Thank you, yes."

They entered the woman's house, and she gestured toward the living room. "Go ahead in and make yourselves comfortable. Would you like anything to drink?"

When they declined, the woman followed them into the living room. Once they were all seated, Metzger began.

"What is your name?"

"Sara Jenkins."

"How well do you know Judge Humphrey?"

"Pretty well. We've been neighbors for fourteen years."

"Do you ever socialize with him or his wife?"

"Yes, with both. They're our friends."

"Have you ever seen the judge display a temper?"

"Heavens, no. He's the gentlest man."

"Ever hear him disparage any racial, religious, or ethnic group?"

"Of course not."

"Do you know any of his friends?"

"Some. He has a large July Fourth party every year. We've met some of his friends there."

Metzger opened up his briefcase and withdrew a picture of Roger Wilcox. "Ever see him at one of the parties?"

Sara took the picture from his hands and looked at it closely, then placed it down on the cocktail table. "No, I don't recall seeing him."

Metzger handed her another picture, one from the files, a man he knew had no relationship with the judge. "How about him?"

Once again, she looked the picture over, then shook her head.

"What one word would you use to describe the judge's character?"

Quickly, she answered, "Thoughtful."

"Did there ever come a time when you thought his personality changed?"

"No."

"Perhaps around three years ago?"

Sara's eyes narrowed. "My husband always tells me I'm too trusting. How do I know you're really with the FBI?"

"Ma'am, here's my card. You can call and ask for my supervisor. Or you can call information and confirm that this is the right number for our office. I'd be happy to wait while you do that."

Sara giggled. "Oh, I'm being silly, I guess. Of course you're who you say you are. I just never had an FBI agent question me before."

"You're smart to be cautious. Now, going back to three years ago. Did you notice any change in him then?"

"No, he's always been very pleasant."

"Thank you, Mrs. Jenkins, I believe we have enough. I just want to remind you that these checks are confidential, and you're not to discuss this with anyone, including the Humphreys."

"I won't. I promise."

After they left, they went up and down the block and the results were the same. The judge was "caring," or "kindhearted," or "intelligent," or "considerate." No one recognized Wilcox's picture, and no one saw any change in him three years ago.

"That's it for today," Metzger said. "Tomorrow we hit the courthouse."

Dani nodded. There was nothing more for them to do.

———

Dani couldn't believe it. She'd called in for messages, and Carol had told her that the appellate court had scheduled oral argument in Frankie's case in one week. Normally, it took months. Despite her confidence that the law was on her side, she knew courts were unpredictable. If they decided the case as quickly as they scheduled it, and the ruling went against Frankie, he could be back at Eldridge much sooner than she'd anticipated. Too soon for the Justice Department to have come up with something solid against ML Juvenile Services and Judge Humphrey.

This wasn't an official HIPP case, yet it was taking up so much of Dani's time. Time that should be spent helping free an innocent man or woman already behind bars, sometimes for years, even decades. She knew she should back off, perhaps ask a junior associate to argue the appeal. After all, it should be routine. But she knew she wouldn't, and she knew Bruce wouldn't want her to. Since she'd begun working on Frankie's behalf, every night when she arrived home and looked at Jonah, she was awash with gratitude that he was safe. How could she turn her back on a twelve-year-old? She couldn't. She walked over to the desk in her motel and began preparing her oral argument.

—

Dani, Tommy, and Metzger arrived at the circuit court just before nine a.m. and headed to the rooms of the chief justice. Metzger flashed his badge to the assistant sitting in the outer office, explained that they needed to ask the judge some questions, and were led into his chambers. Herman Silverman had been on the bench for more than thirty-five years, yet except for his wavy white hair, he looked like a fit fifty-year-old who'd just come off the tennis court.

"How can I help you?"

Metzger went into his routine about a federal appointment for Humphrey.

"That's interesting. He hasn't said anything to me about it."

"He doesn't know he's under consideration for the position. An offer isn't made until after preliminary due diligence has been completed. Of course, if everything goes well, and he's made an offer, and he accepts the position, a more thorough check will be done. Because an offer hasn't been made yet, I have to ask you to refrain from discussing our visit with Judge Humphrey."

"Of course. I understand."

"What's your assessment of his judicial abilities?"

"I'd rate him as one of our top judges. Very intelligent. Understands the law inside and out. And fair."

"Let's talk about that for a bit. We understand that he's considered a hard judge. That he comes down strong on the juveniles before him."

"Well, I think it's because he believes a firm hand now will help them later. Better that they get a dose of reality with detention centers than end up doing hard time when they're older."

"Do you agree with that?"

"I don't handle the juvenile cases myself. I think he's seen a lot over the years where kids were given a warning and just ended up back before him. Or worse, before me, being treated as an adult."

Metzger looked down at some papers in his hand and scanned through them—Dani knew it was for show—then said, "It seems like his rulings started to change around three years ago. That's when he began sentencing more kids to detention centers. Do you know if anything specific happened that changed Judge Humphrey's views around that time? Maybe with a particular case?"

Judge Silverman reclined in his high-backed leather chair and scrunched up his face. Slowly, he began to shake his head. "I can't think of anything. In fact, he'd just returned to the bench after a three-month leave around that time, so I don't think any case could have had that impact. No, I think just in general, he felt it was in the interest of the children to be sterner. In the long term, that is."

"What was the purpose of the leave of absence?"

"Personal reasons."

"I need you to be more specific."

"I don't think that's my place. You should ask him."

"Sir, I believe he would want you to be forthcoming. This is an important position he's being considered for."

"It was a medical issue. Beyond that I believe you need to discuss with him."

"If he had a problem that required rehab, or psychiatric care, it's essential for us to know."

"No, no, nothing like that. He had surgery."

"Are the judges here required to provide any conflicts information?"

"What do you mean?"

"Well, for example, do they provide a financial statement that shows significant investments to make sure they're not deciding any case in which they have an interest in one of the parties?"

"We provide a copy of all our investments. Beyond that, if anyone comes before the court where there could even be a potential conflict of interest, the judge recuses himself from the case."

"Can you make a photocopy of Judge Humphrey's investments for me?"

"Am I allowed to do that? Isn't it an invasion of his privacy?"

"Sir, anything given to us remains in the strictest confidence. It's only used for the purpose of screening out any potential conflicts. I can assure you that if an offer is made to him, we'll be looking far more closely at all his finances."

"I suppose it's okay."

Silverman walked over to a file cabinet in the corner of his office, opened the top drawer, and pulled out a folder. "I keep the sensitive files in my own office." He buzzed his assistant and asked her to make a copy.

They finished questioning the chief judge, thanked him, then left. Once outside, Metzger took out the papers Silverman had given him. He scanned the pages, then looked up at Dani and Tommy. "There's nothing here. No mention of ML Juvenile Services." Metzger stuffed the papers back into his briefcase. "I don't think we're going to find anything more here. I'm sorry to say this, for Frankie's sake, but he looks clean."

"What do you think that medical leave was about?" Tommy asked.

"Just what Silverman said. He had surgery."

"Maybe. But his referrals to ML facilities began around the same time. Shouldn't you look into that?"

"How? We need subpoenas to get medical and hospital records, and no judge will sign one with what we've got. Yours and Dani's speculation just isn't enough."

"Maybe we can go back to that first neighbor—Sara Jenkins. She said they were friends. She might know what it's about."

"Look, Tommy, I'd really like to help, but I think it's a wild-goose chase."

"Never dismiss something without investigating—the smallest clue might lead to the answer. That's what the FBI taught its recruits, remember?"

Metzger sighed. "I have to get back to the office. I'm testifying in another case tomorrow. But I'll free up my calendar next week. We can go back then."

Dani thought briefly about more time away from the office. But she'd be back in Florida next week for the oral argument, anyway, and hoped they could coordinate with that. She thanked Metzger and told him how grateful everyone at HIPP was for his help. She just hoped it wouldn't be too late.

CHAPTER 39

One week later, Dani was back before the Second District Court of Appeal. She greeted Warren Camden outside the assigned courtroom, and noted he wore a different suit but it was still wrinkled. They went inside and waited for Frankie's case to be called. The same three judges who'd granted her emergency petition were on the bench. Dani hoped that was a good sign. When an hour later, Frankie's case was next up, she and Camden took the seats at the tables in front. The bailiff called *Bishop v. State*, and Dani stood and walked to the podium.

"Your Honors, my name is Dani Trumball, and I represent the petitioner, Francis Bishop." Once again, Dani gave the court a recitation of the circumstances that resulted in his placement at Eldridge Academy, the beating he endured, and the injuries he sustained, resulting in his transfer by ambulance to a hospital. For good measure, she threw in the stonewall Jessica Bishop had received at Eldridge when she tried to visit her son.

"While in the hospital," Dani continued, "no guard was posted outside his door, and no restraints were used on him. The night before he was scheduled to return to Eldridge, and in great fear that on his return he would receive further, potentially fatal beatings, he left the hospital and attempted to make his way to his older brother, a Marine at Camp Lejeune. As I informed you during my previous appearance, on his way there, Francis was abducted by sexual predators. After he escaped his captor, the FBI placed him in protective custody as a material witness. The State of Florida subsequently filed escape charges against him. The juvenile court found him guilty and sentenced him to an additional year at Eldridge Academy.

"It's well settled in Florida that criminal statutes are to be strictly construed, and any ambiguity should be resolved in favor of the accused. The statute in question states that in order to be guilty of escape, it has to be from a secure detention facility, a residential commitment facility, or from transportation to or from such facilities. Crescent Hills Regional Hospital is simply not one of those facilities. At the time he left, he wasn't being transported to or from it. He was a patient. An unrestrained patient."

"Ms. Trumball," interrupted the judge in the center. "Can't one say that the hospital, in this case, was an extension of the residential facility?"

"To say that would be to read something into the statute that isn't there. But even if that were the case, Florida Statute 944.40 requires that the person who escaped intended to avoid lawful confinement. That's not the case here. Francis Bishop was a frightened twelve-year-old boy, who had good reason to believe he was in danger of serious physical harm if he returned to Eldridge."

"He didn't go to any authority to explain himself, did he?" the same judge asked.

"He never had the chance. Remember, he's just a child. To him, his brother had always looked out for him, and that's where he was headed. His brother, no doubt, would have notified authorities of Francis's fears. But he never made it there. Even if leaving the hospital could be considered the same as leaving a residential facility, the judge should have considered his defense that he was in fear of serious bodily harm. That wasn't done. For these reasons, the State failed to prove that Francis was guilty of escape. Thank you."

Dani sat down, and Camden stood and walked to the podium. "Good morning, Your Honors. My name is Warren Camden, and I'm an assistant state attorney. There is no question that Francis knew he was in a custodial situation and wasn't permitted to leave. He didn't announce to the nurses that he was going. Instead, during the wee hours of the morning, he snuck out, careful not to alert anyone. That alone shows his intent to avoid lawful confinement. Now, my adversary has argued that it doesn't matter what his intent was, that because he wasn't in a residential facility or being transported to or from Eldridge Academy, he can't be charged with escape. That would turn the escape statute on its head, and I do not believe that was the legislature's intent. Rather, I believe that the court can view his stay at the hospital as part of a lawful transportation from and then to Eldridge. His escape then was during the course of that transportation. The trial court was correct in finding that Francis was guilty of escape, and this court should uphold that ruling. Thank you."

That was it. The bailiff called the next case, and the only thing left to do was await the decision. Dani hoped they'd take their time.

T ommy waited in front of Sara Jenkins's home, Clyde Metzger by his side, for Dani to arrive. When she did, Tommy asked, "How did it go?"

"I think well. We ready to go in?"

Metzger nodded. "Remember, I do the talking."

Both Dani and Tommy agreed, then Metzger rang the front doorbell. Moments later, Sara Jenkins opened the door.

"Oh. You're back."

"We just have a few more questions. May we come in?"

"Of course." Sara gestured them inside and pointed to the living room.

Tommy could smell the inviting aroma of a pie baking in the oven. "I hope we're not interrupting something."

"No. This is a good time. I've just put an apple pie in the oven and was starting to clean up. It can wait."

After they were all settled, Metzger took out his pad and pen. "I understand that Judge Humphrey had surgery around three years ago."

"That's right."

"Can you tell us what the surgery was for?"

The woman frowned. "Now, what would that have to do with qualifying for a new position?"

"Depending on the nature of the surgery, it could have great relevance."

"I don't see how."

"Let's say, for instance, that he was operated on for a brain tumor. We'd be concerned about what impact that might have on his critical-thinking abilities. Or, he had a liver transplant because years of heavy drinking had destroyed the one he had. It would be important for the government to know those things."

"Well, it wasn't either of those."

"I've just given you examples. Unless we know exactly what he was in for, we'll have to assume it's something that would disqualify him for the federal position."

Sara took a deep breath, then leaned back in her chair. "I suppose it's okay to tell you. It's just . . . Howard doesn't like to talk about it."

Tommy's muscles tensed. His gut had told him the surgery was important. It was too coincidental that the judicial rulings changed around the same time. And he didn't believe in coincidence.

"Howard had a kidney disease, an inherited one. PK something."

"Polycystic kidney disease?" Dani asked.

"Yes. That sounds right. It was diagnosed around ten years ago and became progressively worse. He needed dialysis because his kidneys were failing. He was on the transplant list, but nothing was happening. Finally, he found someone who agreed to donate a kidney. That's what the surgery was."

Tommy could feel a rising excitement. It started to make sense. They couldn't find a money trail because money wasn't involved. He'd bet a bundle that Roger Wilcox found a kidney for Humphrey, maybe someone desperate for money. From everything he'd read, Wilcox was sleazy enough to do that. The payoff to Humphrey wasn't in dollars. It was a kidney.

—

"Holy cow," Dani said when they exited the house. "But how can we find out if that's what happened?"

"I'll get a warrant for Florida hospitals," Metzger said. "One of them had to do the surgery. Even with a private organ donation, records should say who it was from. Then we can track down that person and see if Wilcox brokered it."

"Holy cow," Dani repeated. She couldn't wrap her head around it. She'd been convinced that Humphrey was dirty, sending kids to ML facilities in order to line his pockets. Now, if they were right, he was still doing something wrong, still ruining children's lives, still for a selfish reason. But, she realized, he'd been a frightened man facing death and had made a shameful decision. It was still inexcusable, but the anger she felt toward him had diminished. It hadn't gone away but lessened. Assuming they were right, that is.

Dani called Bruce to fill him in. When they got to the airport, she tried to return to the brief she'd been working on but was too excited to concentrate. She felt like celebrating. It wasn't over yet for Frankie, but at least now the path was illuminated.

Two weeks passed, and still Dani hadn't received any word on the search for Humphrey's medical records. She knew that the feds had hit all the hospitals in Florida, then decided to extend the search, heading north, state by state.

Dani was busy reviewing inmate letters for help when her assistant brought in the mail. She had a smile on her face. "There a decision from Florida on top. Thought you'd want to read it first."

Dani grabbed the top document, saw from the caption that it was the decision on Frankie's appeal, and began reading.

"Petitioner Francis Bishop, a twelve-year-old boy who'd been adjudicated a delinquent and sentenced to four months at Eldridge Academy, was brought to Crescent Hill Regional Hospital with injuries sustained from an attack by other residents. He was admitted to the hospital, and subsequently left before returning to the residential facility. He was charged with escape and found guilty, and he appeals that ruling by the juvenile-court judge.

"Petitioner argues that he cannot be found guilty of escape because at the time he left, he was not in a secure detention facility, or a residential facility, or being transported from any such facility. We agree.

It is well settled that penal statutes are to be strictly construed. The purpose is to ensure that everyone is fully aware of what conduct may result in the deprivation of his liberty. Here, the statute specifies only three environments from which an escape may be made. If the petitioner had been confined at the hospital with a guard posted outside his room, perhaps an argument could be made that his hospital room was an extension of the residential facility. Absent that, the statute in question simply does not consider a hospital a location from which one can be charged with escape.

"As a result of our decision, it is not necessary to address petitioner's claim that the court below failed to address his intent. Nevertheless, we agree that it should have been done. Considering the age of the petitioner, and the severity of the beating he had suffered, we find that it was reasonable for him to believe that he was in danger of further serious physical injury upon his return and thus did not leave the hospital with the intention to avoid lawful confinement but rather to avoid further harm.

"Finally, we note the original sentence seemed unduly harsh given all the circumstances. For all these reasons, we hereby vacate petitioner's conviction for escape. The ankle monitor may be immediately removed."

The decision was unanimous. Dani thought she would cry as she read the ruling. Cry from happiness that finally a court recognized the ludicrousness of Frankie's original sentence. She let Bruce know of the ruling, then called Jessica and relayed the good news.

"I really can cut the ankle monitor?"

"Yep."

"And he can return to school?"

"He's free now." Dani paused. "There are no legal matters hanging over him. But . . . I don't know if . . . if—"

"You don't have to say it. He still may not be safe."

Dani could hear soft cries on the other end of the phone. She understood. After a few moments, Jessica asked, "When will it really be over?"

"Maybe soon. We have a lead."

"I can't thank you enough. You and Tommy have been a rock for me. With Alex gone, I don't think I could have gotten through this by myself."

Dani finished the conversation and hung up. She'd told Jessica the legal fight was over, but it wasn't finished for Dani. Frankie still had a record of delinquency, one that could follow him for a very long time. She wanted that gone. And she wanted Frankie to go back to school without fearing that he was in an assassin's sight. To do both, she needed to expose Howard Humphrey.

It's time to get maternity clothes, Dani thought as she looked down at her enlarged belly. She'd had a hard time getting dressed that morning. Even her clothes with elastic waists were too tight. She'd finally squeezed herself into what was once a loose-fitting dress and made it to the office, but now baby Ruth was clearly unhappy with the close quarters. She hadn't stopped kicking all morning.

As Dani tried to get comfortable in her office chair, her phone rang. She glanced over at the caller ID, saw it was Cosgrove, and picked it up herself.

"Josh, any news?"

"Yes. We've got it. Humphrey had a kidney transplant at Duke University Medical Center three and a half years ago. It was probably done in North Carolina because the donor lived there. You're not going to believe who the donor was."

"Who?"

"Roger Wilcox. Turns out, he's Humphrey's half brother. Different fathers. We found the birth records. When Humphrey was nine years old, his mother entered the hospital, gave birth to a baby boy, and relinquished him for adoption. It was the same birth date as Wilcox's. We followed the trail and located the adoption records. There's no doubt."

Dani was stunned. She'd been looking for a connection between Humphrey and Wilcox, but never suspected a familial one. "What now?"

"It doesn't matter if it was a kidney and not money that motivated Humphrey. It was still a bribe, and Humphrey's rulings are all tainted. We're going to send Metzger and Jacobs down there with a warrant, but given your involvement, I thought you might like to join them."

"I'd love to. I'm sure Tommy would as well. Is that all right?"

"It's fine. They're going to do it at his home, not the courthouse. Can you get there by seven tonight?"

"We'll be there."

———

A few minutes before seven o'clock that evening, Dani and Tommy met up with Jacobs and Metzger down the block from Humphrey's home. Together, they walked to his house and rang the bell, waiting silently until Humphrey opened the door. As soon as he spotted Dani, he said, "What are you doing here? I can't have any ex parte communications."

Metzger whipped out his FBI shield. "We're not here on a specific case. May we come in?"

Humphrey stared at each of them in turn. "Unless you're here to arrest me, the answer is no."

"We do have a warrant for your arrest," Jacobs said. "We can handcuff you now, and take you away in front of your neighbors, or you can invite us in and perhaps we can work out an arrangement for you to turn yourself in tomorrow."

"This is nonsense. What is it about?"

"May we come in?"

"No, you may not. Now tell me, what am I supposed to have done?"

"Howard? Who are these men?"

Humphrey spun around. "Doris, it's just some misunderstanding."

"Sir, this is not a misunderstanding," Jacobs said. "Either you invite us in now, or we're taking you in."

Humphrey stepped outside. "If you insist, I'll go with you, just so we can clear this up."

"Hold out your hands, please," Metzger said.

"You're going to cuff me?" Humphrey asked, his tone incredulous. "I'm a respected judge."

"That may be, but you're under arrest. You have the right—"

"I know my rights. And I'm not saying a damn thing until my lawyer's with me."

"Smart man," Jacobs said. "You're going to need him."

—

Two hours later, Dani and Tommy watched through a one-way window as Jacobs began his questioning of Judge Humphrey. Humphrey's lawyer, Barbara Hastings, was by his side. She was a heavyset woman, with a face that looked like it was chiseled in stone, and a mouth that looked like it had never learned how to smile.

"So, what is my client supposed to have done?" Hastings asked.

"He's being charged with racketeering, bribery, and extortion."

"Are you joking?" Humphrey said.

"Let me do the talking, Howard. You have me here as your lawyer for a reason."

"No, sir, we're not," Jacobs answered. "You bribed Roger Wilcox. In exchange for him donating his kidney to you, you populated his juvenile prisons with children. Children who should never have been sentenced to residential facilities."

Dani watched as Humphrey's face drained of color.

"That's absurd. I did no such thing."

"Howard, be quiet. We're here to listen now."

"We know Roger Wilcox is your half brother. We know he donated a kidney to you. We know your record of sending juveniles to residential facilities before the transplant and after. We know you began sending substantially more children to Wilcox's facilities immediately after you returned to the bench following the transplant. It won't be hard for a jury to connect the dots."

"It sounds like all you have is conjecture," Hastings said.

"We don't see it that way. And we don't think a jury will. Now, here's the thing." Jacobs leaned over the table and looked directly at Humphrey. "We could put you away for twenty years, and we're prepared to do that. But we're more interested in Roger Wilcox. If you agree to testify against him, we're willing to make you a deal. "

Humphrey remained still in his chair, his back erect, his face grim.

"Judge Humphrey hasn't done anything wrong," Hastings said, "but out of curiosity, what are you offering?"

"One count of conspiracy. Three years in a minimum-security federal prison."

Dani had known Jacobs would offer this sentence in exchange for Wilcox, but still bridled at the thought of him spending so little time incarcerated. Whatever his motivation for meting out the unfairly harsh sentences to young boys and girls, he'd still ruined many of their lives.

Hastings leaned over to Humphrey and whispered in his ear. He shook his head as she spoke. Finally, she straightened herself and said, "Sorry, Judge Humphrey stands by his belief that he's done nothing wrong. And, even if he did what you say, I think jurors would be sympathetic to the position he was placed in. Hypothetically, of course."

"I'm sorry to hear that, judge. Our offer to you is a generous one, and it's only made because your half brother is a bad man. A very bad man." Jacobs stood to leave the interview room. "Think some more about it. I'll be back in ten minutes, and that's as long as my offer lasts. Then, you can take your chances with a jury."

He left the room, switching off the sound inside, and joined Dani and Tommy.

"Do you think he'll come around?" Dani asked.

Jacobs just shrugged. "He's got a good lawyer, and she's right about juror sympathies. It could go either way for him. If it were me, I don't think I'd take a chance at trial, but he seems pretty dug in. It wouldn't surprise me if he's deluded himself into believing that his harsh sentences actually benefited the kids he sent inside."

Dani could appreciate the conflict Humphrey felt. Not from loyalty toward Wilcox, she suspected. But admitting to a crime and spending even one year in prison would destroy the reputation he'd built during a lifetime of public service. He would end his career in disgrace.

"Noah," Dani said, "do you mind if I go in there with you and talk to him?"

"I suppose it'd be all right." He looked at his watch. "Let's give them another five minutes."

When the time was up, Dani and Jacobs entered the interview room.

"Who's this?" Hastings asked as soon as she saw Dani.

"This is Dani Trumball. She's worked closely with one of the boys sentenced by Judge Humphrey."

Humphrey sat still in his seat, his face pale and his eyes looking downward, unwilling to meet Dani's gaze.

"Judge," Dani said softly, "your half brother is a terrible man. I don't believe you know quite how terrible. He hired someone to kill Frankie Bishop, to keep him from talking about atrocities in Eldridge."

Humphrey lifted his eyes up and looked at her, unable to speak. Finally, his voice barely a whisper, he said, "No, no, he told me it wasn't him."

"Yes, it was. He wanted to ensure that Frankie didn't tell the authorities about a boy who died in prison. Died because of abuse by the guards. The beating that sent Frankie to the hospital? It was ordered by the warden."

Humphrey's face had now turned chalk-white, and he slumped down in his chair, his head hung low. Hastings leaned over and once again whispered in his ear. This time, he nodded in response to her.

"Take prison off the table," Hastings said. "One count of misdemeanor conspiracy with probation, and the judge will tell you what he knows about Roger Wilcox."

Jacobs looked over at Dani and gave her a quick smile, then turned back to Hastings. "If he tells us useful information about Wilcox and agrees to testify at his trial, then we'll go down to eighteen months. Final offer."

Once again, Hastings whispered in her client's ear. Humphrey bowed his head, then looked up and nodded.

"Agreed," Hastings said to Jacobs. "Go ahead, Judge. Tell them."

Humphrey looked up, and his eyes were moist. With his voice soft, he told Jacobs that he'd never known he had a half brother. His father, who'd abandoned him and his mother when he was two, never sent a dime to them. It was hard, both for his mother and for him. When he was seven, his mother remarried Stan. A year into their marriage, his mother got pregnant, and five months later, Stan died in a car accident. They were on their own again. After his mother gave birth, she told everyone—including Humphrey—that the baby was stillborn.

Many years later, when Humphrey was grown, his mother ran into his father's sister, who told her that his father had died two years earlier of polycystic kidney disease, the same thing his own father had died from. Humphrey had some tests done and learned he had the beginning stages of the disease. Over the years, it became worse. His kidneys began to fail; he started dialysis and was put on a transplant list. His name never came up.

Eventually, Humphrey's mother told him the truth about his half brother. It was difficult enough being a single mother with one child. She couldn't handle doing it again with a baby. She lied about giving her son up for adoption because she was too humiliated to tell the truth. He started the process of trying to track down his brother. It took years. Finally, he found him: Roger Wilcox.

At the time, Wilcox owned other private prisons in other states. He already had a reputation for abusive practices in those prisons. Some had already cancelled or failed to renew his contracts; others were threatening to do so. Within a year after Humphrey found him, he'd been shut down everywhere but Florida.

When that happened, Wilcox finally agreed to be tested to see if he was a match. He was. Then he dropped the bombshell: he would give Humphrey a kidney only if he agreed to send a hundred children each year to his juvenile prisons.

"At first, I said no and walked away. But when the disease worsened, and dialysis wasn't going to keep me alive, I told Wilcox I'd do it." Tears ran down Humphrey's cheeks as he recounted the story. He pulled a handkerchief from his pocket and wiped them away, then took a deep breath. "After the first year, I told Roger I wouldn't do it anymore. He said if I didn't, he'd notify the authorities about the bargain I'd made. Even if that hurt him, too."

There was silence in the room. Finally, Jacobs spoke. "Every one of the cases you decided since then will have to be reviewed by an independent panel of judges. Every biased decision will be overturned. That won't give those kids back the normal life they'd had. It won't erase from their memories the horrors they endured. And I suspect there will be hundreds of civil suits against you. You'll have to step down from the bench, of course. But you're doing the right thing now. Wilcox belongs in jail."

Humphrey nodded.

Dani almost felt sorry for him.

———

Dani and Tommy traveled with Jacobs to Tallahassee, where ML Juvenile Services was located. Metzger met them outside its building, an arrest warrant in hand. Together, they walked into the two-story building, showed their credentials, then made their way to Wilcox's office. An attractive young woman with red hair and rosy cheeks sat at a desk outside the owner's office.

"Is Mr. Wilcox in?" Jacobs asked.

"Do you have an appointment with him?"

"No, ma'am."

"I'm sorry, he's very busy. I'd be happy to make an appointment for you if you let me know what it's in reference to."

Metzger whipped opened his wallet and showed the woman his badge.

"Oh!"

"Now, I'll ask you again. Is he in?"

The woman nodded and pointed to the closed door opposite her desk.

With Metzger leading the way, he opened the door, and they all followed him in.

"What's going on here?" Wilcox said as he stood up.

"Sir, we have a warrant for your arrest. Please step out from the desk."

"Susie, call Herb. Tell him to get up here right now," Wilcox called out to the woman outside his office.

Although Dani showed no emotion on her face, inwardly, she beamed. She'd encountered many awful people in her years, both as a prosecutor and a HIPP attorney, but never had she been as disgusted as she was by this sad excuse for a man. She'd known police who'd lied on the stand, and prosecutors who'd withheld exculpatory evidence, but every time it was because they believed the man or woman they'd arrested was guilty. What they did was wrong, but at least they were driven by pure motives. Wilcox saw children only as dollar signs, a means to personal wealth. It didn't matter to him that they were subjected to Dickensian conditions, often turning them into bitter, angry adults who, because of their treatment in his facilities, continued to act out once freed, thereby continuing their cycle of incarceration. He didn't care. He took the State's money, and the children's souls.

"You need me?" A short man dressed in a suit and tie stepped into the office.

"Herb, thank goodness you're here. This man says he has an arrest warrant for me."

"May I see that, please?"

Metzger handed him the piece of paper, and Herb looked it over. "You're charged with bribery, racketeering, and extortion."

"Well, do something about it."

Herb handed it back to Metzger. "Can we agree that Mr. Wilcox will turn himself in tomorrow morning?"

Jacobs answered. "Sorry, we're taking him in now."

Metzger took out his handcuffs.

"Is it really necessary to parade him through his offices like that? He'll go with you willingly."

"Herb, what are you saying?"

"Don't worry, Roger. I'll follow you and have outside counsel over there as soon as possible. You'll be back home tonight, latest tomorrow."

"I doubt that," Jacobs said. With that, Metzger slapped on the handcuffs, and they all marched Wilcox out of the building. Dani no longer held back. She broke out a huge smile.

Three weeks after the new school year began, Tony Cuen ran up to Frankie in the hallway as he was walking to his locker. They were in different classes now, and it was the first time Frankie had seen him since returning to school.

"Hey, you know, I'm really sorry about what I did. Everything."

Frankie stared at him. "Okay."

"I mean it. I was a dick. Can you forget about it?" He held out his hand to shake Frankie's.

Frankie wanted to scream. *Forget all the horrible things I saw at Eldridge? Forget getting beaten till I almost died? Forget that I was kidnapped and might never have seen my family again? Forget the terrible things that happened to Daisy?* He knew lashing out at Tony wouldn't change anything. Even if Tony hadn't lied on the stand, Humphrey still would have sent him away. And it was his own fault for bringing the joints to school.

He shook Tony's hand. "Sure. It's forgotten."

Tony smiled and lightly slapped Frankie's arm. "Thanks."

Frankie had grown four inches since he'd last been in school. He wasn't the new kid anymore. He had friends now. His mom had arranged for his teachers to give him advanced work. He'd made the track team and ran the mile, winning every meet they'd had. He played soccer as well. It was a new start for him. Tony deserved that new start, too.

—

Dani felt like an elephant as she waddled to the lunchroom. If Ruth was on time, she still had eight weeks to go. Not soon enough. She'd just settled herself back behind her desk with her bottle of water when Noah Jacobs called. "I thought you'd like to know, the panel has finished its review of Humphrey's cases post–kidney transplant."

"What did they find?"

"In a little more than three years, the panel concluded that 237 adjudications were an abuse of discretion by the judge. And that only counts the ones that weren't overturned on appeal. Sadly, too many parents can't afford to appeal."

"It's sickening."

"Even more sickening, the State of Florida paid ML Juvenile Services an average of $34,700 for every child placed in one of its facilities. They have a fifty percent profit margin. So Wilcox pulled in over $4 million in profit because of Humphrey."

"Are you sorry you let Humphrey off so easily? I still feel sick when I think how little time he's doing."

"Nah. He wasn't in it for the money. It's hard to say what anyone would do when they're facing death. His testimony will put Wilcox away for a long time. The Florida DJJ has already cancelled his contracts for breach. The company is kaput."

"What will happen to the kids?"

"We can't take back the time they spent locked up, but for many, their records will be wiped clean."

"Thank you, Noah. I really appreciate everything you did."

"Hell, I'm the one to thank you. We might have been able to close Wilcox's facilities after we finished our investigation, but he just would have moved on to another state. That's what the bad ones do.

But you alerted us to Humphrey. Wilcox's extortion of him is what will land him in prison."

After Dani hung up, she realized she'd forgotten to ask Jacobs what the panel decided about Frankie. Although she was happy about the other children, it was Frankie who had a special place in her heart. She quickly called Jacobs back.

———

Two weeks later, Bruce called Dani into his office. "Got anything pressing tomorrow?"

"Not really," Dani said.

"Are you still able to fly? I mean, is it okay for the baby?"

Dani patted her swollen belly. "Yes. I still have one more week before I'm grounded."

"Good. I have just enough frequent-flyer miles left to take you and Tommy with me to Florida tomorrow. Judge Silverman is going to order Frankie's record wiped clean. It wouldn't have happened without both of you. I thought you'd like to witness it."

"Oh, Bruce, yes. Thank you. I'd love to be there for it."

The next morning, the three flew into Tampa International Airport, then made their way to the courthouse. They arrived at two o'clock, searched through the crowded corridor, and finally found Jessica and Frankie. Jessica hugged each one, then turned to the young man in uniform at her side. "Bobby, these are the two I've told you about. Dani and Tommy."

Bobby shook their hands. "I'm sure Mom has thanked you many times, but I want to add mine. Frankie's such a great kid. He didn't deserve any of this. So thank you from me."

Together they all walked into the courtroom, which was already packed. Dozens of children and their parents filled every seat, with more standing along the back wall. Dani knew this was just a portion of the kids whose adjudications were being overturned. Another group had been there for the morning session. Still more would be there tomorrow, and each day until the end of the week.

Judge Silverman presided over the proceedings. They waited patiently for Frankie's name to be called. The courtroom doors kept opening and closing as the children whose sentences had just been stricken left with their families. The noise was loud enough that Dani almost missed hearing Frankie's name called. When it was, Frankie, flanked by his mother and brother, walked to the front of the courtroom.

"Francis Bishop," began Judge Silverman, "you were charged with possession of an illegal substance, namely, two marijuana cigarettes. Upon review of the trial transcript, this court finds that there was insufficient evidence for a delinquency adjudication. Therefore, that ruling and your sentence are hereby vacated."

A big grin broke out on Frankie's face. "Thank you, sir."

"You're welcome, young man. I understand you have a bright future ahead of you. Keep learning, and do your best to make a difference in this world."

"I will."

"There's one other thing, Mr. Bishop."

"Yes, sir?"

The judge nodded to the bailiff, who was standing by the door leading to the judge's chambers. He opened it, and standing there, in full dress uniform, was the man Dani had seen in Jessica's pictures of her husband—Alex Bishop. Jessica broke out in tears as Frankie ran to his father. Alex enveloped Frankie in a hug, then walked over to Jessica and Bobby and wrapped his arms around both. Bruce stepped into the circle and grabbed his brother's arm.

"You're here!" Jessica whispered as she buried her face in her husband's chest. "But, how?

"Doesn't matter right now," Alex said. "I'm back. I'm home."

Maybe it was the hormones, but watching the family reunited, Dani couldn't hold her own tears back. They were happy tears. Happy that Frankie's record was cleared. Happy that she'd played a part in helping him. Happy that his family was reunited. And as she felt that familiar kick in her belly, happy that, just as Alex held on to Frankie, soon she would get to hold her new daughter in her arms, her Ruth.

ACKNOWLEDGMENTS

First Offense was a difficult book to write. As I researched private, for-profit juvenile prisons, I was constantly disturbed by the reported abuses that took place in many of those facilities. Some of the worst-offending operators have had their contracts canceled, and I hope the amount of abuse has lessened. But the profit motive—which depends upon lowering overhead in order to increase the return to shareholders—still results in prison workers who, because of the lower pay, may come to the job with lower skills. Although the specific abuses described in the book are fabricated, they are similar to real cases that have occurred in juvenile prisons throughout the United States.

As with each book I write, I value the input of the members of The Villages Creative Writing Group. I'd like to give special thanks to the following people from that group for their insightful critiques: Linda Dickson, Mike Doyle, Pat Fagan, Millard Johnson, Dave Maurer, Mark Newhouse, Frank Ridge, Mary Lois Sanders, Mitch Smith, Penny Thomas, and Tom Zampano.

Thanks to retired Air Force Lt. Col. Jon Williams for educating me about military matters, and to Richard Pallaziol of Weapons of Choice for teaching me about guns. Thanks also to Henry Hack, who answered my questions about law-enforcement matters. Any mistakes in those areas are purely my own.

I'm grateful to my agent, Adam Chromy of Movable Type Management, for his invaluable advice on the first draft. And big cheers go to my developmental editor, David Downing. Thanks also to my copy editor, Valerie Kalfrin, and proofreader, Jill Kramer, for making the book readable.

I'm also thrilled to be part of the Thomas & Mercer family, and greatly appreciate the work of my editor, Kjersti Egerdahl; Marketing Manager Jacque Ben-Zekry; and Author Relations Managers Tiffany Pokorny and Sarah Shaw.

As always, I want to thank my terrific and supportive husband, Lenny, for always being my rock. I would not have become the person I am now without him by my side for five decades. Our two sons, Jason and Andrew; their wives, Amanda and Jacqueline; and our five grandchildren, Rachel, Joshua, Jacob, Sienna, and Noah, round out my wonderful family; I'm so grateful for the support from each and every one of them.

Finally, I want to thank my readers. You are the reason I keep writing, and I hope I continue to entertain you with my stories.

ABOUT THE AUTHOR

After receiving her master's degree and her professional certificate, both in school psychology, Marti Green realized that her true passion was the law. She went on to receive her law degree from Hofstra University and worked as in-house counsel for a major cable television operator for twenty-three years, specializing in contracts, intellectual property law, and regulatory issues. She is the author of the legal thrillers *The Price of Justice*, *Presumption of Guilt*, *Unintended Consequences*, and *First Offense*.

A passionate traveler, mother to two adult sons, and grandmother to five grandchildren, she now lives in Central Florida with her husband, Lenny, and cat, Howie.